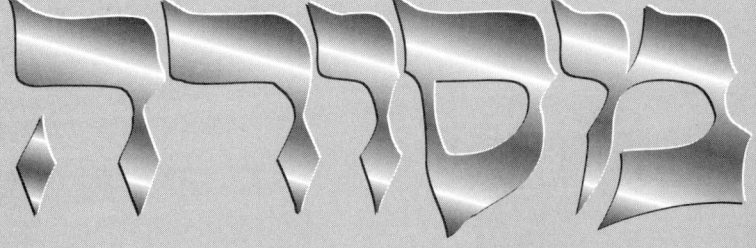

ArtScroll Series®

Rabbi Nosson Scherman / Rabbi Meir Zlotowitz

General Editors

Chance

Published by

Mesorah Publications, ltd

Encounters?

Stories that are hardly by chance

by M.L. Mashinsky

FIRST EDITION
First Impression ... April 2000

Published and Distributed by
MESORAH PUBLICATIONS, LTD.
4401 Second Avenue / Brooklyn, N.Y 11232

Distributed in Europe by
J. LEHMANN HEBREW BOOKSELLERS
20 Cambridge Terrace
Gateshead, Tyne and Wear
England NE8 1RP

Distributed in Israel by
SIFRIATI / A. GITLER
10 Hashomer Street
Bnei Brak 51361

Distributed in Australia and New Zealand by
GOLDS BOOK & GIFT SHOP
36 William Street
Balaclava 3183, Vic., Australia

Distributed in South Africa by
KOLLEL BOOKSHOP
Shop 8A Norwood Hypermarket
Norwood 2196, Johannesburg, South Africa

Typography by CompuScribe at ArtScroll Studios, Ltd.

Printed in the United States of America by Noble Book Press Corp.
Bound by Sefercraft, Quality Bookbinders, Ltd., Brooklyn N.Y. 11232

Table of Contents

Look to the Mountains

I T WAS THE BEST OF TIMES — UNTIL IT BECAME THE worst of times.

As the 19th century turned into the 20th, Frankfurt am Main presented a self-assured and hopeful face to the future. And in this long-established Jewish community, one of the most serene and well-regulated households was that of Herr Selig Schachnowitz, esteemed editor of the *Israelit*, the weekly German-language newspaper which linked European Jewry with all the continents where their co-religionists dwelt, telling of their triumphs, and all too often, their disasters.

In the Schachnowitz home, however, all was calm and order. The well-established routine never varied: After *shul*, Reb Selig came home to breakfast with his wife and their three daughters, Erna, Tilla, and Trude. The meal, served by the white-aproned maid, always consisted of a white roll with butter and an egg, with coffee for the adults and milk for the children. If the girls were very good, they received a spoonful of marmalade with their *kaisersemmeln* or *kipferl*.

Punctually at 9, Papa went to his office, while Mama saw to

the complicated household affairs, which were symbolized by the bunch of keys almost hidden within the folds of her voluminous, floor-length skirts — keys to the linen press, the wine cabinet, the china and silver closet, the pantry. Although the household employed a maid and a laundress, there was a tremendous amount of physical work, since every bit of food was prepared at home. *Barches* [which we call *challah*] and cakes were mixed and kneaded by hand and baked in a big black coal- and wood-burning stove. Meat and chicken were *kashered* at home, a good morning's work. Noodles were dried on a wooden rack, fruits and vegetables were preserved at the end of summer; and winter found the female family members knitting sweaters, gloves, and socks, mending and darning, with a thimble on the finger and a precisely measured thread in the needle.

"Langes fädchen, faules mädchen ..." went the saying — "Long thread, lazy girl ...."

Life proceeded at the same placid, leisurely pace, as regular as the pendulum clock ticking away in the parlor, until ....

The great World War! It began with the assassination of Austrian Crown Prince Ferdinand at Sarajevo, in what is now called Yugoslavia, and quickly spread to involve most European countries, bringing with it fear, hunger, and destruction. Jewish young men were drafted to fight for the Kaiser and the Fatherland.

Food became scarce and very precious. Clothing was patched again and again, or ripped apart and re-sewn. Coal and wood were strictly rationed. To find fuel for heating and cooking, the young girls went to the parks and forests to gather twigs from the ground. A whole day's labor might result in only enough kindling wood to boil a pot of potatoes, which had been obtained from the peasants by bartering household items and jewelry.

Hunger stalked the land, not as on a fast day when a bounteous meal is served at the end, but a steady, gnawing, all-consuming pain that was boundless and endless.

The *Israelit* reported one tragedy after another. Jews suffered in every European country — Poland, Russia, Austro-Hungary, Belgium, France. Although they fought bravely in all the opposing armies, they were blamed for every shortage, every setback, and every defeat.

Then came the greatest tragedy of all for the Schachnowitz family: Frau Schachnowitz collapsed while waiting in line for the family's meager ration of bread. A few hours later, it was all over — another victim of hunger.

Young Erna now struggled to take her mother's place in running the household and raising her younger sisters. Like little girls the world over, the younger sisters resented and often resisted their oldest sister's efforts at discipline, and occasionally staged small acts of rebellion, which were quickly quashed by a word, or even a smiling glance, from their father. But that was not the biggest problem: Finding food and preparing it became a constant preoccupation. Clothing, also, posed challenges. Old sweaters had to be unraveled, the kinky wool washed and straightened, to make shawls, mufflers, and mittens, worn in the house to keep from freezing. Little by little, they sold their possessions to stay alive. There were no more friendly visits or afternoon strolls in the park, no more girlish games and giggles — sheer survival took all their strength and energy.

R' Selig still tried to maintain an atmosphere of cheer and optimism, no easy matter when every day the dispatches brought bad news: Frankfurt's sons killed or wounded in action, often while fighting against their own Jewish brothers, soldiers serving other countries. Every day brought news of revolutions and pogroms, of Jewish suffering the world over. But at home, the day's troubles were not mentioned. In every possible way, the father tried to maintain for his daughters the secure and loving feeling of the past.

The war drew to a close, but nothing was ever the same again. Many of the best and finest never returned; others were maimed or blinded, defending Germany, the "beloved Fatherland." After a while, Herr Schachnowitz remarried, for the sake of his motherless children as well as his own. The girls readily accepted their new stepmother, who treated them as if they were her own.

Erna, the oldest, found herself in an odd position. For years, she had had the responsibility of running a busy and complicated household, as well as exerting authority over her lively younger sisters. Now she was again relegated to the position of a child — and she was not prepared for the change. Her father, always sensitive to her feelings, decided to offer Erna a trip to Switzerland.

"I can arrange for you to stay with some good friends I made during my years in Artigan, and you'll get a real vacation in very pleasant surroundings. You'll have a chance to meet new people and enjoy new experiences. Remember, Switzerland was neutral; they didn't suffer the way we did. So — what do you say?"

Erna needed no persuading. "Papa! How wonderful! I can't wait to go — but will Tilla and Trude be all right without me? And what about Auntie and the baby?"

"Don't worry, my dear. You'll need to have some new clothing made, and a sturdy pair of walking shoes — I'm sure you'll do lots of hiking in the Alps. I'll write to the Rosensteins and arrange the date, and have them meet you at the station."

Erna went off, full of happiness and high hopes. Even the train ride was exciting — the Swiss lakes, the trees and sunny meadows, the Alps rising into the clear blue sky. What a difference from flat, dreary, overcrowded Frankfurt! Here it would be easy to forget the ravages of war and the situation at home. Yes, this would be a really perfect vacation, the first she had had in years and years!

She was met by a coachman who tipped his hat respectfully to the German *fraulein*, and loaded her heavy trunk —

she was expected to stay for several months — into the horse-drawn coach. With a crack of the whip and a yodel, off they went, Erna sitting very straight on the plush seat, trying to look like a poised and worldly young woman, though this was her first trip to the *ausland* — out of the country.

The Rosensteins received her graciously, introducing her to the members of the household: Herr Rosenstein, a businessman with a neatly trimmed beard; his wife, rather fluttery and distracted looking; Rose, the oldest daughter, a bit younger than Erna herself; and what seemed like a whole troop of little boys. Besides an assortment of servants, there was a young tutor, who taught religious and secular subjects to the boys of the family, as was the custom at the time among well-to-do Jewish families.

Erna happily settled into the small room assigned to her, and soon fitted into the routine of the household. The first days, Frau Rosenstein said, she should rest up from her journey; there would be time enough later for visiting and exploring.

Yet, somehow, to Erna's surprise and disappointment, that time never came. First, one of the boys took sick, and Erna volunteered to relieve the exhausted mother, staying up half the night with the feverish child. Then the cook quit, and Frau Rosenstein just couldn't manage. Skillful and efficient, Erna spent hours in the kitchen, assisting her hostess. Soon Erna was put in complete charge, to the relief of Mrs. Rosenstein and the sincere appreciation of all the family members.

One day the young tutor, Jacob Eisenberg, entered what had become her domain, and asked for a glass of water. Somehow, the cup broke in his hand, and splinters of glass mixed with puddles of water covered the kitchen floor.

Sie hat ihm gut angeschrien — she gave him a good scolding — he had messed up her immaculate kitchen. The tutor mumbled a weak apology and retreated to his books.

Erna continued in her self-imposed household duties.

Although this was not what she had expected, she had no complaints; it was not in her nature to be idle.

Papa Schachnowitz, however, sensed from afar that all was not as it should be and wrote her an affectionate letter, asking if Erna was ready to return home. This decision was quite easy for her, and soon she was on the train to Frankfurt.

Now started a new phase in her life. Erna was, after all, a girl of marriageable age. Few suitable young men were available; the war had taken a terrible toll. Anyone considering marriage first had to prove his ability to support a family; in those confused post-war years, this was a most difficult task.

Suitors began to arrive; though carefully screened by R' Selig, some proved quite unusual, to say the least. One arrived wearing short leather pants with embroidered suspenders, in typical mountaineer fashion. Another brought his dearest companion, a huge German shepherd who sniffed and snuffled around Erna, while she sat with her feet tucked under her on the sofa; she was terrified of dogs. There were also some rather nice young men, but nothing came of these meetings.

Finally R' Selig said, *"Sag mir, Erna, was wird denn sein mit Dir?* Tell me, what'll be with you? You don't seem to like any of these candidates. Isn't there anyone who pleases you?"

"Well, Papa, there was this young tutor at the Rosensteins who I thought was very nice — I wouldn't mind somebody like him."

Herr Schachnowitz, ever the man of action, immediately dispatched a letter to Artigan, inquiring about Jacob Eisenberg, the tutor. A few days later, the reply came — they considered him a fine young man, very religious, intelligent, kind, from an excellent Polish family. However, he had left some time ago, perhaps to the United States, but they weren't certain.

That was a disappointment, far greater than either father or daughter would admit, even to themselves. Finding a

Jewish immigrant on that vast unknown continent was harder than finding a needle in a haystack, since ships constantly carried to the New World young men seeking their fortune. The name was not an unusual one, and there was no clue as to friends or relatives who might have contact with him.

They resigned themselves to this missed opportunity, and another *beschau* was set up with a local young fellow. This one was very musical — he came with his cello, and only wished to know if Erna could accompany him on the piano. And so it went, week after week. Until ....

One fine day, a letter arrived from America, addressed to Herr Schachnowitz at the newspaper office. The date stamped showed that it had been underway for a long time — there was no airmail in those days. "Probably someone who wants to subscribe to the *Israelit*," said the office boy, and it was put in the pile of business correspondence. However, when opened, the envelope proved to have another one inside, marked, "Private — Herr Selig Schachnowitz."

"*Sehr geherter Herr Schachnowitz* — Very honored Mr. Schachnowitz —" it began conventionally enough. "I have had the great honor and pleasure of meeting your esteemed daughter, *fraulein* Erna, at the home of the Rosensteins in Artigan, and have ever since entertained hopes of being considered worthy of applying for her hand in marriage." Then came some details of family background and future prospects. The letter ended, "*Hochachtungsvoll* — with the highest regard, Jacob Eisenberg."

The rest is history. However, the story does not end here.

So they were married, and despite the great troubles and adversity of their era, lived happily after.

This story, like all true stories, has a sequel, in fact, several of them. The young couple settled in Vienna, where Mr. Eisenberg became a teacher in the Talmud Torah on Malzgasse. Later they acquired a hotel, called Aue-Meadow, — in the beautiful Semmering Mountains near Vienna. It became a popular summer resort, where many Jewish families spent happy vacations.

In the winter of 1934, a terrible diphtheria epidemic swept Vienna. This disease, almost non-existent today, is extremely contagious and often fatal. Many sweet little Jewish children died that season.

All those stricken with it were placed under strict quarantine. Mrs. Felsenburg, a young Viennese mother whose family had stayed at the Eisenberg's hotel, locked herself in her apartment with her three older girls; the youngest, 5-year-old Ruth, who was not sick, was sent with her father to stay at the kindhearted and hospitable Eisenbergs. There she encountered their son, Benny, who was several years older than her, but, as an only child, quite unused to the teasing prevalent in larger families. Ruti enjoyed all the attention she got in this male-oriented household. For Benny, it was a new and rather daunting experience, but he took it in stride. When the epidemic was over, Ruti returned home with her father.

The Germans invaded Vienna; Ruti's parents escaped by way of Czechoslovakia, Hungary, and France, and ended up in Williamsburg, Brooklyn. The Eisenbergs, too, left when their beautiful hotel was taken over by the Nazis. They traveled through Switzerland and France, and through great miracles, also wound up in the United States. After many years, Ruth and Benny met again — and married.

Divine Providence is openly revealed in their story. Jacob Eisenberg had to leave Poland and come to Switzerland, and then to the United States. (His "first papers" from that brief stay saved the family's lives.) Erna needed a vacation, and after countless twists of fate — a glass broke — *mazel tov*!

And *mazel tov, mazel tov* for generations to come!

Made in Heaven

ALTHOUGH SHE HAD PASSED HER 21ST BIRTHDAY, Mindy had never been on an airplane before, and she was nervous. But it was her friend's wedding, in California; no way would she miss it!

She had planned to take only a carry-on and a garment bag containing her pink silk suit and matching shoes, specially purchased for this great occasion. But then the bride herself, her friend Miriam, had called frantically — the caterer could not get certain items that were absolutely essential for the smorgasbord. Only in New York could these delicacies be obtained, and since Mindy was arriving the day of the wedding, could she, please …?

"Okay. Fine. No problem. Glad to do it!" said Mindy. But it did turn out to be quite a problem. The caterer said that everything would be ready and packed the morning of her departure. She could easily pick up the items on the way to the airport, since the caterer's place was in Queens, not far from LaGuardia Airport.

So Mindy allowed an extra half-hour for that, but when she arrived at Celestial Caterers, the big pots had just been placed on ice to cool.

"Just a few minutes, Miss. It won't be more than a few

minutes," the chef kept saying. But it took much more than that. By the time the food had cooled and been carefully packed in boxes of dry ice, and then in the big borrowed suitcase Mindy had brought along, she was trembling with anxiety. Would she get to LaGuardia in time?

At the airport she had only minutes to check in the heavy suitcase of food. As the departure time flashed on the screen, Mindy dashed up the steps of the airplane. A moment later, the plane began to move. Exhausted, her knees buckling, she fell into her reserved seat. Oh, just to close her eyes and sleep and sleep until the plane reached Los Angeles!

But it was not to be. A furious voice behind her was screaming: "I want my rights! You promised me an aisle seat! And you stuck me in this awful place where I don't even have room for my feet!! Gimme an aisle seat or else!" The yelling went on and on.

It was an elderly woman, her face mottled with fury, brandishing a cane. The stewardess tried to placate her, offering even her own seat on the crowded plane, but "No! No! NOO!" It sounded like a bomb exploding.

Mindy tried to block out the sound by huddling into her pillow and wrapping the blanket over her head. But nothing helped.

"I will never fly this airline again! I will report this outrage to the media! I'll sue you! You'll be sorry!"

The stewardess, nearly in tears, consulted the supervisor. He too tried to persuade the furious woman to take another seat, but no sale. He went up and down the length of the plane, begging passengers on the aisle to exchange their seats, but no one budged. Most of them simply turned away and ignored him. All the while, the difficult passenger screamed and screamed.

Mindy couldn't stand it any longer. "Poor thing," she said to herself. "It's so important to her! Let her be comfortable; I don't really need this aisle seat."

She staggered to her feet — her leg had fallen asleep, but the rest of her was wide awake — and told the stewardess that she was willing to change seats. With a smile of immense relief, the stewardess carried the screamer's bundles and bags to Mindy's place, seated the new occupant, and handed her a big drink. Silence prevailed.

Mindy was left to haul her garment bag and carry-on to the new seat, *not* on the aisle. She stowed her things overhead and squeezed past a stout lady. She started to sink into her seat, when — horrors! — she realized she was sitting on a plastic cup full of ice cubes, apparently placed there by her new neighbor. The woman said, "Shoot! You spoiled my drink. Now I'll have to get fresh ice!"

Mindy closed her eyes. Only 20 minutes into the flight — what would be next?

When she opened her eyes after a brief, unsatisfying nap, the first thing she saw was an open *sefer Tehillim*, the Book of Psalms, identical to the one in her large pocketbook. Had this person opened her bag while she was asleep? But who would steal a *Tehillim*?

She reached for her bag under the seat. Its contents were intact, including the *Tehillim*. She opened it and started whispering the psalm for the day. To her left, a rather pleasant voice was reciting the very same words.

This passenger, too, was an older woman, but what a difference from the screamer and the one with the ice cubes on the right! Her new neighbor had a calm face with laugh lines radiating from her eyes. Mindy realized that she was not just rattling off the words of *Tehillim*, but every word expressed deep feeling.

Repeating the familiar words had its usual soothing effect on Mindy, and lulled by the hum of the engines and her own weariness, she drifted off into a sweet slumber.

"Thwack! Crack! Ugh!" The back of Mindy's seat banged against her spine, sending shock waves through her body. A freckle-faced boy behind her was kicking the seat with all his might, with what felt like hob-nailed boots. She leaned forward, trying to escape, but he only kicked all the harder.

"Little boy, please stop that. It bothers me —"

"So what? Good for you! If you don't like it you can get off! Ha, ha, ha!"

Weren't there any adults with this little monster? Apparently not, or why didn't they stop him?

"Please," Mindy tried again. "I'd like to speak to your father or mother. Where are they?"

"My pop is the mayor of New York City, and my mom is in the zoo in San Francisco, and they let me go everyplace by myself. Ha, ha, ha!"

Were the kicks growing fainter? Or was she just getting used to them?

"Would you like to go to sleep, little boy? You must be very tired by now!" (Child Psychology I to the rescue!)

"Okay — gimme your blanket and your pillow and wake me up when it's time to eat."

Mindy passed back two blankets and pillows. Wrapped in the blankets, the child cuddled deep into his seat and quickly fell asleep, with the most angelic smile on his face.

"I think you handled that very well." The woman at her left spoke in a low, modulated voice. "I felt like slapping him."

"So did I." Mindy smiled. "But then I thought he must be very tired, and hungry, and scared of being alone. He doesn't look more than 8, and he's flying cross-country all by himself. I almost feel sorry for him."

The older woman introduced herself as Mrs. Rachel Spiegel, originally from Brooklyn. She had been living in Los Angeles for the past 15 years, and had raised her family there. Yes, she agreed, the climate was delightful, except for the floods, earthquakes, and fires, but she did miss her friends and family back East. In fact, she had cut short her visit there because of a wedding.

The food carts were rolling through the aisles, and suddenly Mindy felt faint with hunger. She remembered that her last meal had been yesterday. In all the rush of packing and getting to the airport, she had quite forgotten to eat, and she looked forward to the kosher meal ordered for her by the travel agent.

She waited patiently. All the passengers had been served, including her nice neighbor on the left. Finally Mindy asked the stewardess for her meal.

"Sorry, miss, I don't see any kosher meal order for you. Would you like the regular dinner?" Apparently, this was a routine occurrence.

"No, no, of course not." Mindy's stomach was doing somersaults. She was starving.

Mrs. Spiegel was indignant. "How can the agent slip up like that? That's nerve — letting people get on a plane without providing food!"

Mindy said it might have been a computer glitch. Mrs. Spiegel offered her an orange which Mindy accepted gratefully. "Anyway, it's just a short flight," she comforted herself.

Just then the stewardess came rushing up with a broad smile on her face. "I'm so sorry — I just found your tray. It was on the bottom of the rack. Here," and she presented a sealed package.

At the same moment, there was a terrific kick which seemed to go right through Mindy's spine. It was the *enfant terrible* behind her, wide awake now, and angry.

"You didn't wake me up like you promised! I'm starving! I'm gonna pass out!" and he gave a dramatic imitation of just that, sliding down his seat to the floor. Apparently, the flight attendant had placed a dinner on the sleeping child's tray, and then removed it while he was still asleep.

Mindy said, "Here, dear, here's a delicious meal all ready for you!" and passed her tray to the back.

In a second, the boy was back in his seat, grabbed the package, ripped it open, and gobbled the food voraciously, without even a look or word of thanks. When he finished, he handed Mindy the wrappings. "Here, get rid of this."

Mrs. Spiegel and Mindy looked at each other; each knew what the other was thinking. "Don't you think that boy should be taught some manners? You're too kind to him. He's spoiled rotten!" Mrs. Spiegel kept her voice low.

Mindy answered in an equally soft voice, "We don't know what this child goes through every day. Probably his parents ... well, they don't give him much affection, and he has to fight for everything. So he acts like this because he's starved for love and attention. And a 5-hour flight is not enough to change him. At least now he slept and he ate; maybe he'll behave for the rest of the flight."

Mrs. Spiegel had to agree when the next hour passed without any more disturbances. She asked Mindy all about herself and why she was flying to L.A. When Mindy told her that she was on the way to the wedding of her best friend, Miriam Golden, Mrs. Spiegel got very excited. "I'm going to that wedding, too! How do you know Miriam? She's a local girl, and you've never been to L.A."

"Well, we went to Bais Yaakov together, and then to Seminary. And we still are very close. In fact, I'm bringing some of the food for the smorgasbord." Mindy described the tense scene at Celestial Caterers, which seemed quite funny in retrospect.

Except for a few requests from the back for toys, for peanuts, and for drinks, the remaining hour of the flight passed quietly.

When the *Fasten seat belts* sign flashed on in preparation for landing, the boy leaned over to Mindy with a scared look on his face. In a very little voice, he asked, "Could you — just in case — take care of me? I mean just in case ... if no one comes to meet me?"

"Of course I will." Mindy's answer came immediately, without hesitation.

Mrs. Spiegel was amazed. "After all this kid put you through, you're still willing to look out for him?"

"Since he asked me to, I feel it's *bashert*. I was put on this particular plane to help this child, and it's fine."

"Hmm — there may be more than one reason," Mrs. Spiegel spoke softly.

"Of course — do we ever know why things happen the way they do? And you see, he's just a scared little kid underneath it all."

The boy put his hand in Mindy's and they walked off the plane together. There *was* a woman waiting for him; his mother had sent the maid. Happy and relieved, he started to run toward her, but then he paused and turned back to where Mindy and Mrs. Spiegel were standing.

"Thank you," he said. "Thanks for everything, and I'm sorry about before."

Mrs. Spiegel offered to take Mindy to the Golden's home. "My husband should be waiting outside with the car."

He was, and they took Mindy to her friend, promising to drop off the smorgasbord valise at the caterers.

As soon as Mindy had left the car, Mr. Spiegel turned to his wife and said, "She seems like a very nice girl. You met her on the plane? Maybe for our Shmuel …. Can you ask around and find out about her, her character, her background?"

His wife said, "I don't have to. I know everything important about her already, and I agree — our Shmulie would be fortunate …."

At the wedding of Mindy and Shmulie Spiegel, everyone made the same original joke: "This is a *shidduch* made in heaven."

And it is.

Haircuts

JEWISH MEN TAKE HAIRCUTS ON FRIDAY AFTERNOON.
This has been the custom since time immemorial; the barber shop, besides providing tonsorial services, is also a social center where the news of the week is broadcast and amplified.

So it came as a big surprise to Dave Greenberg when he met his long-time acquaintance, Abe Fradin, in Sam's Barber Shop on Lee Avenue on a Tuesday morning at 10 a.m.

"Hello, Abe. How are you? And what brings you here in the middle of the week so early in the morning? You retired already?" This was a joke, since it was well known that Abe worked long hours in his small grocery store six days a week, and even opened on *Motza'ei Shabbos* in the winter.

"I could ask you the same question, Dave. Maybe you won the Irish Sweepstakes?" Abe was aware that Dave had not acquired anything recently but a sprained back, caused by lugging heavy cases of seltzer bottles up the steep stairs of the three-story Williamsburg brownstones. (In fact, he could see the loaded truck outside, waiting in front of the barber shop like a patient steed for its master.)

"No, no Irish Sweepstakes — I didn't even buy a ticket. But my son Yankel *did* win the lottery!" With a brief pause for dramatic effect, Dave continued, "He's getting married tonight! What a girl he's getting," and Dave smacked his lips. "What a girl!"

"Well, she can't be any better than my little girl Henny! And she's also getting married tonight, at Gold Manor, to a wonderful boy. So that's why I'm getting a haircut now, but why you need one for those few hairs on top I don't know — okay, okay — you just want to keep Sam in business."

"Next!" Sam didn't like that kind of joke. He treated all his customers alike, giving exactly 12 minutes per haircut, whether it was a full bushy head of curls or a thin fringe of gray in back. Sam was different from most barbers in another respect: He was not a talker. He heard and absorbed everything that went on in his shop, but never commented, never took part in the steady hum of conversation that accompanied his work.

"Next customer!" And Abe took his place in the chair, putting an end to the friendly banter.

A year later, Dave and Abe met again in Sam's Barber Shop, early Monday afternoon this time.

"So, Abe, what brings you here? You came to read the *Morgen Journal*, maybe? You could buy your own — it's only five cents."

While Abe was known to every *shnorrer* in the vicinity as an easy touch, he was equally famous for his thrift in small things: knotting and re-knotting torn shoelaces, wearing the same threadbare gray suit year after year, and reusing an ancient celluloid shirt collar to save on laundry. A local wag had reported that Abe lost his hair early on purpose, to save on haircuts.

"Hah! No, I'm here to take a haircut. And you better get one too, Dave — you prob'ly weren't here since before Rosh Hashanah, and you got so much hair on your head, your hat from your Bar Mitzvah don't fit any more."

Dave fingered his elegant new fedora.

"This hat happens to be for my Genendel's wedding tonight and cost $6.98 on Roebling Street, so don't make fun. And it's getting late," he said, looking at his watch, "and I still got to pick up my son Yossi from the tailor with his new suit. He grew so much in the last couple months, everything got too short. It wouldn't look nice, a *chasan bachur* like him should have short pants by his sister's wedding."

"*Mazel tov, mazel tov,* Dave! And you know what? My Heshy is also getting married tonight, at the Little Hungary, and I still got to go to the cleaner's for my Goldie's dress what she wore to her high school graduation, and something spilled on it. Anyway, *mazel tov*, and you should have loads of *nachas*!"

"And the same to you, Dave."

"Next!" Sam was in a hurry. "Next customer!"

There was only time for a brief handshake. Abe hopped into the barber chair and leaned back. The cotton cape was fastened around his neck and the scissors were clicking away when Dave left the shop.

Another year passed. Abe and Dave had both become grandfathers by the time they met again in Sam's Barber Shop. Abe was leaving just as Dave walked in on a Friday afternoon.

The store was crowded. Sam's scissors kept up their usual quick snip, snip, snip above the buzz of the customers' talk. Suddenly the sound stopped. Sam called out, "Abe! Wait — I got something to tell you!"

This was most unusual. No one had ever heard anything but "Next customer!" from the lips of the taciturn barber. Rumor had it that he was a former pupil of the Chofetz Chaim, and situated as he was to hear all the gossip, he had pledged not to talk in the shop except for those two words.

Abe turned back, startled. Sam took a deep breath.

"Listen, Abe. You got a nice daughter, Goldie, that she already graduated last year, a real good girl. And Dave here has a Yossi, a very fine *bachur*. He also gets his hair cut here for years, so I know all about him. You couldn't find better. So what do you say, Abe? And you, Dave?"

The next moment, the scissors resumed their regular rhythm.

The two men looked at each other. A great light dawned in their eyes.

"Yes!" said Dave.

"Yes!" said Abe.

"Next customer!" Sam called out.

On a Wednesday morning after Shavuos, the men met again in Sam's Barber Shop. They would both be going to the same wedding that night — Goldie Fradin to Yossi Greenberg.

A Matter of Time

POOR ARI LEVENE! HE'S THE OLDEST BACHELOR IN the whole Kopolner Yeshivah.

He's all of 23!

Many of the students in this Baytown, New Jersey, *chassidishe* establishment become engaged by age 18, and are married, or even fathers, at 19 or 20. So Ari, as well as some other holdouts, has become rather an object of speculation and even pity among his peers.

Not that he feels himself at all pitiable — on the contrary. He's a fine, *frum* student, with an excellent family background. Ari is of good appearance and capable in many fields. He is careful about his clothing, and the orderliness of his dormitory room mutely testifies to an orderly mind. He feels he has a lot going for him.

So why isn't he married yet? There are many good reasons, but only one that really matters: The right girl, the one who *he* feels is right for him, hasn't come along yet, and Ari is willing to wait. True, he gets many suggestions, as well as lots of gentle teasing from his fellow students, but he dismisses them all with a wave of his hand or a shrug of his shoulders: "Just wait, and you'll see...."

Despite this seemingly cavalier attitude, Ari *is* getting a bit tired of waiting.

One winter day a neighbor appears in the yeshivah, a somewhat older man who often comes to *daven* there on Shabbos and Yom Tov. But this is a weekday morning, and Berel Borag has not come to pray, but to transact some business: He is looking for a partner. Since they all know that he earns his living by *safrus*, the writing of Torah scrolls, which is essentially a one-man operation, and since they also know that he does not receive an excessive number of commissions, his quest causes rather a stir in the yeshivah; but it turns out that he is looking for a different kind of partner — a study partner — and he is willing to pay!

That makes it far more interesting, and several of the young men decide to apply. However, Yankel, the first prospective partner, can't give the hours that Berel asks for; Chaim is studying a different *mesechta*; Leibel wants more money; and Kalman, his last best hope, claims that it is absolutely impossible for him to be on time.

So it goes, although there are many who are willing and able to take the job, no one proves to be quite the right choice for what Berel had in mind … at least, not until Ari hears about it.

He had always liked and even admired Berel, who overcame terrible odds before finding a safe haven in Baytown. Born in a Displaced Persons' camp in Germany, Berel lost his father at a young age, and experienced hunger and loneliness. It took him a long time to find a suitable livelihood, and then a wife; and it seemed to Ari that Berel was still struggling — why should it be so difficult for him to find a study partner in this vast yeshivah with its hundreds of students?

So Ari goes over to Berel. "You know what? I'd like to be your *chavrusa*, but not for money. It happens that I've learned the *mesechta* in *Kodshim* that you want to study, and this would be an excellent chance for me to review it — in fact, it'll be a great favor to me! So what are the hours you want to learn?"

Berel is thrilled — one of the best boys in the yeshivah is

willing to learn with him, the exact topic he wants, at the time most convenient for him, and ... he's even doing Ari a favor!

"Done! Every day from 11 to 1. Just one thing: Make sure you're on time. I have a very tight schedule."

So, starting the next morning, the partners meet every day in the *beis hamidrash*. It's an excellent combination — one is sedate and thorough, the other quick and far-ranging, always seeking implications and drawing parallels. Although different in age, character, and background, they become close friends, linked by their daily togetherness and deep commitment to their studies. Berel sometimes talks of times past, of the father he lost, of his sad history, and also becomes well acquainted with Ari's family, just by hearing him talk about them. But — and this is another reason why the younger partner so enjoys learning with Berel — he never pries or teases Ari about his state of singleness. He gets enough of that from his other friends, and his family too; everyone has something to suggest or something to criticize, everyone has a relative or a friend of a friend: "Oy, this Chaya'la, or this Devorah, or that Roizie — she's just exactly what you're looking for."

One day Ari does not show up at 11 or 11:30. It is almost 12 when he finally arrives.

"What's the matter, Ari? You're late — you're not feeling well, maybe?" asks Berel.

"No, I'm fine. Just a little tired, that's all — had a hard time getting up this morning. And then I *davened* late, of course, and the time just ran away."

"You're usually so punctual — what happened?"

"Well, I went to a wedding last night. I was dancing a lot because the music was very *lebedig*, and by the time it was over it was already 2, and till I got back here, it was almost 3, so ...."

"Ah! Dancing all night! What a *mechayah*!" Berel exclaims. "What a pleasure, those young years before you're married!"

"No, it's not such a pleasure at all — I wish it was over already," sighs Ari. "You probably forgot what it's like, but it's not fun at all!" Ari has become very sensitive on the subject. "Now let's not waste any more time — it's late enough already. Let's see, we're up to ...."

That day, Berel goes home deep in thought.

"No, it's no fun being single when everyone your age is already married. Now what can I do for poor Ari? I would do anything, anything to help my good friend. I'd better ask Tzipoiry."

When his wife comes home from work in the evening, Berel immediately brings up the subject which has occupied his mind most of the day.

"Tzipoiry, you know Ari Levene that I learn with every morning? Well, the poor boy really needs a *shidduch*. I feel so bad for him — he must be the oldest *bachur* in the yeshivah by now. Maybe you know of someone for him?"

Her day has been a long one — up early to do the food shopping and start cooking for Shabbos, then working in a noisy factory all day. Tzipoiry is cold and tired, and she still has to get supper on the table.

"Listen, Berel, that boy can't be more than 23, so what's the big deal? Better help me put away these bags and turn up the steam — I'm frozen."

Knowing when to drop a subject is part of the art of being happily married, and Berel busies himself as directed, then sets the table. They settle down to their regular Thursday night supper — fried flounder prepared that morning, and reheated, mashed potatoes from a box of instant potatoes, string beans, canned pineapple. Berel praises the food inordinately, "The fish was delicious — how do you get it so crisp and brown? And the mashed potatoes were so fluffy, even better than my mother used to make!"

After the dessert, Berel leans back, and being a perceptive husband, judges it to be the right time to bring up the subject again.

"That was a great supper! Imagine, poor Ari, eating the yeshivah's food day after day."

"You're right, Berel. It's time he was married and in a home of his own. But ...."

"So you agree. Maybe you know of a nice girl for him?"

"I was just going to say that I don't know *any* girls. All day I work at the machine with non-Jews — they're the only girls I ever see, and that's not what he's looking for."

"What about the neighbors, or the ladies from *shul*, or in the stores? Or maybe your friends from our old neighborhood?"

"Come on, Berel, you know I never get a chance to meet anybody, and besides, there are only little kids around here. If there are any grown-up girls around, I haven't met them. It's funny, but do you realize I don't know a single marriageable girl in the whole America?"

Berel and Tzipoiry sit for a long time, quietly thinking. Suddenly — it is like a light bulb flashing on — Tzipoiry exclaims, "Berel! Mr. Warshawiak!"

"What do you mean, Mr. Warshawiak? Isn't he the man who answered my advertisement in the Yiddish paper about a *Sefer Torah* for sale? That must have been three or four years ago already. So what about him?"

"Don't you remember? Such a nice man — he invited us to the *Hachnasas Sefer Torah* in his house, and there was this sweet little girl who stayed home from school to help her mother serve the *seudah*, and you know what? She even looks like Ari! She must have been 15, 16 then. I'll bet she's ready for a *shidduch*. Let's talk to them about it!"

So that's what they do. First the Levenes are called, since one usually starts with the boy. They think it's a fine idea.

The Warshawiaks also like the suggestion. Mr. Warshawiak

makes subtle inquiries, and the replies prove very satisfactory. Mr. Warshawiak decides to check out the young man in person, just as he had done when buying the *Sefer Torah*. To find a time and place where he could meet the prospective groom without being conspicuous, he calls Berel Borag, who suggests the yeshivah's annual dinner, which will take place next week at a large hall in Brooklyn. Mr. Warshawiak does not need Berel's assistance in spotting Ari. "Doesn't he look exactly like my Hadassa'le?" he says in wonder.

Ari and Hadassah meet several times, get engaged, and are married a few months later. For the *bris* of their firstborn, Tzipoiry Borag bakes specially beautiful braided loaves, since it's two days before Pesach, and no bakery is selling *challah* that close to the holiday.

After the *seudah* and the speeches on this festive occasion have run their course, Berel makes a private little speech of his own to Ari's friends:

"You see, if Ari hadn't been such a good guy and started to learn with me."

Then Yankel says, "Well, he probably had nothing else to do."

Chaim says, "That *mesechta*? Hardly anybody wants to learn it."

Leibel says, "If you'd have offered more money ...."

"But what if he'd *always* been on time? Now you see it's not good, this being so punctual," says Kalman.

He always has to have the last word.

Languages

"**A**NYU, I MUST SPEAK TO YOU — RIGHT NOW. IT'S very, very, very important!"

Raizel raised large dark eyes swimming in tears to her mother, who was methodically shelling peas into an earthenware bowl.

"What's wrong, darling child? You don't feel well?"

Mrs. Weiss felt her daughter's forehead. It was cool, despite the oppressive heat of midsummer. "Hmm . . . no fever, at any rate," she thought. She had always worried about her older daughter. Raizel, she felt, was too attached to home and family, too sensitive to every nuance of word or facial expression, even to her surroundings. If a piece of furniture or one of the many knickknacks decorating the tables and shelves should be moved, she was upset and it took her a long time to adjust to the change.

"*Anyuka*, I'm so worried. How can I bear to leave you and *Apuka* and Feigy and my little brothers? Even our *meshores*, old Ilonka — she's been with us forever, and even the house and the garden ... it's so beautiful now, with the roses and poppies and cornflowers. I just don't know...."

"Raizele, you're 21 years old. It's time you got used to new things, and you'll be going to the best place in the world."

Mrs. Weiss put the bowl aside and took her daughter's hand.

"It's like *Gan Eden* there in Eretz Yisrael, with blue skies all summer long, and date palms and figs and oranges, with flowers like you never see here in Kopolny. You should be the happiest girl in all of Hungary, to have such a chance! And the young man — why, everyone we asked says only good about him! And they say he seems just right for you too!"

"But mother...," Raizel was sniffling, "those people don't know me! How can they be so sure that he's right for me? And how can I go off to a strange country with a stranger? I'll probably never see you again!" With that, Raizel burst into tears, sobbing and gulping noisily, like a little child.

"But Raizele — you never said a word about this before, and he's already on his way here. The telegram today said he left Yaffa after Shabbos." Mrs. Weiss was wringing her hands. She felt like bursting into tears herself.

"But that's why, *Anyu*! When the telegram came, I suddenly knew that this is real, that I'd have to make up my mind. I'll have to leave here and maybe never see you again." This outburst was accompanied by a fresh flood of tears.

"There, there, Raizele .... Don't cry — I'll speak to Papa. I'm sure he can do something. Anyway, it'll take another two weeks 'til the young man gets here, and maybe you'll change your mind by then." Mrs. Weiss spoke softly.

"No, Mama, never! Never, never, never!" Raizel's jaw set in that stubborn line her mother knew so well, just as when she had refused to wear the blue pleated dress that had been made for her from the most expensive silk.

"It's not my style," she had said then, and there was no budging her. After long and fruitless arguments, the dress was passed down to her younger sister, who wore it happily.

"Well, we'll see ...." With a sigh, Mrs. Weiss resumed shelling the peas. She felt a migraine headache coming on, but continued to work. Dinner must be ready when Shmiel came home at noon. Raizel had returned to her room, and her mother heard the key turning in the lock. She was probably lying on her bed, still crying.

Mr. Weiss arrived punctually at 12 o'clock. The table was set, with the children gathered around.

"Where's Raizel?" he asked, after washing his hands and partaking of a slice of the round, homemade loaf. "I haven't seen her since last night."

"Er — she's not feeling so well. I'll tell you later. *Nisht far dee kinder.*" Yiddish was saved for secrets in the Weiss household, because the younger children and the servants knew only Hungarian.

Mr. Weiss was in a happy mood. After much searching and many inquiries, he had settled upon a most estimable young man, Nosson Herman from Eretz Yisrael, as a prospective husband for his oldest daughter. Both families had agreed that it seemed a perfect match, and Raizel had consented to a meeting, to be held in Vienna at Montzy *Neni's* house. It would be quite impossible to meet in their own town, since everyone would immediately know all about the proposed match, and would be ready to voice comments and opinions. And if the outcome were negative, there would be endless speculating, often quite fantastical, as to the reason why. No — in Vienna, the big city, a stranger, even from far-away Palestine, would not be noticed. And Raizel would be thrilled at her first visit to lovely, lively Vienna, so different from their quiet little town. Yes, everything was going according to schedule, *baruch Hashem!*

The younger children, having bentched, kissed their father's and mother's hands, and with a murmured, *"Kezi tchokolom,"* ran out to play. The maid finished clearing the table, folded the checked linen cloth and put away the napkins in their initialed rings.

"Nu, Shari, you want to tell me why Raizel wasn't at the table? She doesn't like the menu maybe?" This was said in a joking tone, but it was no joke — Raizel ate a very limited selection of food, and it had to be prepared and served exactly as she liked it — one shred of onion in the goulash and it was declared unfit for human consumption. Bread from the day before? Raizel would rather do without. And Raizel would try half a teaspoonful of an unfamiliar food, but only after much pleading from her mother.

"Shmiel, have your nap now. I have a migraine and also need some quiet."

Mrs. Weiss rested her pounding head on the armrest of the horsehair sofa while her husband retired to his old lounge chair on the veranda for his 20-minute after-dinner snooze.

After what seemed like only a few moments of rest, Mrs. Weiss reluctantly opened her eyes. Her husband was walking up and down noisily, cracking his knuckles.

"Shari, I looked for Raizel; her door is locked, and when I called her, she refused to come out. What's going on?"

"I was going to tell you later, and also I was hoping she would change her mind, but you know how stubborn she can be, and anyway ...."

"Please stop talking in riddles, my dear, and come out with it. What's wrong?"

"Shmiel — first promise me you won't get upset."

"When am I ever upset? I promise, I promise anything you want — just tell me!"

"Well, she says . . . she says that she doesn't want to marry this Nosson Herman or even to meet him. She says — "

"What? He's on his way already! I — she — what?!"

Shmiel Weiss's face was beet red and he was clutching at his chest.

"Shmiel! You promised! Your blood pressure!" Shari was wringing her hands. She had become very pale.

"Blood pressure, shmud pressure! This is an emergency! I'm going to bang on her door 'til she changes her mind!" And Mr. Weiss stamped off in the direction of his daughter's room.

His wife was making shushing noises, pressing her fingers to her lips. "Please, Shmiely — remember, she's so sensitive!"

"Sensitive, shmensitive — she's got to act like a *mentch*! And if she can't at age 21, I'll — I'll —" His voice trailed off, sputtering.

Arriving at Raizel's door, her mother knocked softly.

No answer. Her father started banging with both fists.

No answer.

Then the parents both knocked together, calling to Raizel to open the door. After a long time, they heard a faint voice.

"*Anyuka! Apuka!* Please stop ...," and they did.

Mr. Weiss shouted through the keyhole. "Come out and explain yourself, miss. I've never heard of such behavior."

"I'm very sorry, *Apuka*, but I'm not coming out 'til you promise me that I don't have to leave here, that I don't have to marry that — that foreigner!" Raizel spoke almost hysterically. She wished to avoid a confrontation with her parents, but she could not bear the thought of leaving her familiar home, and her fear overcame her usual *derech eretz*.

Husband and wife looked at each other in silence. They knew from previous experience that once Raizel made up her mind, she couldn't be budged — a good trait in many instances but now...!

"But what about the young man?" Mrs. Weiss whispered. Without talking, husband and wife had agreed that trying to persuade Raizel to change her mind would be useless.

"Maybe ... maybe Feigy?" It was a desperate croak from Mr. Weiss.

Their younger daughter was only 18, quiet and rather shy, but with an adventurous spirit. She was the only one in the family not scared of the big gander that frightened even the peasant housemaid. She was the one who went to watch the milking at the gentile farmer's stable, a task that the others hated because of the smells, as well as the many dogs one encountered on the way. She never followed the traditional embroidery patterns that all the other girls stitched, but designed her own fantasy flowers and leaves. Maybe … maybe ….

"Raizele? Come out and eat something." Her mother's voice was soothing, gentle.

"We won't talk to you about this any more, and you can go back to your room later if you want."

Her face blotchy from crying, Raizel emerged, not looking at her parents.

Shmiel nodded at his wife: "It's no use. Just let it go . . . and tell me when Feigy gets home. No — send her down to the store — I'll talk to her there." He slipped on his jacket and left.

Mrs. Weiss rolled out a fresh batch of yeast dough. She had just taken the first pan of coffeecake out of the oven when Feigy breezed in.

"Feigy, *Apuka* wants you to go to the store. Take along some of this *kokosh* cake — he likes a little *nosh* in the afternoon — and fix your hair! Isn't it time you got rid of those braids? They make you look like you're 15."

"Mama, I don't want to look older — I'd rather run and jump and have a good time. Wouldn't I look funny, chasing the geese with a big bird's nest piled on my head?"

Feigy made a neat package of the fragrant slices of cake, threw a kiss to her mother and ran out the door.

"Always running, doesn't care how she looks . . . chasing geese! No, it's impossible!" Mrs. Weiss turned back to the big, black wood range — another pan of yeast cake was ready to be taken out.

Mr. Weiss was pacing up and down nervously, hands clasped behind his back, when Feigy entered.

"Ah — *Anyu* sent *kokosh* — good! Here — let's go in the back — I hardly ever get a chance to talk to you, Feigele."

Father and daughter sat on a long wooden bench piled

high at one end with bolts of fabric, munching the fresh cake. Mr. Weiss didn't know how to begin.

Finally he said, "Feigele, how would you like to go to Vienna with me? You've never been ...."

"Oh, *Apu*. I've always wanted to go! The lights and the automobiles and the trolleys and all the people! Do you really mean it? And when, and why?"

"When? Soon, very soon — probably one day next week, *be'ezras Hashem*. And why? Well ... you see ... there's a very fine young man who'll be coming to Vienna then. He's good and kind, a *talmid chacham*, from a very good family in Eretz Yisrael and he knows many languages, and you know ...." Mr. Weiss couldn't bring himself to say the words, but Feigy, ever perceptive, didn't need to have it spelled out for her.

"*Apu* — you want me to meet him? And maybe ... get married to him? But what about Raizel? She's older ...."

"Never mind — I'm asking you — are you interested?"

"But *Apu* — does he know Hungarian? I won't even be able to talk to him, though I'd love to see Palestine; I read so much about it and you have all those pictures and the pressed flowers in the album. But still . . . it's so far away, and how could we talk? He'll laugh at me."

"Feigy, I'll teach you all the Yiddish you have to know. Just say that you're willing to meet him, and I'll take care of the rest." Mr. Weiss was mopping his brow, although the back of the store was dark and cool.

"Yes, I'm willing." The answer came too quickly to suit Mr. Weiss.

"Feigele, please understand — it's not just spending a few days in Vienna. If you like each other, it's leaving home, it's marriage, children, responsibility. This is serious!"

"I know, *Apuka*, and I am taking it seriously. Yes, I'm willing!"

Father and daughter sat opposite each other in the otherwise empty first-class compartment. Mr. Weiss had paid the higher fare so as to have privacy and quiet; his usual second-class ticket entitled one to a noisy and crowded space for the long trip, and the third class — peasants with baskets full of salami and garlic, squalling babies, and squawking chickens. He had made the right choice, and did not regret the extra money. It would enable him to concentrate, to accomplish twice as much on the long journey.

The Yiddish lessons were proceeding slowly. Counting on his fingers, Mr. Weiss enunciated clearly: "*Ayns, tzvay, dray, feer* — that's one, two, three, four."

Feigy repeated after him, with a heavy Hungarian accent, "*Ayenz, tzavay, daray, feeyer* — good, *Apu*?"

"Well — pretty good. Now say *finnef, zeks …*," and so it continued — numbers, colors, names, with Feigy taking notes in her small diary. Finally, she fell asleep, still murmuring, "*Yah, nayen, shvartz, vayes, zibben, acht, nayen, tzayen.*"

Vienna appeared dazzling to the young country girl. The crowds, the bright lights, the cars and trolleys, the multi-storied buildings — her little town consisted of low houses, some roofed with straw, with horse-drawn coaches for the wealthy, and heavy wagons pulled by oxen for the peasants.

"Will it be like this in Eretz Yisrael, Papa? Oh, I can't wait!"

"No, my dear, quite, quite different. But beautiful in its own way. I am sure that you will love it — every Jew loves the land of his Fathers …. But now it's time to get ready." Looking at his pocket watch, Mr. Weiss remembered, "I heard he's very punctual."

Feigy sat stiffly in her chair, careful not to disturb the

pleats of her skirt. Her long hair had been pinned up fashionably by Aunt Montzy, and she felt quite grown-up.

If the young man, Nosson Herman, was surprised at hearing the name Feigy instead of Raizel, and at seeing the very youthful appearance of the "intended," he did not let on! The conversation proceeded smoothly on his part, but Feigy had trouble remembering the right expressions. She spoke slowly, pausing often, with lots of "*yoys*" and "*eezehs*" thrown in.

Speaking formally in the third person, Nosson asked, "And what might be the age of the young lady?"

Thinking long and hard between each word, Feigy answered, "Vell ... by mine lest birtday, I vass ollreddy aydyvun!" She had meant to say 18, but ....

This broke the ice, and a very animated conversation ensued, held in several languages. The young people quickly came to an understanding, and within a week an engagement was announced, followed by a lovely wedding back home in Kopolny.

The newly-marrieds settled in Tel Aviv, which was then just beginning what would eventually be its phenomenal growth. Just as her father had said, Nosson was a truly good man — learned and kind, concerned for others, a most devoted husband and father. Together, they raised a fine family of sabras, without the prickliness, only the sweetness.

To Feigy, the greatest reward for her youthful courage was being able to rescue her entire family, including sister Raizel with her husband and children, from the horrors of the Holocaust, and bring them safely to her beloved Eretz Yisrael.

She will soon celebrate her *real* 81st birthday, surrounded by dozens of children, grandchildren, and great-grandchildren. The congratulations will be expressed in fluent Yiddish and Hebrew, even English — but not in Hungarian.

Queen Victoria and the Rabbi

V ICTORIA, QUEEN OF THE BRITISH EMPIRE, HAD good reason to be grateful to Nathan Adler, who was rabbi of a *shul* in Hanau (Hanover), where the queen had come to visit. Her husband, Prince Consort Albert, was from the duchy of Saxe Coburg Gotha, and her own ancestors had originated in Hanover. The royal couple had arrived there for a vacation before the expected birth of their first child, when suddenly, labor began two months earlier than expected.

The great Jewish *shtadlan,* Moshe Montefiore, a financial advisor to the British government, came to the Court at Hanover at that crucial moment. The doctors and members of the Court were at their wit's end — if the child would be born on German soil, his succession to the throne might be in question, since he would be considered a German citizen and would not be eligible for the crown.

That afternoon, Moshe Montefiore went to *daven* in the *shul* of Rav Nathan Adler, and received a tremendous welcome — not because of his great wealth, but because of his great benevolence to his Jewish brethren all over the world. After prayers, he told Rav Adler about the royal dilemma. It was getting late ....

Rav Adler suggested that the Queen be brought immediately to an English ship, which should then travel out three kilometers from the German shore to international waters. A child born on the British ship would be regarded as having been born on English soil.

Sir Moses quickly relayed this advice to the Court, and Queen Victoria was rushed to the famous British warship, the *Arc Royal*, which was nearby. That night, she gave birth to a son. He duly became known later (much later, since the Queen ruled until her death at the venerable age of 82) as King Edward VII.

A sticky situation was averted by the ingenious rabbi of Hanover, and the Queen did not forget that.

During her long reign, England's glory was at its greatest. "The sun never sets on the British Empire" was truly said, since it shone constantly on some part of England and its possessions — Canada, Australia, New Zealand, India, the African colonies ....

Years later, Queen Victoria's attention was directed to an announcement issued by the Dukes Place *shul* in London, requesting applications to be submitted for the prestigious position of rabbi there. This was publicized internationally, and many renowned rabbanim applied, including Rabbi Samson Raphael Hirsch and others.

The Queen sent a note to the synagogue, stating, "Since Rabbi Adler saved me when I was in trouble, he will certainly be the right guardian and leader for your congregation." And so it was.

When the Queen's advice was accepted and Rav Nathan Adler was chosen as the rabbi of the Dukes Place *shul*, she further suggested that this position was not enough — he should become Chief Rabbi of England, or better yet, of the British Empire! A bill was raised in Parliament in order to decide whether the Empire required a chief rabbi. When put to a vote, a substantial majority chose Rav Adler as Chief Rabbi of the British Empire, a post he filled with honor and distinction for 45 years.

Thus Queen Victoria repaid the good advice of the rabbi of Hanau. Her reign was an era of good feeling toward her Jewish subjects, who prospered and enjoyed more rights and freedom than any of their brethren in the European countries.

P.S. Sir Moses Montefiore, who had received the suggestion and passed it on to the Court, was a proud Jew, completely devoted to the A-mighty and to His people. He earned the respect of gentiles and the gratitude and love of Jews everywhere by his words and deeds, based on the Torah. How different from so many politicians who feel they can succeed only by blending with the mainstream! How good it would be if those who represent Jewry today would follow the example of the man about whom it was said at the time, "From Moses to Moses there was no one like Moses."

(From "THE ADLER FAMILY — ITS GENEALOGY; WITH SOME REMINISCES")

Paper read by Mr. Marcus N. Adler, at the Jewish Institute in London, on the 6th of June, 1909, on the occasion of the Jubilee of the Chief Rabbi. Reprinted from the *JEWISH CHRONICLE*.

"The story of Rabbi N. Adler and the Queen has been circulating in the Adler family but I also heard it from Rabbi Moishe Schneider *zt"l* during one of his *mussar schmuessen* long before I joined the family," writes HaRav Yitzchak Kaufman of B'nei Brak, who is married to a descendant of Rav Nathan Adler. He concludes, "Today, in B'nei Brak alone, there are over 300 *yungeleit*, descendants of the family, learning in local *kollelim* and yeshivos. The patriarch of the family did a favor for the Queen, resulting in his emigration from Germany to England, where he founded generations of Torah-true descendants devoted to a life of Torah and *avodas Hashem*."

A Tale of Tefillin

MAZEL TOV! YANKEL ROTH IS ALMOST 12 YEARS old!

So what's the *mazel tov*?

Why, he'll be Bar Mitzvah in only 13 more months! And it will be the first Bar Mitzvah in the family in years and years, so everyone is very excited. And what's the first thing you take care of when there's a Bar Mitzvah coming up? The *tefillin*, of course!

His parents had been looking forward to this occasion ever since Yankel was born; for the past year they had been inquiring about *tefillin*, and about the men who write them. The *tefillin* had to be very special for this very special boy, so his father, Lazer Roth, had contacted his friends in Jerusalem to find the most pious, the most expert *sofer* who would produce the perfect *tefillin*.

The whole family met to read, discuss, and analyze the reports, and the unanimous choice fell upon Reb Moishe Klavinsky, the chassid, who had been known as a *tzaddik* since his childhood. It was said that his letters were set like jewels upon the parchment, and that the great rabbis in Israel asked for his *mezuzos*. Yankel's parents were advised that *tefillin* from Reb Moishe's hand were a treasure, a sure inspiration for a future of Torah and *yiras Shamayim*. And the cost?

True, they were expensive, everyone agreed. But then — they were worth any price.

So Mr. Roth wrote to Reb Moishe, and requested *tefillin* for his *bechor*, to be ready in a year. As for the cost, he did not even ask — he was ready to pay it, no matter how great it might be.

Soon there came a reply from Reb Moishe. "Yes, he would be glad to make the *tefillin*. They would be ready in six months, and the price would be $1,000."

"A thousand dollars! How can we afford it?" said Mama Roth. But only a moment later, she had already figured out that by cutting some very sharp corners on the food bills, and economizing in various little ways that wouldn't show — not too much, anyway — they would manage. And in just six months, Uncle Raphael from Bnei Brak would be coming for his annual visit to the United States, and he would be able to pick up the *tefillin* from the *sofer* and bring them in ample time for the Bar Mitzvah. Perfect!

And so the order was sent, with a small deposit, and the family settled back to begin the preparations. Yankel studied more and longer hours — after all, he would soon be a Bar Mitzvah! And his *tefillin* were at this moment being written by the greatest *sofer* in Jerusalem! Twice a week, Yankel went to a special rebbi for instructions in *laining*. Alas — Yankel was not musical, but by dint of great effort and constant repetition, it seemed he would be able to read the portion creditably, and make his grandfather proud. *Zeide* always had wanted his son to *lain*; now, at least, he would have that *nachas* from his *einekel*.

So the months passed. Uncle Raphael came.

"Nu? So let's see the *tefillin*!" Papa Roth couldn't even wait until the visitor had set down his valise.

"Sorry — I went to Reb Moishe's place in Meah Shearim

— it took me half an hour to find it — but they weren't ready yet. Another couple of months, he told me."

That was a disappointment, but, as Mama said, "We still have another four months — that's ample time. And *Bobbe* will be able to finish the *tefillin zekel* without having to rush."

I forgot to mention that Yankel's grandmother had made a *tefillin* bag from the softest, richest, dark blue velvet. She had lined it with silk, and was embroidering it with gold thread. Little sister Shulie said, "*Bobbe*, it looks like the sky when Papa lets me stay up for *Havdalah*." And so it did — the gold threads sparkled like stars against the velvety background.

"Heavenly!" said big sister Hadassah.

Soon grandmother would start embroidering the full name — Gedaliah Yaakov Chaim Roth — so big a name for such a little boy! She had already drawn the letters with tailor's chalk in a perfect curve on the front of the bag, and Shulie came every day to check on *Bobbe's* progress.

So no one felt really bad about the delay in getting the *tefillin*, especially since Mr. Levy, their next-door neighbor, was going to Eretz Yisrael in a few weeks. He would be glad to take along the cash and pick up the *tefillin*.

But when Mr. Levy returned from his trip, he did not bring the *tefillin*. They still were not ready. "Next month," Reb Moishe had said.

"Well, that's still more than two months before ...," Papa tried to console Yankel. "No problem — my boss said he's going then. I'll ask him."

And Mr. Goldberg said that of course he would be glad to do this little favor for his valued employee.

Now the family was really busy with the Bar Mitzvah preparations. Mother baked dozens of cakes and hundreds of cookies. Father ordered schnapps and herring — "only from Klamm's — you know theirs is the best!" And Hadassah had shopped and shopped for the perfect Bar Mitzvah outfits for *Bobbe*, Shulie, and herself; mother was wearing her dress from the last family wedding. Yankel was almost letter perfect in his *Haftorah* — and his rebbi said that if he continued like this, he'd be able to *lain* on any Shabbos of the year. Yes, everything was coming along nicely.

Mr. Goldberg returned from Israel on Labor Day. On Tuesday, at 9 a.m., Mr. Roth was in his boss' office.

"And how was your trip, Mr. Goldberg? We missed you here!" he said.

"Fine, fine!" rumbled Mr. Goldberg, "Glad to be back!" And he told in great detail about all the places he had visited and all the meals he had eaten. Mr. Roth was embarrassed to ask about the *tefillin*, but since Mr. Goldberg didn't mention anything, he realized he had no choice.

"Er — Mr. G. — the *tefillin*?" Mr. Roth ventured.

"Oh, yes — in Batei Ungarin — this little kid with long *payos* came out and told me that his *zeide* said next month!" And Mr. Goldberg told Papa Roth all about an art gallery in Tzefas, and about a nursing home in Netanyah.

When Mr. Roth came home, he didn't have the heart to tell his wife. Instead, he got on the phone to find someone who would be going to Israel within the next month. But no luck — everyone had either just returned, or would be going in the spring or summer. Of course, Mrs. Roth soon found out — she had been counting the days even more anxiously than her husband — and she alerted her whole N'shei Chesed group to let her know about anyone going to Jerusalem in the next few weeks. No one was going.

Then came the phone call — long distance from Israel! It was Reb Moishe himself — he had been sick, unable to concentrate for a long time. But, *baruch Hashem*, he was well now, and had finished the *tefillin*.

"And I think they're the best I've ever made, with the help of the A-mighty," said Reb Moishe. "You must have a very fine son."

Tears came into Mr. Roth's eyes, "Yes, *baruch Hashem* .... We'll need someone to pick them up soon."

Now the whole family was making calls, using all the neighbors' telephones. The Bar Mitzvah would be in two weeks! Where, oh, where could a *sheliach* be found?

Finally, there was a ray of hope — and Shulie discovered it! Her friend Goldie was shopping in a grocery store with her mother, and the grocery man said that his brother-in-law, Morris B. Weinberg from Boro Park, was going to Jerusalem on Tuesday. He'd be back five days before the Bar Mitzvah.

Fortunately, there was only one Morris B. Weinberg in the Brooklyn directory, and he turned out to be a very kind, nice man. Yes, he'd gladly take the cash and pick up the *tefillin*.

"I consider it a *zechus* to have part in the *mitzvah*!" he said.

And so it was settled — the money was sent to Boro Park, and everyone heaved a sigh of relief.

Mr. Weinberg's trip was uneventful. On the last day, he went to Meah Shearim. The *tefillin* were ready — and they looked beautiful — perfect cubes, gleaming and black on the white tablecloth. Reb Moishe wrapped them lovingly, accepted the money and gave warm blessings to the Bar Mitzvah boy, to the whole Roth family, and especially to the kind *sheliach* who would deliver the *tefillin* in the nick of time.

Mr. Weinberg packed rapidly and neatly, placing the precious package in his own *tallis* bag, which he then locked in his attache case. He kept it with him on the airplane; the flight time passed quickly — he was looking forward to the pleasure of meeting the Roth family.

The plane arrived on time and made a perfect landing, and Mr. Weinberg was soon speeding home in a taxi. He received an enthusiastic welcome from his wife, children, and grandchildren, and settled back in his easy chair, ready to tell them all about his trip, when suddenly –

"The *tefillin*! I lost them! I left them at the airport!" And Mr. Weinberg remembered exactly where. He had put down his attache case to tip the porter; then he had picked up his two heavy suitcases and walked out of the terminal, leaving the briefcase on the floor next to the entrance.

"I'm going back to the airport right now! Yes, it's late, and yes, I'm exhausted, but I must go back!"

"But a thousand people passed by since then — it's surely gone by now!" said his wife.

"I can't help it — I've got to try, at least!" And Mr. Weinberg went out into the night, hailed a taxi, and was on his way.

"Please do me a favor — wait for me outside the entrance," Mr. Weinberg told the driver, having explained the reason for the trip. "If I find it, I'll be right out. If not, I'll have to fill out forms at the lost-and-found, and I'll have to stay there. But — just in case — promise that you'll wait. I'm too tired to go chasing another taxi."

"Sorry, sir — can't do it," said the driver, "I could lose my license — all the cabs have to take their turn in line. It's just not worth it."

And no matter how much Mr. Weinberg argued, and how much money he promised, the driver wouldn't budge.

"Well, I feel real bad for you. Tell you what I'll do — I'll take you to the nearest parking lot, and wait there for you as long as necessary." And Mr. Weinberg had to settle for that.

The only available space was in a parking lot that seemed miles away from the entrance. Mr. Weinberg was so tired he felt his feet wouldn't carry him back to the terminal, but he had no choice.

The taxi stopped at the edge of the lot, near an overflowing garbage can. As Mr. Weinberg opened the door of the car, he saw, there, on top of the mountain of trash, a maroon *tallis* bag, with his own initials on it. The *tefillin* were inside, intact.

(This is a true story that happened several years ago. Only the names and some minor details were changed. And Gedaliah Yaakov Chaim guards his *tefillin* like the apple of his eye.)

Night of Darkness, Day of Light

～～ Journey to Jeopardy

"**B**UT THESE MUST BE JEWISH CHILDREN!" Marguerite Cohen felt the angry whispers all around her. She clutched Judit more tightly, as if her sheltering arms could protect the frail little girl from the hostile looks of the German soldiers and Austrian travelers crowding around their table in the corner of the Bahnhof Restaurant. The three older children huddled down in their seats, trying to make themselves invisible. The staring, furious faces seemed like masks in a play — a tragedy whose end was not yet in sight, thought the young French woman.

Her French passport had brought her from the security of her comfortable home in Paris, and it was this same passport, Marguerite hoped and prayed, that would serve to protect her and her four young charges through this last and most dangerous stage of their journey. For the hundredth time she glanced at the children — 10-year-old Simchah Felsenburg, the oldest; Ilse and Solomon Schotten, a 6- and 5-year-old sister and brother; and Simchah's cousin, Judit Felsenburg, 2-and-a-half, whose deep brown eyes were filled with confusion and fear, and who whimpered softly, trying to hold back the tears, as she looked up at the strange woman's face.

It seemed impossible to Marguerite that only two days ago she had not known these children — these four who now seemed a part of her, whose lives she would defend at any cost.

The older children were quiet, whispering to each other occasionally, looking down at the breakfast set before them, pushing crumbs back and forth on the starched tablecloth.

Now Judit started to cry in earnest, and the faces of the Nazi officers changed from annoyed to threatening. Marguerite felt her throat constrict, as the blood rose to her cheeks — they mustn't stay there another moment!

"Schnell, kinder, esst auf! Hurry, children, finish eating!" she whispered. Obediently, the children picked up their *kaisersemmeln* and boiled eggs, but were unable to swallow. Marguerite approached the man who seemed to be in charge, an elderly veteran with a kind face. *"Bitte, gnaediger Herr —* is there a quiet room anywhere? I'm afraid my children might disturb your other customers ... and there's a rather long wait for the train to Paris. Perhaps we can stay in some other place until departure time?"

With a smile of understanding, the manager indicated a narrow door near the kitchen. The young mother rose, gathering the little group around her.

"Jacques, do you have all the things? The baby's bottle? Danielle, Phillipe — hold hands now — don't let go! Do we have any toy to stop Françoise from crying? I guess I'll just have to carry her and hope for the best." They followed the manager, happy to escape the glares of the antagonistic crowd.

The room assigned to them was small, full of dusty, discarded tables and chairs, but it was a safe haven from the storm outside. The clatter of pots and dishes from the kitchen covered Judit's crying, which had become hysterical by now; the older children, who had been warned not to talk in public lest their varied accents give them away, could speak freely now, and Marguerite would be able to give them instructions for the final, most hazardous part of the trip, without the danger of being overheard.

"Simchah, if anyone questions you, remember — you are Jacques Cohen, and you are only 9-and-a-half, not 10. Ilse, your name is Danielle, and you're 5-and-a-half and Phillipe is 4-and-a-half. The baby is Francoise, and she's 3. If they ask me why my children speak only German, not French, I'll say you've been staying with your relatives for so long that you've almost forgotten your French. But don't worry — I'll do all the talking. Just remember to call me *Maman* — that's the most important of all!"

"But Frau Cohen … I mean *Maman* … what if they want to know more, like Father's name, and his business, and the names of the relatives where we stayed, and things like that? I'm afraid I won't know what to say."

"Your Papa is Samuel, but everyone calls him Moulu, and he's a businessman. As for the other questions, I have a good idea: When the passport control people come into our compartment, you'll all pretend to be fast asleep. They won't ask Françoise anything — she's too young. And if she'll cry, all the better — they'll want to get it over with faster."

Simchah nodded — he understood. From the time she had picked them up, Marguerite had been amazed at the maturity far beyond their years displayed by these children. After all, they had never before seen this stranger who had appeared one day out of the blue, promising to take them back to their parents in France; yet, they had gone with her, saying goodbye to the relatives to whom they had become so close over the past year. There had been no whining, no crying — the children seemed to sense the danger that surrounded them, and avoided any behavior that might attract attention.

"Again — remember to call me *Maman* whenever you speak to me, but better, try not to speak at all. Does anyone have to go out? No? Good! It'll be better on the train. Just try to play quietly until the train signal."

Time went by slowly in the cluttered room. Games and songs were running short, and a feeling of fear and impatience took over. Marguerite was terribly anxious to get on that train to France, just to be able to sit and think for a few moments. So, well before the time of departure, she got up and, gathering the children and their bundles, headed back to the crowded terminal. The children marched silently before her, through the big waiting room toward the train tracks, again facing the furious stares of the people passing by.

"Jews! Jews! Jewish brats!" Yes, they did look Jewish, Marguerite thought, especially Simchah and Judit, with their big, dark eyes. But, even more — there was a look of pain and fear on their smooth, childish features that seemed to betray their origin to the hostile crowd around them, and infuriate them. "Jews! Jews! Dirty Jews!" The taunts went on and on.

After what seemed an endless walk, the small group reached the train, and — what a miracle! — boarded without being challenged. It was not yet scheduled to depart, but at least they were sheltered from the critical, curious eyes. Now, sitting quietly in the compartment, Marguerite began to pray — for the children and their parents, for herself, for her family in Paris, for all the Jews trapped in the Nazi inferno. The older children sat still and subdued, while Judit snuggled against Marguerite's shoulder, whimpering softly. Solomon was instructing his sister Ilse, "Your name is no more Ilse — now your name is Danielle. Don't forget — Danielle!"

The train started moving, finally, leaving this dreaded station of Vienna. Another miracle — no one came into their compartment! Holding the little one in her arms, Marguerite feigned sleep. The children played, and after some time, fell asleep sitting up, breathing softly to the rhythm of the *wagon-lits* speeding over the rails through Germany toward France.

Marguerite couldn't sleep. Now that she was so near her goal, a hundred fears and doubts assailed her. What if a child blurted out the wrong name or age? What if someone noticed that the descriptions of the children on her passport did not match their appearance? What if ...? A terrible apprehension overwhelmed her. What would happen to her own family if anything went wrong? Why, why had she taken this enormous risk?

"Ayn bereirah! — There is no choice!" That was the answer, and all her youthful experiences, her marriage to dear Moulu, their friendships, their life together, had brought her to this point. No — being the kind of person she was, she had not really chosen to do this — though she could have backed out at any point. This was a challenge she had to meet, a mission she must fulfill!

Marguerite's early life had been so calm, so simple and pleasant ... growing up in the small town of Mulhouse, Alsace-Lorraine, near the border of Germany and France; being raised with her brothers in a deeply religious family, playing with dozens of cousins and friends, helping her mother with household chores — the years seemed to flow by like a broad, peaceful stream.

And then her marriage, in 1928, to Shmuel "Moulu" Cohen, and moving to the capital city, Paris, a tremendous change from her quiet hometown. How gladly she had shared her husband's ambitions and ideas, and his large circle of friends! Their main goal had been to bring closer to the Jewish tradition those who had drifted away, of whom there were so many in pre-war France. How busy they had been, between all the meetings, shows, outings, and educational gatherings for young and old! Their *kiruv* organizations, B.L.E. and *Shema Yisrael,* had been large and vigorous, full of hope for great accomplishments. But by 1933, the coming of Hitler began to threaten French Jewry too, and the movements were swept away. Anti-Semitism was becoming apparent even in "tolerant" France — and there was much reason to be afraid.

Soon, frightening rumors spread from the Eastern European countries, and from those fortunate ones who had fled Germany betimes. But how could they possibly have imagined that the calm, orderly world they knew so well was about to collapse?

Only rumors at first — but then the rumors turned into facts, into a reality of horror beyond description. Streams of destitute refugees who had succeeded in escaping from this hell poured into the neighboring lands. What could one couple with five young children possibly do to help them?

And so it began. The task seemed overwhelming, but one has to start somewhere — and they had begun with a group of families who had escaped to Chelles, a suburb of Paris, after the Nazi invasion of Austria in 1938. Moulu had gone to Chelles often, supplying the refugees with food and clothing, meeting with French police on their behalf, obtaining documents, trying to improve conditions for these hapless emigrants. The Nazi noose was tightening every day ... what would happen to those families who had sent children to stay with relatives in Hungary and Czechoslovakia, to what seemed safety at the time?

These unfortunate parents had planned to establish themselves in France permanently, trusting the future, never suspecting that France, too, would be overrun by the German juggernaut. They were "stateless," without passports or documents; they could not travel, even within France, being restricted by the need for a *laissez-passer*. How could they possibly get their children and together leave France, where refugees would soon be gathered in French concentration camps?

Jewish organizations tried to arrange for the rescue of these children, but their success was limited. The parents were frantic — the situation became more dangerous every day.

Action had to be taken, and soon. "Our own five youngsters are safe and happy here with us in Paris. How can we not tremble at the danger threatening to swallow the children of our friends?" Marguerite had said to her husband late one night after his return from Chelles.

And so it was decided. The names of these four, who were close in age to her own children, would be written on Marguerite's passport, where only the mother's picture was required at the time. The children did not at all resemble the Cohens or each other, but — "No choice!" Moulu had whispered. "We have to try!"

Marguerite had left her brood in Paris in the care of Mme. Felsenburg, Judit's mother, who had become a close friend. Marguerite had boarded the train, a haze of tears obscuring her view, and pretended to be reading, with great interest, the French book on her lap. As soon as the train crossed the border, she began to feel the hostile atmosphere in Germany. In her compartment, the women talked with feverish excitement about the possible presence on the train of their beloved "Führer."

"What an honor, what a pleasure to be so near him!"

"And did you hear what happened in Vienna? Some Jewish children were thrown into the Donau River! Of course, they couldn't swim …."

"Oh, how I would have loved to see that! I would have cried with joy!"

"Plenty of lousy Jewish brats left there! You'll have an occasion, I'm certain." And so on and on ….

Marguerite trembled, turning the pages of her French book, apparently not understanding a word — but each one was clear to her and pierced her heart like a dagger. She felt her face flush and turn pale, tears rising in her eyes, yet she had to appear fascinated by the book in her hands, stolid, unaware of her companions' conversation. So it continued until Vienna, where she had to change trains for Czechoslovakia. Then — Bratislava, formerly Pressburg. The families and friends of the refugees had come to the house of her host, begging for news of their dear ones. But in this winter of 1939, what could she tell them? What hope and encouragement could she give, feeling as she did that eventually France too might fall prey to German might? She trembled as she approached the passport control at each border, but in fact there was no problem — her French passport still afforded some protection.

On to Hungary, to get the two younger children, and finally, finally boarding the train again in Bratislava with all four safely in tow, traveling on to Vienna, the last stage of the journey, but the one that Marguerite had dreaded the most. Again the loud, boisterous talk in German, the comings and goings of Nazi soldiers on the overcrowded trains, the curious looks and sneers at this young woman with her oddly assorted group.

Well, it was almost over now, Marguerite thought. Just a few more kilometers to the border. There had been long stops at German towns, with minute inspections of her passport — who would ever believe that these children, so different in appearance from each other, and from her, could all be hers? And what if …?

The children slept peacefully, huddling against each other. Finally, the train arrived at Kehl, a German town at the border, directly across from Strasbourg — and safety.

A perfunctory check of passports, and then — France! At last, at last they were in French territory! Marguerite, overwhelmed with joy and relief, embraced the children for the first time. The three oldest understood immediately the meaning of this spontaneous gesture! They were safe now, they would soon see their parents again!

They arrived at the Strasbourg station, where they had to change trains for Paris. Marguerite's uncle and her cousin, whom she had notified, were there, waiting for her. When she saw them, she burst into uncontrollable tears. The sudden release of tension was so great that she could only cry and cry. She stood in the center of that pressing crowd, with the confused children holding on to her, shaken by violent sobs, unable to walk another step.

Cousin Lily quickly took charge of the children, offering to take them to Paris, where their families eagerly awaited them; she also called Marguerite's parents in Mulhouse, and arranged for her to get there as soon as possible. When Marguerite at last glimpsed her father's radiant face, she knew she would find peace of mind again ... and the strength she would need to fight the battles still ahead. For now, it was enough that she had escaped the jaws of the beast, and brought the children to safety. Now she wanted only to sleep, to rest in the security of her childhood home.

After sleeping perhaps 24 hours, Marguerite awoke to a hearty breakfast and related the story of her mission to her shocked parents. Her mother then made her promise, against her will, never to take such a risk again. She had forfeited the reward she had promised herself — seeing the faces of the parents and the children at their reunion — but just thinking of that scene was reward enough.

(From *We Who Were Rescued* by Marguerite Cohen, adapted by M.L. Mashinsky)

～๑๛ Epilogue

Marguerite and Moulu Cohen, protected by their French citizenship, continued to defy the Nazis by arranging for the rescue and support of many more Jewish men, women, and children. Finally the Germans caught up with them; Moulu was arrested and dragged off to a concentration camp. The last message to his wife was: "I know where they are taking me. If I don't return, please marry again — I don't want you to be alone."

Marguerite, alone, continued her rescue activities throughout World War II, and survived with her five children; all of them are outstanding in their devotion to the A-mighty and to His people, carrying on their parents' work of returning errant Jews to the tradition of their forefathers.

Many years later, when one of the rescued children tried to offer some words of praise and gratitude to Marguerite Cohen, she said, "I deserve no credit — I really couldn't have done differently."

The Felsenburg and Schotten children were reunited with their parents, who owed a tremendous debt of gratitude to Mme. Cohen. After the end of World War II, they got in touch with her, and there was a sad-happy reunion of Mrs. Cohen and the Felsenburgs in the United States, with many tears shed by the participants. Sad — because Moulu was missing. Happy — because Mrs. Cohen and her children survived.

Many years later, Sarah and Mordechai Perlstein, the daughter and son-in-law of Judit, who had married Shamshon Moller, became close friends with a young couple, the Szmerlas, living in Lakewood. One day, Mr. Szmerla mentioned that his grandmother, Mrs. Cohen, was coming to the States. He then told the story of the rescued children, and said, "She saw the other children, but she never met Judit again. She'd love to see her."

Sarah Moller Perlstein had heard the story of the heroic rescue many times.

"Judit is my mother," she said.

But what happened to the Schotten children? The answers were vague.

"On a kibbutz somewhere ...."

"No, in business in Tel-Aviv ...."

"I think they remained in France."

No one really knew.

Leah, Judit's older sister, went to a niece's engagement party in Bnei Brak. She was seated next to a pleasant older woman, Mrs. Gross, and they struck up a conversation in Yiddish, their only common language.

"You have such a familiar, Viennese way of speaking," said Mrs. Gross. "What's your maiden name?"

"Felsenburg, and yes, I'm from Vienna."

Excited now, Mrs. Gross asked, "Do you know Simchah Felsenburg?"

"Of course — he's my cousin. And you — you must be Ilse Schotten!"

And so she was! Living on Moshav Yesodot for many years, she was the grandmother of the *chasan!*

Leah did not inquire about Solomon, Ilse's brother. One never knew — perhaps Solomon had eventually been caught by the Nazis, or the siblings had become estranged, or perhaps he had died .... No, better not to ask — the answer might be too painful.

A few days later, in Beersheva, Leah told her cousin Shoshanah, sister of Simchah Felsenburg, about the encounter in Bnei Brak.

"Strange you should mention that," Shoshanah said. "I just spoke to Solomon Schotten yesterday."

"What!"

"Yes! I wanted to order some old-fashioned featherbeds, and I called a manufacturer in Tel Aviv. He said my *ivrit* had a familiar accent, and I said, 'So does yours.' It was Solomon Schotten, and he's doing just fine!"

⤳ Mayim Chaim

Moishe Lev was number 58 on the winding line of men that stretched halfway across the muddy yard. He had dreamt about this moment for days now, and it seemed to him that it was taking forever. Good — another man came out of the booth after only three minutes; that meant that there were only 56 more whose turn would come before his.

Strange that everything still looked the same: the same stubbly, dreary field with the same gray barracks surrounding it, the same barbed-wire fences forming a double enclosure around the camp, the same guard towers, the same gaunt inmates in their ragged prison uniforms or in ridiculous castoff clothing that was either too small — or much too big, hanging from the emaciated bodies.

What was different now? The guard towers were empty: the SS men had escaped into the surrounding forest, taking every bit of food, usable clothing, and, worst of all, guns, ammunition, and grenades with them. Moishe was sure that they would return at night and kill him, along with everyone else. Hadn't they tried to do that for the past year-and-a-half, by starvation, by beatings, by heavy labor, by unending cruelty?

But he had survived. Of the 42 boys from his small town in Slovakia, only three were still alive. One, Yossi, was in the temporary hospital set up by the Americans for the typhus that afflicted half the camp, and Moshe would visit him later. The other two were on the line long after him. They had not been able to get up early enough, since they had eaten too much of the warm, heavy food provided by the Americans. Their shriveled stomachs could not tolerate a normal meal.

Only 47 more to go ….

So what made the difference? One word, that hoped-for, yearned-for, prayed-for word — Liberation! When the Americans had come, a week ago, they had found only skeletons — some living, some dead. They had brought food, drink, medicines, but it had been too late for Moishe's bunkmate, Reuven. The food to which he was unaccustomed had killed him. Of all the students who had come with him from Nitra, Reuven had been the closest. But at the end he had been a *musselman*, a walking zombie.

He had weighed 60 pounds, compared to Moishe's 78; they all knew what was in store for him. At least there had been a Jewish burial — the Klausenburger Rebbe had gathered those who could still walk to prepare graves for the *kedoshim*. And at least *Kaddish* would be said for Reuven and for the others.

The line in front of Moishe was getting shorter. Only 28 between him and his goal. The Americans had finished building these booths yesterday; they had been shocked when they discovered that the Nazis had destroyed the primitive plumbing when they had realized that the enemy troops were just a few miles away. So for the past seven days, the water in the camp was to be used only for drinking and cooking, since it was expensively delivered in metal tanks by army trucks. Now even the weekly basin of water supplied by the SS, which had to be shared by 10 people, was not available.

Moishe had always loved the water. As a child he had frolicked in the little pond near his house. How innocent he had been, knowing nothing of the evil to which human beings could descend.

He was only 17 now, but he felt like an old, old man. His arms and hands were thin sticks covered by grayish-white, torn skin, and two of his teeth had been knocked out by a Polish Kapo, but everyone looked like that — so what? At least they were alive.

Only 19 more to go ....

Soon, soon it would be his turn! He would stand under the cleansing shower, letting it wash away all the filth, all the fear, all the pain of the endless months since he had been dragged away from home. He would feel the clean, cool water running down, soothing his wounds, making him feel alive again.

Four more to go ....

Now! It was his turn at last. He lifted the curtain and entered the booth. But what was this? Another inmate had come in with him — an ugly, skinny, repulsive creature.

"Get out! I had to wait in line over three hours — get out

and wait your turn like the rest!" Moishe was very angry.

The person in the booth with him made strange gestures, mocking him, but he did not answer.

"Don't you hear me?" Moishe had been speaking in Yiddish. Now he tried Hungarian. No response. Slovak, broken German, even Rumanian — the queer person only moved his mouth and hands convulsively.

Back to Yiddish again, Moishe yelled, *"Aroys fin dannet, ober shoyn!"* and gave the ugly creature a mighty shove with both hands. His bony fingers almost broke from the sudden thrust — the face in the mirror was his own.

⟶ Rolling Wheels

The two brothers, Nathan and Moishe Feld, arrived at the Zurich train station after a harrowing journey from Paris. At every stop and several times between, they had had to show their *laissez-passer*, the documents issued to stateless Austrian and German refugees by the French authorities. Without them, one could not travel, even between towns, much less across borders.

The Swiss border guards eyed them suspiciously — maybe these Jews planned to stay in Switzerland, adding to the swelling numbers of desperate people entering the country, legally or illegally.

But the brothers had no such intention. Their task was far more difficult. Somehow they had to get Simon, Nathan's 14-year-old son out of Czechoslovakia and to safety in France.

Safety? The Germans, who had invaded Austria in the spring of 1938, and Czechoslovakia not long after, were now getting ready to grab Poland. It was only a matter of weeks, everyone knew that. And then — war! France and England had formed an alliance with hapless Poland. If that country should be attacked, her allies would be forced to declare war on

Germany. Where in all of Europe would a Jew find safety then?

Still, France had a powerful and well-equipped army, at least according to the government propaganda. Its people were protected by the mighty fortification of the Maginot Line. German troops would never be able to break through it, the French generals assured the nation. Yes, France meant safety. And somehow, a way had to be found to bring Simon safely out of Czechoslovakia and to France by way of neutral Switzerland. It was his last chance.

The brothers sat on a hard wooden bench in the railroad station, surrounded by the bustle of travelers, by colorful advertisements for every kind of merchandise, by the blaring of loudspeakers announcing arrivals and departures.

"Nathan, I can't believe how *normal* everything looks here. So prosperous, so calm, so ... so satisfied — don't they know what's happening just a few kilometers away?"

"They know, but they don't want to know." Nathan, the older, was a realist. He had been an Austrian soldier in the Great War. He had survived many battles and had come home safely in 1918, though his older brother, Naftali, had not. He had married and established a family, struggling through the Depression, which set many formerly prosperous citizens to begging in the streets. And a great epidemic of diphtheria in Vienna had swept away his precious little daughter, along with many other children.

Then — the *Anschluss*! The Nazis had entered Vienna triumphantly on the eve of the scheduled election. They met no resistance. Within a few hours, every house was flying the black-white-red swastika flag, although the National Socialist party had been outlawed in Austria. And life in *gemütliche*, comfortable Vienna became hell for its Jews.

The Feld brothers decided they must escape, anyhow, anywhere, just as long as it was out of doomed Austria.

The great Rav of Nitra, Rabbi Solomon Ungar, had advised them to send their children to Czechoslovakia or Hungary, where they had friends and relatives. The parents would then be able to cross the borders secretly, and once settled in France, they would be able to retrieve their children.

At the time, it had seemed a simple and practical plan. In France, the parents tried to contact people with offspring of the same age, gender, and general description as theirs. Using their passports, these French citizens would go to Czechoslavakia or Hungary to bring out the children of the refugees. Within a few weeks, or months at the most, parents and children would all be reunited in France. But now ....

Nathan had endured and overcome so many problems, so many matters of life and death. But now he had used all his contacts, exhausted all his resources, and saw no solution.

Moishe was thoughtful, as always. "Remember, Nathan, the younger children we were able to bring in on other people's passports. Until now, no picture was needed, only age, color of eyes and hair. But now they've got to have a photo on every passport, even of the children. So what do we do? We must find, and we will find, a boy of Simon's age who looks like him. Then we will arrange the passport, bring him here to Switzerland and somehow get him over the border."

Nathan grew more depressed with every word his brother said.

"Look, Moishe — Simon is not your regular 14-year-old! He's tall, looks much older, with dark eyes and thick black eyebrows same as mine, and you remember, he broke his nose when he fell down the steps on Franz Hochedlinger Gasse. So how do you think we'll ever find a boy who looks like him? And if we do, which is impossible, what do you think the parents will say? 'Here, Mr. Feld, please take my son's passport and smuggle in your son?' Hah! They could be arrested and sent to prison — nobody will take such a chance!"

But Moishe was not ready to give up.

"Didn't we bring in the other children? It wasn't easy, finding someone with a passport that matched, arranging the trip, paying and bribing to get them across the borders — but the *Aybishter* helped us every step of the way, and He'll help us now too. Let's get going — sitting here won't get us anywhere."

They walked down the immaculate streets of Zurich toward the house of one Yosef Rothschild, who had been recommended as always ready to help his fellow Jews.

No, not one of the legendary millionaire Rothschilds. R' Yosef was wealthy too, but his treasure consisted of a fine family, and of innumerable good deeds. The Felds had been assured that if anyone could help them, R' Yosef Rothschild was that man.

The brothers walked slowly. It was unfamiliar territory, and they were distracted by the weight of their worries. Occasionally they saw a man with a beard or a boy with *payos*; they were approaching the Jewish section. In Vienna, and in France too, such obviously Jewish individuals had become a rare species.

A tall youngster came toward them with that familiar, slightly stooped yeshivah boy lope. Nathan noticed him first.

"Look, Moishe — doesn't he resemble my Simon? Same height, same dark eyes and black eyebrows; even the nose, and the walk …."

"You're right! Now if we could find out who he is, and persuade his parents to make a passport for him and lend it to us …."

Moishe was so excited that Nathan felt he had to calm him down.

"You've got to be realistic. True, he looks like Simon, but you'll never get his parents to take such a chance. You know the Swiss are sticklers for correctness, and that's asking them to break the law. It's impossible!"

"Nothing is impossible if the Blessed Holy One wills it. We'll get Simon out of there one way or another, you'll see!" Moishe's voice was full of a confidence he did not really feel. He had no idea how this could be accomplished.

After many twists and turns, they arrived at the Rothschild home, a modest house on a side street. R' Yosef received them graciously, offering welcome refreshments.

"*Macht a brochoh*! Make a blessing here in my home, and may all Jews be blessed!"

The brothers had come in worried and downcast. Their host's hearty greeting and the warm food revived their wilted spirits. Nathan told Reb Yosef about his problem, ending with a heavy sigh.

Herr Rothschild stroked his beard, thinking. "Now let's see — he's 14. So he needs his own passport. Hmm — I have an idea."

He pulled a braided bell cord, and in a few moments the maid came in.

"Mitzi, please see if Judah is home, and tell him to come in here."

The hall door opened, and in walked the tall youngster they had encountered earlier on the way to Yosef Rothschild's home.

The two brothers looked at each other, awestruck.

"*Megalgelim zechus al yedei zakkai,*" said Moishe. "Hashem brings merit to those who are meritorious."

Only three weeks later, Nathan and Moishe Feld were again at the Zurich railway station. From the distance they heard the rumbling of the wheels, the hiss of the steam engine. The train slowed down gradually. And there, waving from the window of the first carriage, was Simon Feld.

‿ The Beginning of the End — 60 Years Ago

A factual report of the events of the infamous "Kristallnacht"

November 10, 1938
By Selig Schachnowitz
Translated and adapted from the German by M.L. Mashinsky

At 6 in the morning, Herr Bloch awoke from a restless sleep beset by nightmares. He opened the blinds, but the pale morning light was blocked by fog. There was something heavy and oppressive in the air of the street below, which was just beginning to come to life, that prevented him from shaking off the foreboding caused by his dreams.

Salo Bloch was a sober and realistic man who did not believe much in dreams. But today there were no facile natural explanations to remove the heaviness from his heart, the feeling of something dreadful about to happen. True, the paper he had read last night before going to sleep had brought news about the assassination in Paris and of the sinking condition of the victim. If he should die … the consequences here, in Germany, would be dreadful.[1]

Depressed though he was, he dressed rapidly. He had to get out, fast, before the rising waters cut off his last chance of escape.

For the past 30 years, Herr Bloch had taken the same 10-minute walk to the same synagogue, one of the most beautiful buildings in the ancient town, with its gray marble facade and picturesque gables and domes. He had taken the newspaper from the mailbox before he left, and there, at the top of the page, he found the item he feared: the name of the victim, with a cross next to it! So it was all over now, he thought.

---

1. On November 9, 1938, Herschel Grynszpan, a German Jew, assassinated the German envoy to France, von Rath. This action was the pretext for the vandalism and terrorism which followed.

Perhaps it would be wiser to stay inside today. Who knew what the rabble might do now? But the street was as usual today. In the bakery across the street, hands moved busily under the dim light, shaping the day's loaves and rolls. The little stationery store and the nearby tobacco shop were still tightly closed, and the Jewish greengrocer was unloading baskets of produce with his customary broad smile.

"Good morning, Herr Blumenrot, and how's it going?" Herr Bloch greeted him as he did every morning.

"And a very good morning to you," replied Blumenrot, rubbing his hands.

"Hard times we're having, troubled times. You probably read the paper already — do you think I should go to the market today? There's something scary in the air ...," and he laughed as if he had made a great joke.

A few more steps, and Herr Bloch heard the rattling of the milk cans stacked on the horse-drawn wagon of Blaufuchs, the Jewish milkman, a perpetually grouchy fellow, who was mumbling something into his beard as he poured the milk in a steady stream from the tilted can into the customer's waiting pot. Were his mutterings a commentary on the difficult conditions, or the beginning phrases of the morning prayers? One couldn't tell.

All around Herr Bloch, the town went about its usual activities — delivery boys sped by on their bicycles, carrying orders from the butchers and bakers; girls and women on the way to work in the factories jumped out of their way, throwing smiles and jokes at the nimble messengers. Trolley cars, with their lights still on, braked noisily, while cars and trucks tooted their horns. It was the usual morning clamor of the city, not different from any other day. Yet, there was something in the air — but perhaps it was only Herr Bloch's imagination? It seemed to him that he was still under the spell of last night's oppressive dreams. Suddenly, his thoughts were interrupted by the strident siren of a fire engine racing through the jumble of traffic, scattering pedestrians on all sides. Herr Bloch had reached the clock tower in the center of the city, whence the tree-lined promenade led to the synagogue.

"Where ya going, Jew?" someone shouted at him. "Dont'cha know your synagogue is burning?"

"Yeah, that's a great bonfire you're having," came another yell. Herr Bloch ignored the sneering remarks; hundreds of years of anti-Semitism had taught the Jewish population to appear deaf and dumb in the face of gentile jeers. He continued toward his goal, but a heavy iron chain blocked his way. Errand boys, factory workers, and even policemen stood by, idly watching the show, while more fire engines raced past from every direction.

Now Herr Bloch saw thick columns of smoke ascending from the dome, and drifting toward the promenade, with solitary sparks glittering like jewels against blackness. No one seemed to be concerned with him, but it was impossible to go any farther. Herr Bloch glimpsed the two "early birds" of the congregation leaving the scene; although they were old friends, and were walking next to each other, not a word was exchanged. When he hailed them, they did not reply. Quickly, he turned and began to make his way back home, meeting others silently hastening away from the conflagration. A solid, well-dressed woman spoke to him. "Nice times we're having, eh? So they're burning the synagogues now! Just because one man got killed over there by a crazy fellow, they want to kill everyone!"

Salo Bloch did not reply. She waited until he had opened his front door and gone in. "May G-d be with you!" she called out. He had never met her before, nor did he ever see her again.

Herr Bloch woke his wife and children. "When it's burning," he told them calmly, "it's better to get up."

"Where's the fire?"

"Everywhere! There's something evil in the air! May G-d

be with us!" Almost mechanically he repeated the last words of the unknown woman. He did not want to mention the worst of all, the burning synagogue.

Outside, the dawn had turned into full daylight. Traffic in the streets had increased, and masses of office workers and businessmen crowded the sidewalks. And still, fire engines rushed through the streets; police cars, one after another, seemingly without any order or direction, passed by the flaming edifice as if it were invisible.

Herr Bloch went to the telephone to call some friends. There was no answer to most of his attempts; occasionally some distraught, inarticulate voices whispered a few words, and then fell silent. Only sobs were heard at his next try. "Where is your husband?" he asked.

"Where all the men of the Jewish council are today — they came for him!" And quickly, frightened of the information that had been given, the telephone was hung up.

The coffeepot stood steaming on the table as always, the little rolls in their basket, the jam in its porcelain dish — all was as usual. Only the butter was missing — there hadn't been any for a long time. But no one felt like eating.

Now came a new disturbance. "No school today! Hurray! They told us to go home! Hurray!" Children's feet came pounding up the steps, their voices full of excitement and joy at this unexpected freedom.

The pale faces around the table stared at each other. "What's going to happen now?"

Nevertheless, Herr Bloch picked up his briefcase as he did every morning, and, out of long habit, prepared to go to work. "You'd better take a taxi today," his wife called to him.

The telephone rang. It was his manager, calling from the office, announcing that, by police order, all Jewish businesses were to remain closed. "And don't worry — the bookkeeper will bring the mail to your house."

Salo Bloch searched through his papers and pulled out the

family's passports. He had arrived in this German city more than 30 years ago, and had been quite successful, even honored; yet, he had kept his Swiss citizenship out of love for the country, its mountains, and its people. A sign which he had prepared years ago, certifying that the house was under the protection of the Swiss consulate, went up on the outside wall. The doorbell rang, sharp and loud. What now? But it was only the mailman, a small friendly person, who came up the steps to claim the foreign stamps for his collection.

Again a ring, but softer now, more careful: some friends had come at this unaccustomed hour, and, slightly embarrassed, refused offer of refreshments. They had been up early and had already eaten, they said. From behind the blinds, they could see that the few Jewish shops were closed and locked tightly. The greengrocer was hurriedly turning the key in the door, as if it were Friday afternoon. On both corners, agitated groups gathered in excited debate, but in between, the street lay deserted. Only the occasional ringing of the trolley bells, the roaring of fire engines, and the sirens of police cars broke the calm.

"Trr! Crash! Trr!" Suddenly a tremendous noise of shattering glass assaulted the ears of the terrified listeners. A furiously screaming mob was gathered on the sidewalk in front of the coffeehouse Markreich, which had become the gathering place of the Jewish middle class when the other establishments were closed to them. The owner was surrounded by a group of young thugs who pushed him out of the shop and threw him to the sidewalk. The vandals remaining in the coffeehouse hurled the trays of cakes and delicacies through the shattered windows. They overturned the enormous urns and howled with pleasure as the brewed coffee poured onto the sidewalk, with pieces of cake and pastries swimming in the thick liquid. "Again! Again!"

Policemen dashed by, ignoring the disturbance. A guard appeared and politely requested, "Please — no gathering here, no standing ...." No one listened, and the guardian of peace didn't seem to care at all.

Pogrom! For the first time, the dreadful word came to the lips of Herr Bloch and his fellow spectators. Kishinev, Chmelnicki, Petliura, Denekin — all those places and people somewhere in far-off Russia. The distant bloody images came to life, moved ever nearer and nearer.

"Close the shutters and gates!" Or, perhaps, better not—it might only incite the mob more and serve as identification of the terrified prisoners within. Orders and counterorders contradicted each other. "No one is to stand at the window!" "No one outside!" "Isn't that someone calling for help?" "Isn't that blood flowing over there?"

No, it was not blood, but a heap of ripe tomatoes which had been thrown out of Blumenrot's shop, and trampled into the gutter, mixed with apples, heads of cabbage, onions and beets. "A typical Jewish dish," someone called out, and the bystanders howled with laughter.

Now a stream of white mingled with the varicolored mess; rivers of milk came pouring out of Blaufuchs' dairy store, whose cans were emptied to the last drop onto the dusty sidewalk, eventually joining the ruined produce in the gutter.

Blumenrot wrung his hands. What had he ever done to deserve this? Whom had he ever harmed? He strictly adhered to all the laws, observed the Sabbath, did not fool or cheat anyone, and had friendly relations with everyone, including non-Jews. Why? What did they want from him?

And his poor customers, who'd have nothing to eat today! No fruit, no vegetables, nothing! There were such shortages anyway — how would they ever manage? Blumenrot loved his customers, far more than was warranted by his small profits. A nervous twitch pulled his features into a grimace which could be mistaken for a smile.

"Look at that Jew grinning, making fun of us!" The angry words were followed by a wild blow, and Blumenrot lay sprawled in the gutter, among his smashed vegetables.

"Now, clean it up Jew — clean up every bit of that mess — and do it fast!" Blumenrot obeyed in silence, his face never losing its customary expression of benign amusement.

Next door, books, papers, fountain pens, copy books and slates were hurled from the stationer's into the road. "The Talmud!" the crowd screamed as a thick volume hit the cobblestones. "Let's make a fire and burn the Talmud!" But a secret dread held them back. Instead, the windows were broken with a few quick blows, and more and more books went sailing into the filthy street.

Weinheimer, the owner of the small shop, was a great Talmudic scholar who used the many quiet hours in the store for his deep research into all the paths of the Torah. Just last night, in the pre-dawn hours, he had awakened his wife with the joyous cry, "Rivkah, I've got it!" having found an answer which reconciled all the contradictions he had found in the portion he was studying. This morning he had been on the way to prayers, carrying his *tallis* bag as usual, when he realized that it was impossible to go on. So he had donned his *tallis* and *tefillin* in a room adjacent to his store, and had begun the morning prayers with intense concentration. The screaming mob dragged him outside, still clad in his prayer vestments. "Hey, look at St. Paul!"

"Nah, he's Judas!" the crowd howled and jeered, and fists were raised, but — "Don't touch him! Let him collect all his junk — fast! Hurry up, Jew — get your papers and Talmud rags together!" And now Weinheimer lay stretched out in the gutter and, with his delicate scholar's hands scraped up splinters of glass, shreds of paper, and torn books. His neat gray beard swept the ground like a broom. The crowd went wild with excitement. "What a show! Just look at him!"

Weinheimer seemed not to hear or see the mob. His lips moved silently, "Rivkah, I've got it!" His eyes closed and he continued to work mechanically. He had probably been in the middle of the *"Shema"* when they dragged him out into the street, and he would have to start from the beginning now.

This is how the Jewish martyrs of ancient Rome must have appeared when they entered the arena, clad in their white prayer shawls, to do battle with wild animals.

An elderly gentleman with a gray goatee and the dignified air of an academician or a clergyman passed by, observed with disquiet the white-clad figure cowering in the gutter, and the mocking rabble pressing closer. "And you dare to call yourselves decent Germans?!" he murmured.

"Jew servant!" came the instant reply, along with threatening words and raised fists, causing the passerby to turn rather quickly into a side street, and to continue on his way at top speed.

From the house opposite, in which the Bloch family resided, there came a woman, dressed in apron and slippers; she was the custodian, often irritable and usually ready to scold anyone in sight. She never read the newspapers and was ignorant of current events, but when she witnessed the scene in the street, she began to scream hysterically.

"What do you want from that poor man, you hoodlums? There's no food to be had, and you just spoil and ruin everything!" She was unable to continue; a wild crowd surrounded her, belabored her with their fists, and dragged her by the hair to the nearest police station.

"Put her in jail, that rotten Jewess! She insulted our country and our party! Let her have it!" commanded the young fellows who had seized complete control of the streets.

The woman was in tears, wiping her eyes with a corner of her apron. When her captors had left, the policeman accompanied her to the corner and let her go, with a bit of fatherly advice: "Go home in some roundabout way, if you want to stay alive, my good woman. We all have to be careful now."

In Salo Bloch's home, the telephone shrilled. "Is that Salo Bloch? Report to the secret police immediately!"

"Does it have to be right away?"

"Immediately!"

Herr Bloch looked into the chalk-white faces of his family, and exerted every bit of control he could muster to appear calm, even attempting a little joke: "You know, my dears, this morning all the prominent people were taken away; it would be almost an insult if they left me out. Besides, the way things are going now, maybe it's safer, being held there. And anyway ...," he tapped his pocket where the Swiss passport rested, for his own and his family's reassurance. As an additional precaution, he pinned the Swiss coat-of-arms to his lapel.

After some telephone calls, he succeeded in getting a taxi. It was not advisable to go that long way on foot, and much less so to take the tram. The trip dragged on endlessly. In the center of the city, the main business artery was almost entirely blocked. Vans, cars, trucks, and trolleys were tangled in a tremendous traffic jam, and the screaming, tumultuous mob had entirely taken over the streets in a pagan celebration illuminated by a radiant fall sun. Small groups, armed with sticks, clubs, and iron bars, smashed windows and doors and threw valuable merchandise into the gutter, to the sound of inhuman howling and crazy laughter. Although the chauffeur guided the taxi skillfully through the dark masses, Herr Bloch dreaded being attacked by the vicious crowd. He breathed more easily when the cab finally turned into a quiet side street. Surely no one had ever been so eager to reach that place, whose motto, like that of the Spanish inquisition, was: "Whoever enters here seldom returns!"

The cab driver inquired if he should wait. No, thought Herr Bloch — it might take too long — perhaps a few months, or even years. He paid, and, gasping, mounted the broad stone staircase, which seemed to afford a certain security.

A smoothly courteous young employee greeted him

politely, asking to see his identification papers in order to set a legal process in motion. Would Herr Bloch be willing to sign this document, which would end the publication of the Jewish newspaper of which he had been the editor for the past 30 years?

Herr Bloch signed and was dismissed. The feeling of relief experienced by those who were able to leave that place did not materialize. How would he get home? The taxi was gone, and there were no others in sight. The porter barked: "This here's the Gestapo, and not a telephone booth!"

Slowly and painfully, Herr Bloch made his way to the nearest taxi stand. The driver of the first cab turned away, ignoring his polite request. Herr Bloch entered a small coffeehouse and asked to use the telephone. "Didn't you see the sign?" he was asked. On the way out, there it was: "Juden Unerwunscht! Jews not wanted!"

Now an old acquaintance crossed his path. It was a uniformed member of the city guards, who had often come to Herr Bloch's home, spouting political jokes and orations in favor of Jews. Only a few days ago, Herr Bloch had given him a generous tip, asking him not to tell any more political jokes.

"Could you possibly get me a taxi to take me home?" Herr Bloch inquired. The guard looked to the side, embarrassed and frightened. He was really awfully sorry — an urgent errand and so forth. "And anyway, the number 14 takes you almost to your house. Danger! Nah, not a bit! Silly young people having their fun, that's all!" The brave fellow spoke with his face averted, so no one would catch him speaking to a Jew.

Herr Bloch followed his advice and jumped into the overfull trolley car. It moved slowly down the streets, jingling its way through the congested Old City, the stage for a thousand years of tragic Jewish history, from the Crusades to the Fettmilch rebellion, to extortion, robbery, and murder. History seemed to be holding its breath here, before the thousand-headed monster that filled the plaza. The crowd was densest around the giant dome of the synagogue, which flamed like an enormous torch, throwing clouds of smoke and glowing sparks up against the autumn skies. Smoldering fumes, arising from other parts of the city, united with the dark columns mounting from the synagogue to cast a black pall which covered the city like a roof. People stood on fences, wagons, and chimneys to better observe the spectacle. Some young fellows daringly climbed to the uppermost branches to get a closer view.

A few people left the tram and Herr Bloch was able to squeeze himself onto the corner of a seat. Some of the people turned away from him, while others held a lively conversation of which he was the subject. An elegant lady murmured, "Well, it's quite understandable — they're taking vengeance, that's all!" No one replied.

Salo Bloch felt like a prisoner, but to get off here was tantamount to suicide. He only wanted to close his eyes and ears, but could not look away from the flames.

"The Roman legionnaires threw a torch through a window, and the Temple went up in flames." Here, the legionnaires were the firemen who trampled upon the ancient graves in the cemetery behind the synagogue, and directed fiercely hissing streams of water at — the outbuildings. The green dome shone and glittered under a crown of flames. Through the burned portal, he saw the Eternal Light shining dimly, trembling under the onslaught of the blaze. It flickered, was almost extinguished, but flared up with renewed vigor.

Finally, the tram began to move again. Soon it arrived at a coffeehouse which had been plundered that morning. There was nothing left to destroy, and the rabble had moved on to greener pastures. This might be a good place to get off, reflected Herr Bloch — the street was quiet, and in a few moments he would arrive at his own house.

A friend who lived outside the city hailed him, and asked him to accompany him a bit. "You shouldn't have come to town today, Herr Blumer," remarked Herr Bloch as they walked along.

"I didn't come for enjoyment, you can be sure of that," answered Herr Blumer. "We have an appointment at the American consulate in Stuttgart, and there are still some formalities to be taken care of here."

They had only gone a few steps when a boy on a bicycle approached them, weaving from one side of the street to the other, and nearly running over their feet. Suddenly they realized the purpose of this maneuver — for behind the novice cyclist loomed two giants in civilian dress, who were obviously members of the dreaded S.S., having removed their uniforms for this special mission.

"Another pair of Jewish swine!" bellowed one of them. An enormous hand grabbed Herr Bloch's collar. He pointed to the Swiss emblem for protection. "Who cares about that?" shouted his attacker in mounting fury. "You're a Jew, arent'cha?"

"Even worse — a foreign troublemaker!" yelled the other one. "We'll teach him to make trouble here!"

What happened after that seemed to Herr Bloch almost like a dream. He felt that he was flying a great distance, pursued by furies, high, high, into the clouds. After a while he fell, unconscious.

When Herr Bloch finally dragged himself up with his last remaining bit of strength, his head was splitting and he was not able to move his limbs properly. Otherwise, he felt no real pain. No blood had been shed, and there was no sign of external injuries. His hat was gone, as if it had escaped under its own power, and his eyeglasses were missing. The street was empty; the giants had disappeared, and there was no trace of his friend. He heard his name being called from an upstairs window, but with his nearsighted eyes he was not able to determine the source of the summons. Half-blind, he ran into the nearest gate. On the ground floor there was no sign of a *mezuzah*. The first floor — was that a Jewish name? Probably not. The nameplate on the second floor and the sign on the doorpost attested to Jews living there, but there was no answer to his repeated ringing. A door opened on the third floor, and a stocky man in a wagon driver's smock came down. "You can ring and knock as long as you like," he said. "Those people were taken to the border in the 'Polish action' ages ago."

"Are there Jews living upstairs?"

There, where the door was standing wide open, children were crying in panic: "Mama, did you hear? They're coming! They asked if we're Jews!"

A woman descended the stairs and called him by name. He was with his own people now, and was safe for the moment.

No questions were asked. He was guided to the couch, and given a sedative. An hour later, heavy footsteps ascended the staircase. The doorbell rang shrilly. The children ran to their mother, clutching her skirt. But it was the wagon driver, bearing the lost hat. The glasses were gone, he said. The proffered tip was refused with thanks. "Those fellows outside are hired thugs and arsonists. I can't take money just for doing my duty as a human being." Thus spoke the simple man, who all his life had dealt only with horses and heavy loads. He offered to find transportation for Herr Bloch, and when, after an hour he had succeeded in finding a cab, he sat protectively at the side of the exhausted passenger, to make sure he got home safely.

Soon the traffic came to a stop again. There was a smell of burning in the air. His *shul*, to which he had gone this morning, all unsuspecting, was still in flames. Salo Bloch closed his eyes, and only opened them when the car stopped in front of his house.

The entrance was blocked. A bunch of young fellows, with the jubilant encouragement of the crowd, was throwing the furniture and equipment of the photographer, Arnsberg, from the ground floor, into the street. The custodian, still in apron and house slippers, stood by, crying hopelessly. She dared do nothing more.

Arnsberg was the son of an old-time teacher, and had expected to follow the same profession. However, due to the changing times, and in line with his artistic inclination, he had started a photography business, which soon enabled him to support himself and bring a bride from his hometown. It seemed as if everyone needed to have a picture taken, whether for settling in Palestine, or emigrating to America, or to any corner of the world that would admit a hapless Jew — a visit to Arnsberg came first.

A baby boy had been born to the Arnsbergs after five years of marriage. The child cried loud and often, perhaps in protest against all the sad and worried faces that surrounded his cradle. And now, in barely ten minutes, all that Arnsberg had built up through years of unremitting toil lay smashed in the gutter. No equipment, no furnishings, no curtains and linens; also, no window panes, no doors, no table or beds.

Half-carrying Herr Bloch, the wagon-driver guided him through the howling mob, into the vestibule, and up the two flights of steps. The people were so engrossed by the spectacle downstairs that they barely noticed. And again the man refused to take any money.

Arriving home, Herr Bloch found much going on. The Arnsberg family, husband, wife and child, had taken refuge upstairs, together with Arnsberg's 80-year-old father. The friends who had come in the morning were still there. The infant, bedded on the sofa, cried constantly.

In their happiness at seeing their husband and father again, the Bloch family almost forgot his earlier summons. They wanted to know what had happened at the Gestapo, what they wanted from him. "It went pretty well," reported Herr Bloch, "except for a bit of trouble on the way home. The eyeglasses are ruined. But what difference does that make, when there's tons of broken glass lying all over? The hat got lost, but its back now, as you can see, and the head's intact, too. I guess I won't be able to lecture this Sunday — how can I, without using my hands?"

These jokes fell flat, and Herr Bloch tried another tack. "Well, let's get down to business now. It's time for dinner. You've surely made something good in honor of the day?" Herr Bloch knew he had to make some sort of beginning, or no one would think of eating. "And of course you'll all join us at the table!"

The long table, with all its leaves inserted, was quickly set with all the dishes and silverware in the house; and in what seemed like moments, a meal of potatoes and green beans appeared, thanks to Frau Bloch's forethought in shopping early in the morning at Blumenrot's. Silently, the guests spooned down the food, perhaps only in order not to shame their hostess. After a while, an almost cozy atmosphere began to pervade the room.

Suddenly, the phone rang.

"Who is it?"

"None of your business! It's your husband we want, immediately!"

"What do you need him for?"

"You'll find out soon! Where is the business and where is the private residence?"

A quick glance at her husband, and she remained silent. "What? You refuse to tell us?" a furious roar came over the receiver. "We'll find out anyway, and you'll regret you ever answered the phone!"

Husband and wife looked at each other in silence. Only a few hours ago, Herr Bloch had decided to remain; but now he realized they were on a rapidly sinking ship, and everyone who could had to save himself. While his wife and oldest daughter attempted to pack the most essential items, he went downstairs, leaving behind him — without a backward glance — the bookcases with the irreplaceable volumes and the small closet which held his Torah scroll. The pendulum clock which had accompanied him for 40 years through joy and sorrow struck 5.

From the home of a friend, Herr Bloch called the Swiss consul. "Do you know what's happening in town? And what do you propose to do to protect us?"

"You may give me your suggestions," answered the consul.

"I am not suggesting — I *demand* that an employee of the consulate pick us up from our home within half-an-hour and take us to the train, at our expense."

"It shall be done!"

When Herr Bloch and his family passed the border after midnight, the Friday morning newspapers were already proclaiming: "Pogroms in Germany! All synagogues burned! Mass arrests of Jews!"

Herr Bloch purchased some papers and found out that what he had experienced in 12 hours in his town had happened in much greater measure to hundreds of thousands of his co-religionists in all the towns of Germany and of the former Austria.

On Friday morning, new refugees arrived from all directions, and they began to realize that the destruction of that day was only a prologue. The real tragedy was beginning — Dachau and Buchenwald. The piles of shattered glass and ruined household goods were followed by piles of millions of broken bodies ... and broken hearts.

AUTHOR'S NOTE:

R' Selig Schachnowitz, editor of the *Israelit*, the famous weekly paper of European Orthodox Jewry for 30 years, wrote this story about himself. He would have been able to escape Germany long before, since he was a Swiss citizen, but he refused to do so and remained at his post until the last moment, in order to help his brethren trapped in Nazi Germany.

R' Selig was a constant source of help and encouragement to the refugees who were interned in Switzerland. Modest and self-effacing, he was a true hero of his time.

Never Say Never

SYLVIA WAS AN ONLY CHILD, AND CLAIRE WAS THE oldest of four. They had been friends, it seemed, forever. Well, not quite that long! They had played in one crib as babies, had started kindergarten together, had enjoyed the good teachers and endured the not-so-good ones through elementary school. Together, they had run away from their respective homes (their parents refused to let them stay up past 8:30 at age 11!) for one whole afternoon. When it got dark and they got hungry enough, they slunk home. The worst part was that no one had missed them, because they had neglected to leave the dramatic farewell notes they had composed in school during afternoon recess.

In high school, Sylvia moved across town, but that made no difference in their friendship, since they spent all day attending the same classes, and most afternoons and evenings in one another's homes, talking, laughing, nibbling, and occasionally doing homework — but always together.

After completing high school (graduation speech by local politician: "Your education is never finished. You young people, the hope of our great country, the hope of the future, you must keep learning, you must keep growing ...") they both looked for work, and to their immense satisfaction, found jobs located only five blocks apart — Claire as a girl Friday in a publisher's office, Sylvia as a dental assistant and secretary in her uncle's practice.

They met during lunch hour, consuming their sandwiches brought from home, sometimes even trading as they had done throughout their school years, laughing and talking as if they hadn't seen each other for a year. Actually, they often met at the bus stop in the morning, before work.

Until ... Sylvia shyly confessed to Claire that a nice young dentist had been mentioned to her by her uncle, who had met him on the first day of a convention. Sylvia and Sam were introduced at the final session, and met again a few days later.

"He's a *really* nice, smart, pleasant young man, and I think he's interested in me ... though he hasn't said anything ...," Sylvia related.

"So what makes you think he's interested?"

"Well, Uncle Morris told me yesterday that he asked lots of questions about my family, and that he's thinking of establishing his own office. And ... oh, I don't know. It's just a feeling I have."

Claire nodded her head judiciously. "You're right — it definitely looks like he's interested!"

The friends had each been dating for a while, but this was the first time that someone had appealed to either one — appealed enough to be taken seriously.

The next working day, Monday, the friends met again — they hadn't seen each other for four whole days. Sylvia was rather quiet and thoughtful, and Claire teased her, "Are you thinking about uppers or lowers? Molars or incisors? Or maybe about a certain young dentist?"

Sylvia blushed. "Well, he told Uncle Morris he'd like to meet my parents, and they said okay ... so *Motza'ei Shabbos* he came over, and he made a great impression. But I wonder — does he really like me, or is he looking for an experienced dental assistant? Okay, okay, Claire, you know I'm just joking!"

"You'd better be! How could he possibly help liking you? Do you really, really think he's serious?"

"Yes, I guess so — he wants me to meet his father, and … Oh, I'm sorry, Claire."

There was a moment of silence between the friends. Claire's father had died of a sudden heart attack only three months before; the wound was still fresh, very fresh, and Sylvia was afraid that the word "father" might have caused her friend added pain.

But if it did, Claire did not show it.

"Of course I miss Daddy terribly — we all do, and Mom most of all. He was always such a happy, cheerful person, joking and telling funny stories. The house is so quiet now — even Ellie and Lisa have stopped clowning around. But at least Sue is engaged, and we're so glad that Dad still lived to see it. No, Syl — there's no reason for you to feel bad, mentioning his father. Anyway, I'm sure they'll like you, and you them. Anyone would be thrilled to have you in their family."

"Thanks! But tell me, Claire, do you mind that Sue will be getting married before you? You're the oldest, you really should go first."

"No, not at all. I haven't yet met anyone that I really feel is right for me, so why should she wait? And Dad was so happy about the engagement, and we all like Dave. Mom says he's almost like a son."

A few weeks later Sam proposed and Syl accepted. The happiest girl at the wedding, aside from the bride, was Claire, her good and faithful friend. The friendship continued, became even closer, especially when Sam was drafted into the Army Medical Corps and sent to Vietnam.

Syl and Claire talked to each other almost as often as before, only the subjects changed.

Sylvia read to Claire the weekly letters she received from Sam, telling of his loneliness, his fear, but also of his daily triumphs — putting on *tefillin*, keeping kosher, even looking into a *sefer* occasionally between arduous hours at the field hospital where he was repairing shattered jaws, replacing lost teeth, and not only mending broken bones, but restoring hope and confidence to broken spirits.

Sylvia was proud of him, proud of his courage, his ability to separate his army life from his spiritual life.

"That's enough about Sam — tell me, anything new in your life?" Syl didn't want to pry, but her friend seemed abstracted, not as responsive as usual. "Claire?"

"I guess everyone has their worries, and mine seem so petty next to yours. You worry about Sam staying alive, coming back in one piece, and my mother worries why I'm not married yet. Every time I meet someone, she stays up until who knows when, and the moment I walk in it's, 'Nu? Did you like him? What did he say?' I wish I could say 'Great! Wonderful!' — but I can't. There's always something wrong, something off. Lately, I'm wondering if maybe there's something wrong with *me*."

"Oh, Claire — *you* are all right … it's just that the right one hasn't come along. But maybe — anyway, at the end of this letter, Sam mentions a nice young medic he works with, Joseph Keller, and he says he's a great guy, and just right for you –"

"Come on now!" Claire was laughing. "Sam thinks you're just about perfect, so naturally I must be the same, so his perfect friend is perfect for me! It's just silly — I know he means well, but he doesn't know me at all, so let's just forget it, okay?"

Sylvia was a little hurt — any idea of her husband's seemed wonderful to her — but she knew that trying to get her friend interested in an army doctor in a field hospital in 'Nam was — well, not very realistic. So she kept her peace.

Sam's letters kept coming — he was working hard, he had lost a little weight but was feeling fine, hoped the war would be over very soon, missed her terribly — and somewhere there was always a mention of his good friend, Joe Keller.

In his letters to Syl, Sam spoke so highly of Joe; he seemed just right for his wife's friend, Claire. "Shouldn't she at least write to him, out of simple *mentchlichkeit*?" Sam asked.

"Please tell Claire he doesn't have anyone — maybe she'd just send him a card or something. It would mean so much to him."

After many appeals, Claire relented. Sam had informed them that Joe's 27th birthday was coming up, and the coincidence was too much — hers was a week later — so she sent him a funny card, selected with much care: not too personal, but friendly.

Thus began a correspondence between Claire and Joe Keller — very tentative at first. Joe wrote about his lonely childhood. Having lost his mother at an early age, he had been placed with his grandparents; his father traveled all over the United States as a salesman for a coat and suit firm. *Bobbe* and *Zeide* had been good to him, but over-protective: He was not allowed to swim, or ride a bike, or stay up late.

When Joe was 16, his grandfather died, followed only a few months later by his grandmother. After the funeral, his father asked Joe to come live with him; he was getting too old for traveling and was ready to settle down.

Joe moved to the Bronx to share his father's tiny apartment. A new school, finding new friends … but the toughest part was that since his father had stopped traveling, he had lost interest in living. He was tired all the time; he refused to go out, even for a little walk or to shop. Running the house and taking care of his father became Joe's responsibility. For over a year, Joe had watched his father slowly deteriorating.

When he finally agreed to see a doctor, the diagnosis was devastating: The same fatal illness that had taken his mother was now destroying his father.

When it was all over, Joe was on his own. He had only one burning desire: to become a doctor, to battle the terrible disease that had robbed him of both parents. With enormous struggles, he had achieved his goal, but the scenario was different than he had planned: Now he was repairing shattered limbs in the jungles of Vietnam.

Claire continued her correspondence with Joseph Keller, but it was fitful. Sometimes weeks passed without a letter from Joe, and she worried a little then, but since most of her free time was taken up with meeting and going out with "fellows," as she thought of them, she didn't dwell on Joseph Keller. The pressure to marry became greater — after all, she was almost 28, and her youngest sister was engaged — but her lack of feelings and respect for the young men she was meeting prevented her from taking this major step with any of them.

The war was over! The boys, now battle-scarred men, were coming home!

Sam returned, with several medals, and was very happy to resume married life and his interrupted career. He begged Claire to meet his best friend Joe, but she refused.

"Look, Sam — as long as he was in the army, I felt I had to write to him, give him encouragement — after all, he was risking his life every day. It was the least I could do. But that's all over now, thank Heaven."

There was no budging the stubborn girl.

So it was all the more surprising when a letter addressed to Claire came from Joe Keller, who was in Cincinnati. He wrote that he was coming to New York for the following weekend. He wanted to meet Claire and her family, and of course his good buddy Sam.

Panic! It was Friday when the letter came — he was surely on his way already! There was no way to cancel the visit.

Claire was thoroughly angry. "That was a mean trick he played! Just because Sam and Syl nagged me so much to write to him … Mom, I just don't want to meet him. Maybe I should stay at Sue's while he's here?"

"You can't do that!" Claire's mother, usually so calm and softspoken, was visibly upset. "To hurt a person who went through so much already — Claire, you'll stay here and act pleasant and gracious to him, or … or …." Tears stood in her eyes, ready to spill over.

"Okay, Mom. But I'm telling you right now — don't expect me to go out with him or anything. Never!"

"I don't expect anything. Just don't shame him … or me."

Mother and daughter flew into action. They quickly arranged for a room for Joe in a nearby apartment building, since Sam and Syl lived in a two-room apartment on the other side of town, and for sister Sue and her husband Dave to come to Claire's mother for Shabbos. After all, there had to be a man in the house.

Joe's letter was discussed and analyzed at great length.

"See — he writes 'weekend.' Shouldn't it be 'Shabbos'? How religious can he be? And Dave better make *Kiddush* — Joe probably doesn't know how, and he'll be embarrassed."

Joe arrived an hour before Shabbos. Dave was delegated to keep him busy until it was time to go to *shul*. When the family sat down to eat, Dave asked Joe if he wanted to make his own *Kiddush*, but Joe politely declined. He did join in the Shabbos songs, singing the familiar melodies in a pleasant baritone.

Claire avoided both looking at and talking to Joe. She went to bed soon after dinner was over, pleading a headache.

The next morning, the two men went to *shul*. Home again,

and this time Joe made *Kiddush*. The meal passed pleasantly enough.

Afterward, having recited *Bircas HaMazon*, Joe turned to Claire, and in a cracking voice, said, "Miss — er — Claire, would you care to go for a little walk with me? The weather is beautiful."

Claire couldn't disagree with that. After a pleading look from her mother, she fetched her coat and she and Joe went out into the winter sunshine.

It turned out to be quite a long walk, and it was two hours or so before they returned to the house. Joe bade a polite farewell to Claire and her mother, who immediately asked her daughter, "Nu, Clairele, what do you think of him?" She barely listened to the answer. When had Claire ever liked any of her dates?

Claire's eyes were shining.

"Mom — if he wants me — he's all I could ever ask for — "

Just as Sam had predicted, Joe turned out to be *exactly* right for Claire, and she for him.

The dental practice is flourishing, but, as Sam says, "In case I ever run out of teeth to fix, I can always fix up some people with *shidduchim*."

All's Well

THE WELLNER HOUSE IN MONSEY WAS OVERFLOWING with excitement, redolent of delicious baking and cooking, noisy with telephone calls back and forth about what to pack, about traveling arrangements, and about predicted weather conditions this gray winter afternoon.

They were going to Lakewood, Mrs. Rochel Wellner and all nine children, to the Bar Mitzvah celebration of their cousin Yankel. It would also be a gathering of the tribe, since the numerous members of the Wellner family seldom had a chance to be together for a whole Shabbos.

The father, Avrohom, was already on the way to New Jersey. He worked in Manhattan, so it made no sense to go north to Monsey, and from there south to Lakewood. Rochel's nephew Berel, who had recently received his driver's license, was driving Rochel and the children to Lakewood in a big borrowed station wagon.

"Berel, are you sure you know the way? Did you get good directions? It's getting late, and if there's a lot of traffic we're in trouble."

Rochel was not exactly worried, but still — by the time the children came home from school, changed clothing, and helped to load the car — the timing might be tight; it's about two hours to Lakewood from Monsey.

"Don't worry so much, *Tante* Rochel. We'll get there with time to spare. Why did you prepare so much food anyway? And why not pack it now, before the kids come home?" Berel, a bachelor, had no idea of how things work in large families.

"I sure hope you're right, Berel. I'm taking food 'cause I don't want my sister Mindy to have to prepare so much, and I can't pack it until the kids come home. There's also a case of frozen meat that'll have to go in at the last minute. They'll have to hold the bags of challah and cake on their laps. Here they come — ready, get set, go!"

The car was loaded in record time. The children climbed in, little ones wedged between the older ones, with boxes, bags, and pots fitted into every nook and cranny, and off they went.

"Lakewood, here we come!"

The Wellners were bouncing up and down happily in their seats. No one noticed that the driver, instead of turning north and then south, had taken a direct route south — after all, Lakewood is in that direction, isn't it? Only when they came to a bridge with a big sign did they realize the error. There was nothing to do but turn around and go back almost to the beginning.

Now they followed what they thought was the correct route — and again wound up at that selfsame bridge!

This time a relative in Lakewood was called. He assured them that they could still make it in time. That was a relief; and they set out afresh, with only slightly dampened spirits.

The station wagon was rolling along smoothly when it began to snow — small, hesitant flakes at first, becoming fatter and fatter, falling faster and faster. The windshield wipers flailed back and forth, but it was soon difficult to see the road. The whirling snow obscured signs and landmarks, changing the landscape to a dazzling white sameness.

Berel kept checking the directions, but they gave no clue; they were completely lost on a strange highway, and the sky was turning dark. It seemed that they had been following the road for hours, without knowing where they were going. The car crawled along steadily, while the hands of the dashboard clock raced inexorably toward Shabbos. They couldn't possibly reach Lakewood in time.

One of the children noticed a sign above the highway: *Union City.*

"Ma, look! We know people there! Maybe we can get there before Shabbos."

They pulled off the highway at the Jersey City exit. At the first gas station, Mrs. Wellner jumped out to call her Monsey neighbor's daughter, in Union City, but the rude station attendant refused to allow her to use a phone book.

On to the next garage, whose owner graciously offered the Union City directory, but Bayla Enten was not listed. Half-an-hour until Shabbos ....

Would they have to spend the festive day in a roadside motel? A nightmare vision of being turned away — since she had no credit card and very little cash — flashed through Rochel's head. They would have to sleep in the car. Luckily, she did have food — but Shabbos!

Desperately, Rochel thumbed through the telephone book. She *knew* her friend's daughter lived in Union City, so why wasn't her name listed?

More frantic flipping of pages with trembling fingers. Maybe there would be a familiar name among the clergy listings.

There was. Suddenly the name Mandel, Rabbi David leaped before her eyes. But how could she ask this couple, with their own large family, to accommodate her crowd? But this was no time to speculate — only 15 minutes to Shabbos!

The telephone rang and rang. At last there was an answer! "Hello?"

"Hello? Hello?" Rochel's voice was a croak. "This is Mrs. Wellner from Monsey. We're stuck here in Jersey City, and we have no place to be for Shabbos. Could you — would you — ?" Her hands were shaking.

"Sure — come! Come right now!"

"But I'm here with nine children, and me, and the driver. How can you possibly have room ... and aren't you going to ask your wife?"

"I'm sure it's fine with her." The voice on the telephone sounded far away, as the man continued, "Union City is quite near. You can be here in a few minutes — here are the directions. I'm putting the *blech* on the stove and leaving the door open. I have to leave now, so — *a gutten Erev Shabbos!*"

Back into the car, zooming down the road, tensing at every red light — but they made it!

They came to a neat brick house with a small front yard. It was a funny feeling, coming into a strange house with no one home. The children streamed in, carrying bundles, bags, pots and jars. Berel brought in the heavy case of frozen meat. Rochel still had time to call her husband in Lakewood and assure him of their safety.

There were the candles in the polished silver candlesticks on the white tablecloth, with matches prepared. The kettle was on the stove and the fire was on; all Rochel had to do was to put the *challah* on the table and light the candles with a heartfelt blessing.

The children scurried around, stowing the food in the refrigerator and freezer, hanging up their clothing. They came bursting into the kitchen from the back rooms, sparkling with excitement.

"Ma, it's just like Goldilocks! Three little chairs, and a whole bunch of beds, all freshly made. It looks like they were just waiting for us!"

There was a hesitant tapping on the door. It was the lady who lived upstairs.

"Welcome, welcome! I'm Mrs. Nussberg, Henny Mandel's mother, and I'm so happy you made it in time! Please tell me if you need anything; we have plenty. And your driver with some of the boys can sleep upstairs — there's enough room for everyone."

"Mrs. Nussberg, we can't thank you enough. But tell me — why this empty house with all the beds? It's a miracle! We would have been sleeping in the car in Jersey City if not for your son-in-law!"

Mrs. Nussberg smiled. "Well, my daughter Henny is in the hospital in New York for a good and happy reason. Boy or girl? No, no, she's still waiting, but all is well, *a dank der Aybishter*. The children have been sent to friends, so when you called, my son-in-law *knew* it was *bashert* — he had an empty house, and you needed a place for Shabbos. Please just call me if you need me — I'm right upstairs."

Rochel plopped down on the recliner and gave herself up to its warmth and comfort. The boys had gone off to *shul* with Mr. Nussberg; the younger children happily explored the house, which was well-stocked with toys. The candles burned brightly on the table, spreading a radiance of Shabbos peace.

When Mr. Nussberg and his son-in-law, trailed by the Wellner boys, returned from *shul*, David Mandel told the Wellners, "You know, if you had called five minutes later, there would have been no answer. I had gone to the rebbe earlier today to ask whether I should stay with my wife in the hospital over Shabbos or remain here. The rebbe answered that I should stay here. 'Go home and prepare for Shabbos,' he told me, and then he said, '*Toldoseihem shel tzaddikim maasim tovim* .... The children of the righteous are their good deeds.' I wondered what he meant by that. Now I know."

The Wellners spent a delightful Shabbos in Union City. The chassidic fervor of the *davening*, the generous hospitality, and the friendliness they encountered all added up to a unique and inspiring experience.

True, they had missed the Bar Mitzvah, but they had seen the protecting Hand of G-d.

A few days later, the Wellners heard stunning news from Union City that spread through Monsey like wildfire: Henny Mandel, their absent hostess, had given birth to triplets and all was well.

"It seems the righteous are given multiple chances to do good deeds — and in this case, multiple offspring, as well," mused Rochel Wellner. "And how can we possibly thank them?"

After the excitement of the triplets' arrival had simmered down a bit, the Mandels received a beautiful, hand-made *birchas habayis* plaque, with multiple blessings, courtesy of the Wellners. It graces their dining-room wall to this very day.

Fraydeena

MONDAY, APRIL 2

"Hello? Is dis Mrs. Shain? Mrs. Faigy Shain? Good! Here is speaking Mrs. Elke Rubin. You vant to know if it's about 'Fishele and Fraidele'? No, it's about a grown-up girl. Her name? It's Fraydeena. Vat kind of a name is that? Vell, it's really Frayde Deena, but everybody calls her ...."

"Tell me, are you the same Mrs. Shain vat found a vonderful girl for my nephew, Heshy Brody? Sure, sure, and also for my neighbor's daughter, such a doll she is, Suri Grinbom. Yes, she already has three *kinderlach, ken ayin hara.*

"So listen, Mrs. Shain. I have a friend, Riftchu Kestenberg, she comes from my hometown, from Debrecen. You don't know vere is Debrecen? You vere never in Hungary? Oh, you vere born in America. Nu, I suppose there's *heimishe Yidden* in America too. Are you maybe related to the Shain vat used to have a carriage store in Williamsburg? My first carriage for my Yankele I bought there; I had it also for Chayele, Pehree, Hentchy and Avrumy, so cute they vere .... But then they came out with those fancy carriages, that it only lasted one kid, my Shmiely ....

"So listen, about my friend Riftchu, I know her from ven she went to school with me, almost 50 years, *ken ayin hara* — she has such a sweet *einekel,* a real doll! Oh, 18, maybe 19 .... Yes, very nice family. The father? He has a business from feathers on the East Side. Only the best goose down he handles .... He vouldn't touch that cheap duck and chicken garbage .... No, no, no! You should know the best feathers come from Hungary — vite like snow, soft like ... like a feather! They shouldn't tell you that Chinese stuff is just as good ....

"Oh, the girl — she's so sweet, not tall, more like a petite type. Dirty blonde .... No, no, she's a real *balebosteh*, so clean you never saw in your life. She already has a whole *oysshtafeering,* vith a gorgeous hope chest, vit feather quilts like you never saw in your life .... If you vould see those *shtuppgenz* in Debrecen — every goose is twice as big as the next one, and that *layber* and that *shmaltz* — mmm, mmm — vat a *mechayeh!*

"So the girl, her name is Frayde Deena after the Veiss *Neni.* She was from Grossvardein, also a relative of the Erlenboiger Rebbe. You never heard of him? Can't be — vy, people used to come to him from all over — Budapest, Debrecen, Munkacs ....

"Vat school? Vat school? I think Bais Yaakov, by Rebbetzen Kaplan, like my Hentchy .... Yes, very smart, a real good girl, the way she helps her mother, and she made already six Gobelins.

"You think you have a boy for her? Not very tall? That's okay, but you say you vouldn't talk a *shidduch* if you never saw the person? So what's the problem? You'll go see her! Yes — in her house after she comes home from work. It's a very good job, in the garment center. She's only four months vorking there, and already her boss gave her two raises. It's by her uncle Feivish, he's the president from the *shul,* Divrei Chaim Gemilas Chesed Anshei Ungarin ....

"So anyway, you vant to see her? So I'll give you the address, and you'll go after 6:30, and just ask for Fraydeena. *Zeit gezunt*! Bye-bye!"

TUESDAY, APRIL 3

"Shmuel? Where were you? What took you so long to answer the phone?

"Why I'm calling long distance in the middle of the day? Listen — I have to tell you what happened to me just now. It doesn't make sense! I just can't figure it out! Okay, okay, I'm getting to it already.

"You remember about Mrs. Rubin who called from Brooklyn yesterday about her friend's granddaughter? Yes — the one from Debrecen, with the feathers. She gave me the address and said I should go there and meet the girl after work. Well, I went there — it's a big apartment house — and just then a girl comes in the hall, very nice girl, and she sees me looking at the names on the mailboxes, and she asks could she help me. And just like that I ask her, 'Are you Fraydeena?' and she says yes! So I talk to her a couple of minutes and she makes a very good impression, and now I don't know what to do! I just don't know what to do!

"Shmuel — you don't see any problem? Well, if you'd see this girl, you'd know right away! I should stop talking all around the mountain and explain …. If you'd give me a chance to throw in a word already ….

"Remember I told you that Mrs. Rubin said this Fraydeena is petite and blondish, and you had that short Cohen boy in mind for her? Well, this girl from the hall has long black hair and she's much taller than me — without heels, even! So, Shmuel, what should I do?

"Of course it was the right house! And how many Fraydeenas can there be in the world? Maybe that Mrs. Rubin was playing a joke on me, but she acted so friendly, so *haymish*! And if I think she's an okay girl, you think you have a boy for her? Tall? I should call Mrs. Rubin and ask her? Shmuel, a *layben oif dine kop* — that's brilliant! You're a genius! I'll do it right now. Let's see — I have two quarters. That should be enough."

TUESDAY, APRIL 28

"Hello? Hello? Yes, this is Elke Rubin. Oh, hello, Mrs. Shain! Don't tell me you already found a nice boy for my friend Riftchu's *einekel*. So they can meet in my house, it's more quiet here, and all the neighbors don't have to see .... The *tellerbrechen* from the engagement should be in the hall from the Anshei Ungarin. Then, for the vedding ....

"You're calling about something else? So listen, as long as you're on the phone already, I'll tell you about Fraydeena's cousin, she doesn't have a father or a mother, *nebbach* .... It's a big *mitzvah* .... Yes, she also needs a *shidduch*. Oy, was that a sad story! The father, he had such a good business, ladies' dress trimmings, all imported ... From Hungary? How did you guess? So he was delivering in his van, and a *shikker* hit him. That was the end, and the poor mama, from all the aggravation she had a heart attack.

"So what happened to the *kinderlach,* Mirel and Shloimie and Fraydeena? Well, they moved in the same house like Riftchu, but upstairs in a different apartment. Imagine, two Fraydeenas in one building! Oy, that Riftchu, she's such a good Bubbie, she's like a mother to them. You want to know if that nice Fraydeena is tall with long black hair? How did you know that? Are you a *novi*? Oy, she's such a doll also, so sweet, so *geshikt* ... You think you have a *shidduch* for her too? A tall boy? *Gebensht zolt eer zein.*"

MONDAY, MAY 18

"Mrs. Shain? This is Fraydeena. I want to thank you very much again for introducing me to Dudu Feiner. Yes, we met a few times already, and he seems very nice. Yes, I agree, but ....

No, there's no problem really — he's a gentleman, always very polite and his family seems nice too, but ....

"Well, I don't know how to explain it exactly, but after we went out last time, he told me that he feels he knows all about me already, and now he wants me to know him better, and he started telling me all the things about himself that I didn't know. Like what? Well, he's a smoker, and I hate smoking. He drives too fast, he likes to joke around and he'll do anything for a laugh, he's impulsive — and a whole lot of other things like that. So now I don't know what to do.

"All right, all right, I'll stop crying. It's just that — well, everything was coming along so nicely, and I was really hoping that he's the right one, and then he tells me all those things about himself.

"Oh, you think that's a good sign, even a sign of character? Where would I ever find such an honest boy who tells the *emes* about himself, who's so open and doesn't hide anything? You know, Mrs. Shain, you may be right. I went out with a few boys already, and some of them were always showing off how great and perfect they were.

"You're so right, Mrs. Shain — honesty is the best policy, and Dudu Feiner is the most honest boy I ever met. Oh, Mrs. Shain, thank you! Thank you! Thank you!"

TUESDAY, JUNE 2
Dudu Feiner to a friend in Brooklyn:
"Yossi? It's Dudu. I just came back from Israel. Yeah, I was in the middle of a *shidduch*, and no, my mother didn't want me to go — she almost flipped, but I was never in Israel, and Abie Kramer was going, and the fare was low, and you know me — I just got in the mood, so I went.

"Anyway, in Jerusalem we meet up with Shimshy Kornfeld. He's learning there a few years, and he got involved in following *mekubalim,* you know, going to those people in

Meah Shearim that can tell you all about yourself. So just for kicks, we both went with him, Abie and me. You know I don't go for that stuff, and neither does Abie. Yeah, like I said, just for kicks.

"So first Shimshy takes us to a rabbi who does everything by names and numbers. I tell him I'm seeing a girl, so he says her father's number has to match her mother's and the same for my parents, and then they have to match hers, and my parent's number has to match mine, and then our two numbers have to match each other. Of course I didn't know her parents' Hebrew names, but I found out, and guess what? Everything matched the way it was supposed to, so he gives me permission to go ahead and marry her.

"The next one was even weirder. We go up these narrow stairs to the top floor somewhere in Meah Shearim, and there's a very old man sitting by a table with an old *sefer* in front of him. He studies me carefully and then he starts telling me my whole life story, but everything, even stuff I forgot. Then he starts with the numbers business, and I thought I'd fool him, so I gave him a different name. So he says, 'That yellow-haired girl? She's *bichlal* not for you!' Now how did he know that before I met Fraydeena I went out with a bright blonde for about one-and-a-half times? And then — listen to this! — he says, 'You will soon become engaged to a girl who will be very good for you.'

"So now I'm becoming a *chasan*. Tomorrow night I'm getting engaged to Fraydeena. You can come and wish us *mazel tov*!

"You want to know the name of that person and where he lives? This is the queerest part of all — I can't remember it, or the address, and neither can Shimshy and Abe. Isn't that weird?

"Yes, Yossi, if I ever do, I'll call you right away. Bye for now — see you tomorrow!"

WEDNESDAY, NOVEMBER 2

Yossi to Shimshy Kornfeld:

"Shim? This is Yossi. How you doing in the Holy City? Still learning? Great!

"Listen, Shimshy — I need a big favor from you. I went to Dudu's wedding last week. He married this tall dark girl with the funny name .... Anyway, at the wedding I was introduced to a very nice girl, sort of yellow hair, and I need to know about that *mekubel* you took Dudu to — yeah, the one that looks at your hand and tells you everything you want to know, and even what you don't. You know who I mean? You know, but you can't remember ... ?

"Shimshy — that's so weird! Can it be — that he doesn't *want* anyone to remember? That's how it seems to you too? Real weird!"

Fraydeena and Dudu moved to Jerusalem with their children several years ago. Whenever Dudu has occasion to be in Meah Shearim, he looks for the house with the twisting stairs, with the book-lined room at the top. But he hasn't found it — yet.

Learn While You Can

⁓ "Glass"

AARON GREW UP IN A VILLAGE SURROUNDED BY vineyards and orchards, by fields of grain and hay dotted with cows grazing in the sunshine. He remembers his early childhood as idyllic — many other little boys to play with and plenty of time to explore the hills, to swim and fish in the shallow ponds, to make whistles out of willow shoots, to run barefoot on the soft grass of early summer.

When he was a big boy of six, before he had even started school, his grandfather, the glazier, began to take him along on jobs. This was a great privilege — watching Grandpa deftly cutting the sheets of glass into neat straight pieces, fitting them into the wooden window frames — he hardly ever had to trim the glass because it was perfect the first time — then hammering in the little metal wedges that held the panes in place and, finally, shaping the putty into a neat border which would fasten the glass securely for years. Every step of the process was fascinating for little Aaron, and he begged his Grandpa to take him along on his out-of-town trips, two or three miles from the village.

One day he saw his Grandpa kneading a lump of clay — not the usual soft yellowish putty but a dark red, harder substance. Grandpa's powerful hands pushed and pulled at the mass, occasionally turning it over.

"What are you doing, Grampa?" Aaron asked. "That looks just like when Mama makes the dough for Shabbos, but it's such a queer color."

"Come with me and you'll see," Grandpa said. He loaded the small wagon with his tools, a sheet of heavy glass, and the lump of putty well wrapped in a large piece of oiled canvas. Aaron climbed up on the seat. Grandpa took the reins and the horse cantered along as if it knew the way.

They drove for what seemed to Aaron an eternity, until they came to a tall iron gate leading to an alley of chestnut trees. The gate was opened by a wizened old man hardly taller than Aaron himself, and they proceeded down the drive, finally arriving at a stately mansion, three stories high, with many large windows.

"Does a king live here?" Aaron asked. There were no kings in Hungary between the world wars, but he knew all about kings — hadn't he listened to countless stories of mighty rulers — King David, King Solomon — and of their palaces?

Grandpa smiled. "No — only Baron Nesterhazy, but he's almost like a king around here. No more talking now — let's get to work."

A servant conducted them to the site in the back of the house, facing the garden. There was a huge metal frame set in a wall of solid masonry, and the glass inside the frame was broken into jagged shards.

Grandpa put on his heavy leather gloves and removed the broken glass, saving the larger pieces, which might be used to mend the small windows in the village. He took a portion of the red putty and rolled it into long strips which he neatly fitted all around the iron frame. Then — careful now! — he lifted the large pane of glass and placed it precisely in the frame.

It was a perfect fit. More strips of putty were then applied on the inner side, smoothed and beveled with a special tool, and the window was complete, like new.

"Grampa, why didn't you put in nails like you always do?" Aaron asked too many questions, his mother always said.

"Well, you know you can't hammer nails into metal, so I mix this special putty with iron inside, and that will hold the glass maybe even better than nails."

Aaron filed away this bit of information in his mind, together with all the other important things occupying his thoughts — which field had a ripe watermelon, where to catch minnows, his very first day of school at the end of the endless summer.

Eleven years later. The scene is the Terezin concentration camp. Endless lines of skeletal figures dressed in rags shuffle forward at the command of the SS men, who stride arrogantly along the rows, delivering blows and kicks at random.

There are no children, no old people on these lines. They have already been selected — for death. Only those deemed capable of working are here, for another kind of selection: assignment to various kinds of labor in the camp. And woe to the one who has no trade, no profession, no experience — he will be told to go to the left, and they all know what that means.

Aaron is shivering with cold and fear. He is 17. All his years were spent in the *cheder* and then in the yeshivah. All his experience lies in the pages of the Talmud. He has never driven a car or a wagon or handled tools — what can he say?

Now it is Aaron's turn.

"What trade?" the SS Kommandant barks.

Aaron is silent. Suddenly he sees his grandfather's hands, kneading and kneading the red putty.

"I'm a glazier!"

"Ha — that's what you *claim* you are! We'll soon find out. Glass shop foreman, get over here!"

A grizzled veteran of the camp, one of the few over the age of 40, comes forward. He starts to question Aaron about glass.

"How do you fix a broken window?" asks the foreman.

"Well, first you clean out all the broken glass. Then you cut the new glass exactly and put the window in the frame. After it's in just right, you hammer in those little pieces of metal to hold it and then you put a rope of putty around it. In the end you make the putty smooth and tight, and clean it off the window," Aaron trailed off.

The SS officer is not satisfied. "Anyone who ever watched a window being put in would know that. Doesn't prove anything!"

So the glazing foreman asks, "Tell me, how do you repair a window with a metal frame?"

The Nazi guard grins, smug and triumphant.

Aaron croaks, "There's a special red putty — I don't know what it's called in German — that takes the place of nails when you work with metal."

The shop foreman snaps to attention: "Herr Oberkommandant, this inmate is a genuine glazier." And that is how Aaron's life was saved.

～ꙮ What a Doll!

Rechel was the oldest in her family and had much responsibility. Her father, like many others in those Depression years, had gone to America to seek a livelihood, leaving his wife and seven children behind until he would be able to earn enough to establish a home for them in the New World. When Mr. Sitner left, he thought it would take a few months, maybe a year, but times were hard in America, too. He sent money regularly, but it was not enough — the boys seemed to need new shoes almost every month, the girls needed clothing, there were books and school supplies to buy; food was expensive — whatever Papa sent was not enough.

So Rechel, at the age of 13, was apprenticed to a wig maker. She was bright and a fast learner, and soon was able to crochet the hair into the silk foundations just as well as the older, more experienced workers. Her mother was a skilled seamstress; between these two the family never lacked food. Only Father was missing, but they knew he was working steadily toward the goal of reuniting the family.

And then — disaster! The Nazi war machine had overrun Austria, Czechoslovakia, Poland, then Holland, Belgium, France — and wherever the German boots marched, Jews were crushed beneath them. Somehow, Hungary was spared until 1943. Some said it was Admiral Horthy who prevented a German takeover. But eventually the Hungarians too quite happily, became part of the juggernaut of destruction. Jews were pushed into ghettoes, starved, abused. Then came the Final Solution. Deportations proceeded at a rapid pace; the crematoria smoked day and night. Hungary would soon be *Judenrein.*

Rechel's family was lucky — they were taken to a working camp whose inmates assembled bullets for the German army. The work was hard, food was scarce — a piece of bread and watery soup were a day's ration. And if one got sick and could not work . . .!

Another stroke of good fortune — the farms in the area were short of labor; there was no one to plow, or plant, or pull weeds, or pick produce. So on Sundays, the camp inmates were "rented out" to the peasants to work in the fields. Rechel and her mother were assigned to a nearby farm whose owner was fighting the Russians on the Eastern Front. His wife was having a hard time managing alone and she welcomed her new helpers. When she found out that Mrs. Sitner could sew, she set her to mending and making over old garments while Rechel worked outside, stooping to pick the last of the season's beets, potatoes, and turnips from the hard earth. Sometimes she was able to keep a few items to bring to her little brothers and sister in the camp.

How lucky they were — Mother could be inside, out of the cold, and they had all that extra food! Indeed, a family to be envied!

The days grew shorter as winter set in. The cold weather, hunger, and disease reduced the ranks of the camp inmates, but Rechel could still look forward to Sundays and the extra food it provided.

One day, the farm woman complained bitterly "Here it is almost our holiday and I don't have anything to give my little Gertrud! She misses her father so much — he always brought her presents; and now all the stores are empty and there's nothing to buy. Ah, this war, this terrible war!"

Rechel and her mother looked at each other — they couldn't look at the woman. Then Rechel asked, "Didn't I see an old doll in the woodshed? Maybe Gertrud can still have a nice present."

Sure enough, there was a big battered doll with loose stuffing and a bald head thrown in a corner among the logs and kindling. Mother and daughter went to work. Mrs. Sitner neatly sewed all the rips in the doll's body and made her a magnificent dress from scraps of velvet and satin while Rechel knotted new hair into the doll's scalp. Finding hair was no problem — all the women in the camp were losing theirs as a result of starvation.

The doll now looked better than ever before. The farm woman was thrilled, and she gave them bread and potatoes, which they took back to the hungry children.

The news about the rehabilitation of the doll spread quickly, so Rechel and her mother were "lent" to other farm wives. They fixed dolls, they made and repaired clothing, and they received extra food which they could share with others. The family survived, and after the war, the father returned and brought them all together safely to America.

Rechel says that she subsequently had many good, high-paying jobs in exclusive wig salons, but what she earned for repairing that doll's wig was the very best pay she received in her whole life.

∽ The Right Words

Hannah was afraid. Her heart beat loudly — she was certain that the other applicants must hear it, but they all seemed absorbed in their own thoughts.

After all she had experienced in the last years — being torn away from parents and home, the ghetto, the *lager* — why should she be afraid now, afraid of a simple test in reading and translation? But her future, her entire life depended on it.

Hannah's life, until the Nazis came, had been calm and secure. Mama was a good housewife and loving mother, warm and protective toward her three teenage daughters. Papa was a *chazzan*, a cantor, and she was thrilled and proud when all the neighbors stood at the windows to listen to his sweet melodies on Friday nights. Hannah had often thought of writing down her father's songs in musical notation, but she never did; she would rather have a good time than spend so many hours with pen and ink and the ruled music sheets.

But the good time ended before it had truly begun, when the Germans, with the willing assistance of the local populace, began to round up Jewish men, women, and children, young and old, sick and healthy, and ship them off to so-called labor camps, where the final destination was ... the gas chamber.

A veil must be drawn over the horrors of that time. It is

enough to say that within a few months, 100,000 Hungarian Jews were killed, including Hannah's parents and her older sister. The period before and shortly after the Liberation was almost worse than what had gone before — the camp was ravaged by hunger and disease. Hannah's younger sister Blima, who had been with her through all the pain and terror, did not survive.

And her friends, girls from her hometown? Some had been "eliminated" almost immediately — they were too frail, deemed incapable of working; others, for taking an extra piece of bread or for hiding a tiny gold ring, the last reminder of parents and home, or for not running quickly enough, or just for the look on their faces — they were gone, gone forever.

Hannah's neighbors, Devoiry and Suri, who shared the splintery board they called a bed, decided to escape. Even being shot was better than the daily, hungry wait for death! They had begged Hannah to go with them, but she was afraid; the familiar horror seemed safer than the unknown. One night they were gone.

Afterwards she found out that the sisters had succeeded in breaking into an abandoned shack. They had hidden in the attic, and there they found a cache of wine and honey. They washed with the wine, and they ate the honey, rationed by the teaspoon. Thus they survived the few weeks until the Liberation.

Hannah still does not know how *she* survived. At the end, she was so weak that she could not get up for the *appel*, the daily roll call, even though she knew what that meant.

When the Americans came, it was as if the sun had suddenly risen in all its glory in the middle of the blackest night. The survivors were infused with new spirit, new hope. Hannah was sent to the hospital and there, with constant care, her body began to recover. But she could never recover what she had lost — her family, her friends, her home, her youthful innocence, her trust. She felt worn-out, ancient — and afraid.

What should she do now? She had no one to turn to, and no place to go.

The government of Sweden, in a humanitarian gesture, offered to take in refugee girls like Hannah, to nurse them back to health, and to give them homes and a semblance of normal life. Hannah accepted.

Life in the clean, bright northern country was beautiful, even more so after the filth and terror of the concentration camp. Kind faces, food to eat, a bed of her own to sleep in — but it was not enough for Hannah. She wanted to be among her own, to see Jewish faces and hear Jewish voices. That meant America. She had heard that a friend had gone there and married a boy *"fun der heim."* But to enter the United States, she needed an affidavit sent by someone who agreed to sponsor her and pledged to support her so that she would not become a burden on the state, something she had no intention of doing. Most of the girls had relatives to vouch for them, but Hannah was all alone. Wasn't it enough that she and the others like her were alive and safe in Sweden?

Rabbi Dr. Wolf Jacobson did not think so. He realized that life alone was not enough, that these girls must be brought to a religious environment, to have an opportunity for a Jewish life, for marriage, for rebuilding the homes they had lost. Here in Sweden there was no chance — most of the Jews were affiliated with the Reform movement, trying their best to assimilate. A few of the girls, lonely and bereft, found themselves attracted to the kind Swedish boys; some had even found gentile husbands.

Rav Jacobson contacted many organizations in Europe and America, begging them to take at least some of the girls, but the answers were negative:

"There is no money."

"We can't take the responsibility."

"How can these girls possibly fit in, with their different

languages and backgrounds and, worst of all, after their terrible experiences?"

Rabbi Baruch Kaplan of Bais Yaakov High School and Seminary, then based in the Williamsburg section of Brooklyn, replied: "Send me as many girls as you wish. We will arrange for student visas and we will care for them."

Hannah was one of that group. She was ecstatic — to be among Jews again at last!

But then a problem arose. The American consulate did not want to admit these foreigners so easily. "How can all these girls be considered students? Some are too young, some are too old. No — it's just a way of getting into the United States under false pretenses!" So — each prospective student must be tested as to her basic Hebrew knowledge. The test was to be administered by a member of the staff at the Swedish consulate.

Hannah trembled with fear as she waited for her turn. In her native town, Kleinverdan, the girls attended the local Jewish school, which had one hour of religious instruction every day as per government ordinance. She had learned the blessings and *Bircas HaMazon*, the *Shema* — that was the extent of her knowledge. How would she ever be able to pass? And if she didn't, would she be condemned to remain among non-Jews forever?

The secretary called, "Next! Hannah Gross!"

She entered. A dignified gentleman, a member of the consulate's staff, sat at a large table. He opened a thick black-covered book at random and covered the left side, containing the translation, with his hand.

"Read and translate this Hebrew sentence!" he commanded sternly.

Slowly and hesitantly at first, then with more confidence, she read:

"*B'tzeis Yisrael mi'Mitzrayim, bais Yaakov mei'am loez* ....
When Israel went out of Egypt, the house of Jacob from a nation of a foreign tongue ...."

That was the only *pasuk,* the only translation she had ever been taught back home, so many years ago, and that was the only question she was asked!

Hannah wanted to sing and dance with joy. She had survived physically through many miracles, but she credits her spiritual survival to those precious words memorized when she was a child.

Hannah Gross was accepted as a student in Bais Yaakov and was able to come to the United States, where she married and established a beautiful family. She remains forever thankful to Rav Jacobson and Rav Baruch Kaplan whose concern and caring saved her and so many others.

And every Yom Tov and Rosh Chodesh, she cries as well as smiles when the congregation recites these words in *Hallel*, giving praise to the Eternal Who allowed her to survive to this time.

"Learn while you are still young," grandmother used to say, "and remember everything. You never know when it will come in handy." Yes, you really never know. Remembering what they learned as children came in very handy for Aaron, Rechel and Hannah — in fact, it saved their lives!

A Chulent of "Coincidences"

Sometimes we encounter what seem to be a long string of "coincidences" in a short period of time; but a person whose eyes and mind are open will quickly realize that it is not coincidence at all, that even the smallest details of our daily lives are supervised by a Higher Power.

I T WAS AN EXTREMELY SHORT WINTER FRIDAY IN THE Mashinsky household. The telephone rang constantly as desperate people called about utility shut-offs, no food for Shabbos, no water, even eviction notices. Kupath Ezrah, the organization from which they were seeking help, was overdrawn at the bank because huge sums had been paid out during the previous weeks to *prevent* shut-offs. There simply was not enough money to cover the checks already issued. In between answering calls for help and sending out S.O.S. calls to shore up the K.E. account, I tried to clean, shop, cook, polish silver, and do the myriad *Erev Shabbos* tasks.

Finally the cooking was almost done, about three hours before Shabbos, when the phone rang with devastating news: Mr. Sam Nussbaum, the founder of Kupath Ezrah and my husband's 40-year partner in this charity organization, had passed away in a New Jersey hospital. Could we arrange to notify the community?

"Of course!" was the answer. Quickly the decks were cleared for action. Son Yossi rushed over to help. Telephone calls were made, a text for the announcements was written and printed, key people were notified.

Suddenly I remembered that I had not put up the *chulent*, and what is Shabbos without *chulent*? No problem — there were par-boiled beans in the freezer, I thought, and a can or two in the pantry. But there weren't any. Long ago, I had stocked up on this essential item, and somehow thought the supply would last forever. But all good things must come to an end, and now there wasn't a bean to be found.

My husband volunteered to go to the store.

"It's probably closed by now. I'll call Mazal upstairs, maybe she has some."

"They're Sephardim," said my husband. "They surely don't use beans for *chulent*. I'm going to the store."

"I'll call them anyway — you never know."

Sure enough, the answer was "yes" and the neighbor's little boy came down with two full bags of beans. I took out the one cup I needed and my husband took the rest upstairs. A moment later he returned with a big smile on his face, carrying the bags of beans.

"Mazal said she never uses them, and two minutes before you called, she didn't have a bean in the house. A friend had called in the morning, offering her the beans, but she had refused them. But a moment before you called, the friend came and dumped the beans on the table. 'Here, take them, they're yours,' she said. And now they're ours." So my good neighbor Mazal, who never ever uses them, supplied us with pea and pinto beans, just what I like to use for *chulent*.

~ Let There Be Light

The following week was a stressful one. The emotions of the *levayah* and the *shivah* week, the struggle of trying to meet the Kupath Ezrah obligations, calling possible donors to make up the shortfall — yes, a lot of *Tehillim* were said. Then came a ray of light: Rabbi Dr. Kram called to say that he wanted to introduce Kupath Ezrah to a wealthy possible donor. He would be coming to our home with the lady on Thursday at 8 p.m.

After rushing around to clear the supper dishes, arranging some Kupath Ezrah information on the dining-room table, and turning on hall and porch lights, I caught my breath; it was 8:10 already.

Suddenly, everything went pitch black. I looked out the window — the entire block was in darkness, including the streetlights.

I didn't bother calling the electric company, realizing that others would surely be doing that. My husband located the flashlight and with its help, we found candles and lit them.

Just then there was a knock at the front door. There, standing in the blackness, were Rabbi Kram and the guest. We all gathered around the table, which was lit by many candles, and presented the Kupath Ezrah case to the prospective door, Miss Simon.

"When did the lights go out?" was her first question.

"Just before you came."

"And why is Kupath Ezrah so short of funds? Does that happen often?" she asked.

"It's because people call Kupath Ezrah to keep their utilities from being turned off. We spent thousands of dollars in the last few months to keep the lights burning, and that's why the organization is in the present predicament," I said. "Sitting in the dark like this is quite cozy for a few minutes. But imagine being without light or heat, no washer or dryer, no refrigerator! And that's what people have to face every day when they can't pay their bills."

"Yes, to bring light into darkness — it would be a privilege to help!" said Miss Simon.

Just then the lights went on.

What was the cause of the blackout? Orange and Rockland Utilities wouldn't say. But we know!

P.S. On Friday, a few weeks later, a $250 check came from Miss Simon. Shortly after that, about two hours before Shabbos, a man came with an electric and gas bill of more than $1,000. He was embarrassed and apologetic.

"I don't expect you to pay that large an amount. But Orange and Rockland said that if I give them $250 today, they'll give me another week's time. By then, I'll get a pay check and will be able to cover it."

Thanks to you, Miss Simon, and to the One Above Who brought you to our door during that brief blackout — creating light.

‿ Wired

When I told my daughter-in-law in Jerusalem about these incidents, she responded with one of her own:

An elderly neighbor asked me to go to Bezek, Israel's telephone company, to exchange a broken phone for a new one. She also wanted a six-meter wire, not the curly kind, but the straight one that connects to the wall outlet. I knew that the office closes promptly at 4 and had planned to be there earlier, but a series of unforeseen events — a late bus, loads of traffic, getting off at the wrong stop — delayed me and I got there at 4:05. A miracle — the office was still open and they let me in! Another miracle — they politely exchanged the broken phone for a new one at no charge. But when I asked for the extra-long wire, the clerk just shrugged.

"Sorry, we don't carry that."

"But this old lady *must* have it. She has only one phone jack and she has to take the phone from room to room. She can't manage without the six-meter cord!"

"We don't carry that, I told you. And I can't even tell you where to get it. Too bad!"

I thought I detected a smirk on his face.

A woman working on a computer in the back suddenly piped up: "Ilan, we *do* have a six-meter wire. Don't you remember, just when you were going to close at 4, a woman came in to return an extra-long wire. There it is, in the corner under the counter!"

"Wow!" Ilan exclaimed. "*Mikreh!* What a coincidence! Here, take it for free. I guess it was meant for you."

"I guess it was," I answered, "but it's no coincidence. Those same letters — *reish, kuf, mem, hei* also spell *rak mei* Hashem — only through Hashem. That woman had to come in just as you were closing, so the office would be open a bit longer, and the wire would be here, waiting for me. How can you call this coincidence?"

The man listened with great interest. Was he convinced? I don't know, but when I left, he said, "You certainly gave me a lot to think about."

A Smelly Tale

I TOLD MY DAUGHTER SARAH A STORY ABOUT A SHY, insecure girl of whom everyone takes advantage. When a dead cat turns up in front of her house, people give her all kinds of advice on how to get rid of it, but to no avail. Finally she disposes of it herself, and is rewarded with a tremendous feeling of power, enabling her to overcome problems that had plagued her for a long time.

"Ma, what an unbelievable coincidence!" said Sarah. "Almost the same thing happened to me last week, but it was a dead skunk!"

"There are skunks in Lakewood, dead or alive?" I was surprised.

"Yes, indeed. And this one picked the worst possible time and place to expire. It was the morning of the big cornerstone-laying ceremony here, and the street across from us was going to be roped off to accommodate the overflow crowd. When I sent the children off to school, I noticed people walking funny, sort of tiptoeing around a dark pile in the middle of the road. I went to look and it was a horribly mangled skunk, with an even more horrible smell.

"I ran inside and tried to forget about it, but an hour later it was still there. Soon people would be arriving for the cornerstone laying: Something had to be done! And it seemed that I was the one to do it. Well, Ma, you know how I can't stand the sight of blood, but I put on my rubber gloves, and took a shovel and broom and a big black garbage bag and marched across the street. A policeman was directing the heavy flow of traffic, and you remember how scared I always was of police! I asked him to stop the cars so I could remove the — ugh! — object in the road. He smiled graciously and said 'It's being taken care of, ma'am, but thanks for your effort anyway.'

"So I didn't have to do it after all. But the rest of the day, and for quite some time afterward, I felt so strong, as if I could tackle anything."

When we finally deal with something we've been dreading, or overcome an obstacle, we find that great power is given to us to overcome more obstacles.

Oh, Dear!

DAVID MILLER WAS DRIVING ALONG THE HIGHWAY AT a steady clip of 60 miles per hour. It was *Erev Shabbos* and the car was crowded, the kids were fidgeting impatiently, the baby needed a change — every good reason to maintain the greatest speed permissible on that road.

Suddenly there was a queer noise. The rooftop rack was rattling and scraping. From the racket overhead, it seemed about to fall off. David slowed down; luckily, he was in an outside lane, with no cars near him.

As he slowly went around the next curve, he saw a family crossing the road right in front of him. It was a family of deer: a buck, a doe, and an adorable little Bambi. Now hitting a deer is dangerous for the animal — and even more so for the passengers in the car, which was inches away from the animals. At his previous rate of speed, David surely would have hit at least one of the deer.

The rack did not rattle again until they reached their destination. When they got out to inspect the car, they saw that one single bolt was loose.

"I can't imagine why this should have made such a racket." said David.

"Well, I can," answered his wife.

Brave Soldiers

THAT TUESDAY, *EREV SUCCOS*, WAS SURELY THE MOST painful day in the entire life of Avrum Goodman. His 3-year-old son, Ephraim, was about to be admitted to Fairview Children's Hospital. The diagnosis: leukemia.

It had come that morning like a bolt out of the blue. Froyim'l had been complaining for a few days — his head hurt, his back ached, his tummy had a boo-boo — but there was nothing to *see*. Repeated doctor visits and tests were inconclusive.

More tests were taken. Maybe it was Lyme disease, maybe meningitis or hepatitis, or pneumonia, maybe who-knows-what. But now the verdict was in, and little Ephraim was to be hospitalized immediately.

The drive to Fairview seemed endless. Avrum and his wife, Esther, spoke in whispers. They agreed that they would try to keep the illness under cover, to talk about it only to the people directly involved, thus avoiding unnecessary heartache. And besides, they still couldn't believe that their usually so cheerful and active, happy-go-lucky Froyim'l had the dreaded disease. Maybe it was all a big mistake and it would turn out to be just an infection of some sort. So why alarm their relatives and close friends needlessly?

They arrived at the hospital, where a team of doctors and nurses awaited them. Ephraim was quickly whisked off to an examination room. Avrum had to fill out endless forms while Esther went along with her son, but before leaving the lobby, she whispered to her husband, "Remember, Avrum, don't get too friendly with anyone. Don't give your name — we don't need publicity."

Avrum, of course, agreed. He sat down with a *Tehillim* and began reciting the psalms where he had left off — was it only this morning? It seemed like a century ago.

After a while, Avrum got the uncomfortable feeling that someone was staring at him. When he looked up, he saw that a tired-looking, somewhat older man, had taken the chair next to his and was looking at him intently.

"*Sholom aleichem!*" said the stranger. "*Vos macht a Yid?* My name is Gedalyah Cohen, from Boro Park, and my son is a patient here. What's your name? And whom do you have in the hospital?"

Thus directly challenged, Avrum could not refuse to answer, despite his previous resolution not to reveal his name or his circumstances.

"Ah — my name is Avrum Goodman from Passaic. My 3-year-old was just admitted. Yes, leukemia." He could hardly bring himself to say the word.

The other man patted him on the shoulder with an encouraging smile.

"Well, my son is older — almost 15 — and he's been under treatment for five months now. He's doing well, thank G-d, and I'm sure your little fellow will be okay too."

Just then a nurse came in, calling for Mr. Goodman. Avrum went to join his wife and son, shaking hands with Mr. Cohen on his way out. He never saw the man again in the hundreds of hours that he subsequently spent in Fairview Children's Hospital.

Little Ephraim underwent many painful tests, transfusions, and chemotherapy. At first, he screamed and had to be held down for each procedure. Eventually, he became a veteran and endured the pain stoically, with barely a whimper. As the treatments progressed, his face puffed up and he lost all his dark curly hair, as well as his thick eyelashes and brows. His father had a brilliant idea: All the little boys in the neighborhood were given short-short haircuts and were presented with red baseball caps, lettered, "The Baldies," in white. It was a great honor to belong to the team.

Finally, Ephraim received a bone-marrow transplant, with his brother Shauly being the donor. The procedure went smoothly and the brothers had a fairly uneventful recovery.

In that year of treatment, Froyim'l matured far beyond his age.

When he was old enough to attend kindergarten, his parents decided to enroll him in a school with small class sizes, and to acquaint the teacher with Froyim's medical history, since he was still somewhat frail. The next year, in the next grade, they spoke to Froyim's teacher privately so he would be able to watch out for him and to protect him from the roughhousing so common among little boys. This worked out well. His teacher was aware of the problem, and was able to assist in the recovery.

The following summer, Ephraim was a big boy of 6, eager to go to day camp with all its exciting activities. His parents agonized: Should they tell the camp director? The counselor? It was a big camp in their suburban neighborhood, with hundreds of boys. Everyone would know.

Finally, Ephraim himself decided the issue. "Pa," he said, "don't tell anybody I was sick. I'm okay now, and I don't want them feeling sorry for me."

His father promised not to tell, though with a heavy heart. He worried about Froyim — still slight and delicate in body, though strong and determined in spirit, never whining, never complaining.

Throughout that summer, Avrum debated with himself. Had his decision been the right one? Days in the broiling sun, the cold pool, long hikes uphill, the chance of catching an infection or a stomachache — so many possibilities for Froyim'l to get sick again! Maybe he should have told the counselor. Maybe he should still do it, but he had promised!

Avrum did not tell.

Slowly, slowly the hot weeks passed. Ephraim enjoyed every moment of camp. His appetite was good and he gained some weight. Best of all, he truly loved and admired his young counselor, Tuvia, who came from Brooklyn every day to work in the camp.

The last evening of camp was a very special occasion. There was a campfire with songs, stories, and much laughter. In a quiet moment, Tuvia approached Shaul, Froyiml's brother, who was a waiter in the camp.

"Tell me, Shaul, was Froyim'l ever in Fairview Hospital — like a few years ago?"

"Wha — how did you know?" Shaul was astonished. No one in the camp had been told about his brother's sickness.

"Well, Shauly — you see — I was there at the same time, and I kinda thought that Froyim'l was there too. So I asked my father and he remembered the name Goodman. So all summer I was looking out for him — didn't let him stay in the sun too long or let him get too tired. And I made sure he had drinks and extra snacks. You'll see, he'll be fine, just like me."

So Tuvia, who could have gotten a summer job right near home just as easily, had traveled from Brooklyn every day, the only counselor who did. All summer he hovered over Ephraim like a guardian angel, watching his every move and providing for all his needs, protecting him so tactfully that the child was never aware of it.

Avrum Goodman is full of gratitude for the Divine Providence that shelters his dear Ephraim, even in the most difficult circumstances, as it is said in the words of the *Navi*: *"Haben yakir li Ephraim* — Is Ephraim my most precious son, a delightful child … I will surely take pity on him."

Comfort Zone

Elke Friedman met her friend and former neighbor, Susie Goldberg, at the annual N'shei Chesed gathering in Flatbush.

"How are you, Susie? I haven't seen you for ages. And how's that cute little Motty of yours?"

"Cute he is, but not little. He's almost six feet tall, 22 years old, and just about ready to get married."

"You don't say! Well, I know the perfect girl for him. Same background — a little bit Hungarian, a little bit "Poylish," mostly American. It's Chavie Engel, the daughter of my neighbor down the street. Very sweet looking, also tall, brown eyes, brown curly hair — why, she reminds me of how your Motty used to look before he got his haircut! And her parents are the nicest people! Her grandfather was a nephew of Reb Yossele Kopolner, and ...."

"That sounds very interesting," said Susie. "But tell me," and she looked around to see if anyone was listening, and whispered into Elke's ear, "tell me, are they *comfortable*?"

"Comfortable? They're very comfortable! In fact, they're just about the most comfortable family I know."

"All right, Elke, we'll be in touch. I can't wait to get home and tell Sol about this. It sounds great!"

The friends parted amiably, and a few days later, the telephone rang in Elke's kitchen.

"Hi, Elke, it's Susie. Thank you so much for thinking about our Motty. We discussed it and we're very interested in this Chavie Engel. So please get in touch with them. You *did* say they're comfortable?"

"Oh, very much so, Susie. I'll call them and get back to you soon as I have an answer."

A few days later, Motty Goldberg met Chavie Engel. After several more meetings, they knew they were meant for each other.

The Engels invited Motty's parents to their home to get acquainted, and the Goldbergs accepted the invitation with pleasure; they could hardly wait to meet the wonderful girl and her wonderful parents whom their Motty raved about.

They were surprised when they pulled up in front of the Engel's house. It was so small, so — so — ordinary looking. But perhaps the Engels were people of that European type, plain outside, lavish inside?

No. The interior consisted of several box-like rooms, with old furniture that verged on the shabby. The Engels gave the Goldbergs a very warm, friendly welcome. Soon everyone was chatting easily, seated around the broad dining-room table. Mrs. Engel brought in tea and delicious chocolate chip cookies. In the course of conversation, they found that they had many friends, and even relatives, in common.

Motty and his parents stayed much longer than they had planned. After dropping off Motty at his yeshivah for night *seder,* Sol Goldberg asked his wife, "Didn't you say they're comfortable? It sure didn't look like it to me."

"Well, Sol, Elke Friedman said they are, and she should know. Maybe they're the kind who don't flaunt their money ... and the girl seems very nice."

Pretty soon an engagement was announced. A happy, noisy crowd gathered in the small Engel home to congratulate the young couple and their parents. Elke Friedman, whose idea it had been, had a place of honor among the ladies.

The mother of the groom turned to Mrs. Friedman.

"We're very happy with Chavie — she's a darling. But didn't you say that the Engels are *comfortable*?"

"Oh, they are! They are! They make me feel so comfortable whenever I come, so warm and welcome, and just look — I bet everyone here feels the same about them. The Engels are the most comfortable people I know! And did you ever taste her chocolate chip cookies?"

A word can make a difference. If Mrs. Goldberg had asked, "Are they well-off," or more crassly, "Do they have money?" would Motty and Chavie ever have met?

It's like that old joke, "If my grandmother had wheels, she'd be an automobile." But grandmothers don't have wheels.

It was fated that this particular expression should be used by Mrs. Goldberg, and that Mrs. Friedman should understand it in a different sense. When a couple is destined to be united in marriage, not a word or a world will stand in the way.

Emunah

∼⊙∼ **Hide and Seek**

NOCHUM SILVERMAN WAS PROBABLY THE HAPPIEST young man on the streets of Boro Park that fine summer day. One — he was newly engaged to the best girl in the world. (Of course every *chasan* thinks so, but in Nochum's case it was really true!) And two — he was on his way to Eretz Yisrael to continue his studies at Yeshivah Derech HaTorah, where he had been learning for the past three years.

Nochum had come from Monsey to visit his relatives and to do some last-minute shopping. He would get a ride straight from Boro Park to the airport. His parents had given him a large amount of cash to take along, to pay some debts and to give to his yeshivah. Nochum had put the money in an old sock and pinned it securely to his clothing. Every once in a while he would pat his jacket to make sure the cash was still there.

Yes, Nochum had every reason in the world to be satisfied. The smile never left his face as he went from store to store and from house to house, saying his good-byes. He packed his suitcase with the last-minute purchases, crammed his pockets with his favorite cookies, supplied by his grandmother, and was soon on his way to the airport with a friend of his parents, Manny Levy.

The scene at the airport was nothing new to our hero. He waited on the long line until his luggage, bulging with clothing, *sefarim* and gifts for his cousins, was weighed and checked. He joined a *minyan* for *Maariv* and went upstairs as the time of departure neared. He planned to find his seat on the plane and settle down for a good night's rest.

When he took out his passport at the passport control booth, he slapped the pocket where he had stowed the precious sock, but it wasn't there! The pocket was flat and empty.

Desperately, Nochum tried to remember when he had last checked it. It must have been at 18th Avenue, when he had gotten off the Monsey bus. After that he had been too busy and had simply forgotten about the money. There was no way he could go back and look for it now — departure time was only an hour away. And even if someone *did* find it, there was no name or address on the sock full of cash.

How hard his parents had worked to accumulate this money! And now, because of his carelessness, it was gone! Nochum wouldn't, couldn't tell them. What use would it be anyway? He'd only cause them heartache.

He did not call home.

Nochum boarded the plane. His usually beaming face was drawn and pale. Even meeting some former classmates on the plane did not change his somber mood. Trying to laugh at his friends' jokes took a tremendous amount of effort.

One of the boys asked, "What's the matter, Nochum? You look like you bit into a lemon. Are my jokes that bad?"

"No, no — they're hilarious. I guess I'm just tired."

He was, as a matter of fact, completely exhausted. But he couldn't fall asleep.

Back in Brooklyn, little Shimmy Glick sauntered along behind his mother, keeping his eyes out for stray coins. On a windy corner near the bus stop, he spied a dusty sock on the sidewalk. When he impulsively picked it up, he was surprised at its weight and thickness.

His mother said, "Ugh! What do you want with that old sock? Throw it in the garbage!"

"But Ma, there's something inside. Look!"

The sock was stuffed with cash. Mrs. Glick quickly put it into her pocketbook; she would check it out at home.

There was close to $900 inside, but no name. "Oy — that poor person who lost it — he must be frantic!" Mrs. Glick searched for a clue as to the ownership of the money, but couldn't find any. No — wait! Clipped to a $100 bill was a note with the name *Silverman* — nothing else.

How many Silvermans are there in Brooklyn? And why does it have to be Brooklyn? Could be Manhattan, could be Queens, could be anywhere in the world!

Just then Mrs. Glick's married daughter, Mirel, who was visiting from Jerusalem with her husband Chaim, walked in. Mrs. Glick showed her the sock full of cash.

"Wow! That's a lot of money to lose! But look, Ma, this name Silverman — there's a Monsey boy by that name who's a friend of ours. He learns in Yeshiva Derech HaTorah together with Chaim, and he's leaving for Eretz Yisrael today. I bet it's his; you know people often take cash on this trip. Let's get the Silverman's number from Information."

No sooner said than done. Mrs. Silverman in Monsey answered after several rings.

"Yes, I do have a son Nochum who learns in Derech Hatorah. In fact, he's on his way there right now. But why are you asking? Did something happen? Is he all right?"

"No, no, he's fine! I'm sorry if I scared you. But listen — was he carrying any money on him? And if yes, in what and how much was it?"

"But how do you know about it? It was in a gray sock, and it was $875." It seemed a queer conversation, Mrs. Silverman thought. Why would a complete stranger ask about the amount of money her son was carrying?

"Well, my son Shimmy picked up this old sock on 18th Avenue, and then my daughter, Mirel, said she thinks it must belong to Nochum Silverman, and then ...."

Nochum's mother couldn't believe her son's restraint in not notifying them of the loss. And that the money should have been picked up by his friend's little brother-in-law! Nochum's *emunah* had been immediately rewarded. But by now he must be very worried. Maybe she could still reach him somehow. She called the Levy house. Yes, they had just received a call from their father on his cellular phone, from the airport.

"Please — the number — quick!"

In the nick of time, at the last moment before boarding, Mr. Levy heard his phone ring.

"You want to speak to Nochum? He already boarded the plane. But I'll be glad to give him a message as soon as I board."

"Just tell him," Mrs. Silverman was breathless, "about the money — it's been found. And we'll send it tomorrow with his friend Chaim."

Nochum Silverman enjoyed the flight immensely. He laughed at his friend's jokes, and after saying *Shema*, slept like a baby all the way to Lod.

∞ The Bazaar Queen

Gittel is a great organizer, finding masses of merchandise for her school's giant bazaar. She once had directions to a big textile factory, but apparently it was the wrong address — a private house on a strictly residential street.

"Well, if Hashem sent me here, there must be a reason."

Gittel went upstairs to look — nothing. Then she went to the basement. There she found a thriving knitwear business which has since supplied the school with hundreds of profitable samples. No one had ever solicited merchandise from that factory until Gittel came along.

People often ask her, "How do you find all these places?"

She answers, "Sometimes I smell them."

Gittel had been visiting an aunt in Queens when she sniffed a powerful and vaguely familiar odor. What could it be? It was silver polish, but so strong was the smell that it must have come from a bathtub full of it. Gittel followed her nose to the end of the block. There was a big industrial building, and occupying three floors, a silverplate manufacturer.

The owner was forthcoming and generous, but he had one question: "How did you ever find this place?"

"I smelled it."

A Tithe in Advance

Gittel Silverman's dryer was dying. It took ages to dry a load, quite a hardship for someone who had children in diapers and two older ones who loved to play in the mud. But the worst part was that it emitted clouds of smoke during each cycle. Gittel was in constant fear that one day it would catch fire, so she frequently checked on it and would never dare leave the house when the dryer was on.

So why didn't she buy a new one? Simple, she could not afford it, although she needed it desperately. So a good part of the day was devoted to monitoring the ancient machine.

One day her sister-in-law Riva called her in great excitement. "Listen, Gittel — you need a new dryer, don't you? Well, I just got a call from someone — I don't know how she got my name — and she says she has a brand new gas dryer she wants to get rid of right away. Are you interested?"

"Boy, am I interested! But why should she want to get rid of it? What's wrong with it?"

"She says she's allergic to it somehow. It cost her $369.99, and as soon as it was installed in the basement, she started wheezing and coughing, even in the bedroom upstairs. So do you want it?"

"Sure. How much is it?" Gittel couldn't get over her good fortune. Just when she had decided that the old dryer couldn't be used even one more day, along came this wonderful bargain offer!

"She doesn't want anything. In fact, she'll have someone deliver it and install it right away. I'll give her your name and address. Bye!" Riva never wasted words.

The new appliance was delivered and installed the next day. It worked perfectly and no one in the house had any allergic reactions.

A couple of days later, Gittel called her sister-in-law to get the lady's name and telephone number in order to thank her.

Riva answered on the first ring. "I just knew it was you, Gittel! Listen to this — that woman who gave you the dryer, well, she called me to say that you shouldn't thank her, she has to thank you. Why? She said that her husband is a professional billiards player, but he hasn't won a tournament in seven years. The day after she sent you the dryer, he won $3,699 in the playoff— 10 times more than the value of what she gave away!"

⌘ Emunah Car Service

Gittel Silverman is surely the only woman in the world, or at least in the United States, who has her own private fleet of taxicabs, ready to serve her at any time of the day or night. She calls it "Emunah Car Service." Whenever she has to go somewhere, there's a driver ready to take her to her destination, and the best part is that it's absolutely free!

The Silvermans don't have a car, and the distances in their town are great. With her various activities and responsibilities in the home and even more outside, Gittel could spend a fortune on taxis, but she doesn't. All she has to do is call upon her *bitachon* and she's on her way.

A recent instance: It was the day before *bedikas chametz*. That morning Gittel had decided that her kitchen must be painted and had immediately set to work. But halfway through, she ran out of paint. The only place to buy that particular brand and color was at Pelmer's Paints, miles away in another town.

Should she leave the kitchen half done? No, it would bother her all Yom Tov, and anyway, it looked awful. But how could she get to the store and back? She didn't have a minute to spare on that super busy day.

"It has to be done, that's all," Gittel decided. She stepped out of her door with the paint store's address and a sample in her hand. Around the corner came her friend Roizy, driving her old jalopy.

"What are you doing out today, Gittel? Me? I just had to get away a few minutes. Can I take you anyplace? You need to go to Pelmer's? Sure, no problem. I'll wait for you and take you home. Please don't thank me, I needed a little outing anyway."

When they came to Pelmer's, the store was empty, just waiting for Gittel, it seemed! She was in and out in moments.

The paint color matched perfectly, and Gittel's kitchen shines, cheerful and bright in its coat of fresh paint.

Emunah Car Service works for the whole family, not only Gittel. When he was 13 years old, son Nochum needed new eyeglasses. He discovered that they would be considerably cheaper in Brooklyn, so he decided to go there; fortunately, a neighbor was able to take him to the big town and to drop him off on the way to work.

But how would he get back? He had never been in Boro Park alone. The bus would take the better part of the afternoon, and his savings would be swallowed up by the bus fare. Well, worrying wouldn't help. Nochum paid for the glasses. As he left the store, he saw a car stop at the corner. He thought the yeshivish driver looked vaguely familiar, and ran over to the car.

"Are you maybe going to Monsey?" Nochum asked.

"Sure, hop in."

Talking to the driver, Nochum found out that he was a cousin whom he had seen at a family *simchah*; and after a quick and pleasant ride, Nochum was delivered to his home in Monsey — door-to-door taxi service, free of charge.

~ From the Beginnings

The Silverman family seems to experience miracles on a daily basis. Perhaps everyone does, but some of us are more aware than others. That trend was obvious right from the start, even before the Silvermans were married.

When Michael Silverman proposed to Gittel Fass, she said, "I'm so lucky — you're the very first boy I met — for *shidduch* purposes, I mean."

He answered, "You want to know something? You're the first girl I ever met."

"How can you say that? Didn't you tell me you've been going out for almost a year?"

"That's right," Michael smiled, "It's just about a year ago that I started. But you're still the first one, and now *baruch Hashem* the last one. The first date I ever had was with a girl from out-of-town who was studying in Seminary. And, like a lot of these girls, she was a boarder in this very house, on the top floor. So when I rang the bell downstairs, who answered the door? It was you, Gittel!"

She blushed with embarrassment. "That boy was *you*?"

She remembered the incident because she had been wearing scruffy slippers and her mother's oldest robe, just right for cleaning house, with her hair in curlers.

Mrs. Fass had been upset. "That's how you answer the door, a girl of marriageable age?"

"Okay, okay, I'll be careful from now on, Ma. Anyway, it makes no difference — that boy asked for one of the Seminary girls upstairs. He's not interested in me."

"Funny you should have said that." Michael's smile spread from ear to ear. "When the *shadchan* called to ask about the outcome of that date, I said she was not for me. But there was this nice girl who answered the door downstairs ...."

Late Redemption by Divine Intervention

THAT FRIDAY, TZVI HALPERN DID NOT FEEL WELL AT all. His head ached, his nose ran, and there was a lump in his throat the size of a matzah ball. He called his wife from the school where he taught.

"Miri? No, I'm not feeling any better than last night, in fact, much worse. I'm coming home early; maybe, if I rest up a while, I'll still be able to go to *shul* tonight."

"Good! A nap usually helps." His wife's voice was soothing as always. "I'm almost ready for Shabbos. But what about Yossi?"

Yossi Miller was their *Shabbos bachur*, their steady guest at every Friday night dinner and for lunch the next day. The only son of a famous film director, he had come from California the year before and had enrolled in Yeshivah Nidchei Yisrael, a yeshivah for young men who had come late to Judaism, and who were studying with great zeal to make up for lost time. Yossi had immediately felt comfortable in the welcoming atmosphere of the yeshivah; when Shabbos meals with the Halperns were arranged, he felt truly at home.

His hosts never inquired about his background, but after spending several evenings as their guest, he talked freely about his past. Yossi — called John by his parents and friends — had known that he was Jewish only because of his grandmother, a tiny, wrinkled woman born in Poland who clung fiercely to the little she remembered *"fun der alte heim." She* was the one who had insisted that the name of her father, Yosef Chaim, be given to her grandson. *She* was the one who came to visit every year for Passover; she arrived a week early and scrubbed and scoured relentlessly. After *bedikas chametz*, for which she brought her own wooden spoon and feather, Yossi would bring down the Pesach dishes and pots from the attic. The next day she spent at the stove, cooking all the dishes fondly remembered from her youth. Then *she* conducted the Seder, instructing her grandson when to ask the Four Questions, when to dip his finger in the wine, when to make the horseradish sandwich, when to sing, when to eat. His grandmother had not come the past few years; she was too old, too frail. He had tried to conduct a Seder of his own, asking the Four Questions and prompting his father with the answers, but the feeling was not the same.

Then came high-school graduation; like all the other parents in that wealthy suburb, the Millers offered their son an overseas trip of his own choosing before college. Israel was one of the stops on his itinerary. There at the *Kotel* he met, or rather was met by, the irresistible Meir Schuster, who introduced him to his Jewish heritage. When Yossi returned to the States, he chose to go to Yeshivah Nidchei Yisrael instead of the university to which he had been accepted.

Yossi quickly adapted to his new way of life, and as he often told the Halperns, "The Shabbos in your home is the highlight of my week."

"Well, what *about* Yossi?" Tzvi Halpern asked his wife. "He knows he's always invited."

"You're not feeling well; maybe I should call him not to come?" Miri was worried — it might be a thoroughly depressing evening.

"No-o, that wouldn't be fair, at the last minute. Let him come like always. I'll try to act cheerful. Bye now, I'll be home soon."

All that afternoon and evening it rained and rained. Tzvi's *davening* at home was accompanied by coughs and sneezes. When Yossi finally came, his clothes were drenched, his shoes were soggy. Miri tried to make him comfortable in a warm robe and slippers of her husband's. After a hoarse rendering of *Shalom Aleichem*, Tzvi recited a subdued *Kiddush* and the three sat down to eat.

The gray drizzle outside seemed to penetrate right into the Halpern's dining room: no singing, no stories, no laughter. Miri decided she must do *something* to brighten the evening. Oh yes — telling about that interesting event last week should do it!

"Yossi, my husband had an unusual experience recently. A student in his eighth grade had a *pidyon haben* at age 14. He's almost six feet tall and quite husky. I wonder how they got him onto a tray, and who carried him in.

"Oh, you don't know what a *pidyon haben* is? Well, every Jewish boy who is the firstborn of his mother has to be redeemed at the age of 30 days by his father. They put the baby on a silver tray, surrounded by gold and jewelry, and sugar cubes and garlic cloves, and his father redeems him with the equivalent of five *shekalim* that he gives to a Kohen. Then there's a nice meal, and that's the *pidyon haben*. I wish I would have been there. I would have loved to see them bringing in that basketball player on a silver platter."

"Okay, okay, Miri, you know very well that wouldn't happen." Tzvi Halpern was smiling; his wife had a vivid imagination. "And why did he first have his *pidyon haben* at age 14? Well, there's a history behind that. Moshe Marks' parents became observant after they had been married some time. They knew about a *bris* when Moshe was born, of course, but not about this. When I was learning *Parshas Bo* with my class, where it tells about the *pidyon haben*, Moshe went home and asked his parents if he ever had one. The answer was no, and they immediately set out to remedy the situation. They asked me to arrange it, and it turned out to be a very special and moving occasion — even though they didn't bring him in on a tray."

"And that jewelry, sugar, and garlic — what's that all about?" Yossi had been sitting, quiet and thoughtful, hardly saying a word all evening. Miri was surprised; he was usually so talkative.

"The jewelry is to make it *hiddur*, to beautify the *mitzvah*. And the sugar and garlic is an old custom. A *pidyon haben* seldom occurs, since the baby has to be the firstborn of the mother and delivered naturally; his father can't be a Kohen or a Levi. So the guests take home the sugar and garlic as a remembrance. Even in some large families, there hasn't been a *pidyon haben* for generations."

Yossi had listened with great interest. Finally he said, "I'm the only child in my family. Is it possible that I never had a *pidyon haben*? My grandmother made sure about the *bris* and the name, but she may not have known about this at all."

Back in the yeshivah for the *seudah shlishis*, the third Shabbos meal, Yossi told his fellow students about the *pidyon haben* of 14-year-old Moshe. The students looked at each other; most of them came from homes similar to Yossi's, and had never heard of this commandment. During the week that followed, 16 boys in the yeshivah, including Yossi, discovered that they were eligible for the ceremony. A mass *pidyon haben* was quickly arranged and celebrated by the whole community. Miri Halpern *did* attend that one, but all the sons to be redeemed walked in under their own power.

"Isn't it funny," she remarked to her husband on the way home, "if you hadn't had a cold that night I never would have thought of telling that story."

"And if I wouldn't have been teaching *Parshas Bo*, Moshe Marks wouldn't have had a *pidyon haben*, and there'd be no story to tell," said Tzvi.

"But if the Marks family wouldn't have moved to this town ...."

"Miri, it's an endless chain, and each link is necessary. I wouldn't even mind having another cold if that's what it can accomplish."

From Beyond the Grave

MR. SCHWARTZ LOWERED THE TELEPHONE GENTLY, ever so gently, into its cradle. What he really wanted to do was bang it down, scream and yell, but what would his wife think? She would be upset enough when he would have to tell her what happened with the latest *shidduch* for their son, Shimon Tzvi.

"So, Eizik, what did Mr. Weiner say? Are they interested?" Klara had come in from the kitchen. She was drying the two breakfast spoons with a dishtowel she had embroidered when they still lived in the cold-water flat on the East Side.

"I can't take it any more, Klara, I just can't take it any more! That Mr. Weiner — he's just like all the rest of them! He promised me backward and forward that he knows the girl and her family like the back of his own hand, and she's just Shimon's type. He must have called me 20 times, pestering me about this Shirley Klein. Then they want him to come in for the son's wedding so they can look him over. So after we make phone calls all over to check it out, and after Shimon makes a special trip from Toronto, and after you go shopping with him for a new suit and hat, what does Weiner say?"

"Eizik, please, calm down. Your blood pressure ...."

"How can you expect me to be calm after this? He says Mr. Klein decided that Shimon is not Shirley's type after all — she wants someone more outgoing! OUTGOING!! OUTGO-ING!!! There's nobody in the whole world more outgoing than our Shimon — he must have gone out at least a hundred times! And when I think of some of the girls who turned him down — he's much too good for them!"

"But Eizik, don't forget he also turned down plenty of nice girls. That sweet Feigy Bankes ... I wish he would reconsider. And he never gave a good reason why he didn't care for her. I'm sure she would have made him a very good wife. And what about the Rothstein girl? That seemed a match made in heaven, but he wouldn't even see her a second time. And — "

"Listen, Klara, that's old history. Why dig it up? Let's forget about it!"

"Easy for you to talk! *You're* the one who doesn't let me forget about it, Eizik. Each time it doesn't work out, whether he says no or she says no or even when it's a *gleicher shidduch* — they both say no — you just go crazy. Maybe Shimon should just take off a few months from this girl-meeting business, and give us all a break."

"Klara, how can you say that? He's getting older every minute! I just don't understand it. He's smart and good-looking, like me, and of course he's a big *yachsan:* the Kopolner Rebbe on your side, and Reb Yitzchak Eizik Sher on mine. He's a terrific learner, he's quick — remember when he put the succah back up after the hurricane? And put down those spoons already!"

Klara had been polishing and polishing the two spoons, quite unaware of her actions. She felt that keeping her hands busy helped her brain to work better. And it was also a family tradition; she still remembered her mother, her aunts, her sisters — knitting countless sweaters, embroidering table-cloths and pillowcases and dishtowels for their trousseaux, all the while talking, discussing, deciding.

"Tell me, Eizik, why are you so anxious about our Shimon Tzvi? It's all true what you said — he's good, he's smart, he's handy, everybody likes him; so why are you so worried? What's the big rush that he has to get married? He's only 22."

"Only 22? Look, Klara. When we got married, you were 18, I was 20. What was the rush? We had no money, no one to help us, no place to live, but we got married anyway. Why? Because we wanted to have a family, we wanted to belong to someone and someone should belong to us. After the *reshoim* killed my parents, I was alone, alone like a stone. And after the D.P. camp I went back to Nove Mesta, but there was nothing left there — not the house, not the store, not the *shul*, not the Jews. Only the *bais oylom* where everyone goes in the end .... And they're lucky, those old ones buried there, with a stone over their graves and their names on it, not like their children who went up in smoke."

His wife had been silent when he spoke. In the 35 years of their marriage, he seldom brought up the past, those precious souls that were lost. He had wanted to forget, to bury the terrible memories, to build a new life, a new family, and they had struggled together toward that goal.

It was becoming easier. Their three older children were married, with sons and daughters. But Shimon Tzvi — yes, Eizik was right. She was beginning to understand his eagerness to see his youngest son married; it was a deep yearning for continuity, for new generations, for a future.

"Eizik, listen. I have an idea. What you said about your grandparents, the ones from Nove Mesta, and the Tirnauer Zeide too — what about going there? Going to their graves and begging them to intercede for their *einekel*? They were such great *tzaddikim*, and our Shimon Tzvi is named after them. Go, Eizik, throw yourself on their graves, *daven* there, and I'm sure we'll be helped."

Eizik stroked his chin, deep in thought. "You know, Klara, that's not a bad idea at all! I don't know exactly how to manage it, it's the middle of the season and the shop is very busy, but I'll do it! And with the help of the *Aybishter*, Shimon Tzvi will soon find the right one."

Arranging for this trip was easier said than done. Czechoslovakia was still under Communist rule and Americans did not find easy admittance. Much time was spent waiting in consulates; documents had to be produced and money had to be pressed into eager hands, but at last Mr. Schwartz had his visa, his papers, his passport, and his ticket. Klara came to see him off, accompanied by Shimon Tzvi, who had met a nice girl several times over the past few weeks. Last night she had made it clear to him that they were not suited to each other. Shimon Tzvi took it hard; he had been hopeful, in fact quite sure, that this would be the one.

"Go *gezunterheit*, Papa, and come back *gezunterheit*."

"Shimon Tzvi, wish me that I should be *matzliach*, that my holy *Zeides* should look out for you from the *shamayim*. And if you meet the right girl before I even come back ... well, that'll be the best news."

"You're going to the *kivrei ovos*, so I'm sure that Shimon will find the right one very soon. So go in good health, Eizik, and bring us back good news." Klara's eyes were red.

"Good-bye! Good-bye!"

The flight seemed endless. There were few Jews on the plane, not even enough for a *minyan*. Wrapped in his *tallis* and *tefillin*, Mr. Schwartz received some hostile stares, but refused to let them bother him. He was going to the graves of his forefathers, and he shouldn't *daven*?

The hours seemed to stretch during the rest of the trip. There was much too much time for thinking, recalling events he had tried to blot from his memory: The Nazis dragging away his parents, the shots, hiding in the cellar of the peasant Janos Hunya who had later betrayed him for a pair of boots; crawling across frozen fields at night …. And that terrible moment when he was sure the end had come: lying under a pile of corpses, trying not to move, not to breathe, to make himself part of the earth where he lay.

Suddenly he had been flooded by a wave of absolute, overwhelming certainty: "Yitzchak Eizik, don't give up! We are watching over you …. You are going to live! All will be well with you, *b'ezras Hashem*."

It seemed to Eizik that his grandparents' voices were calling to him; he knew that he would live, and his heart filled with reluctant hope.

Eizik Schwartz had many more narrow escapes after that, but he had never been able to recapture this feeling of complete and perfect faith. Now, returning to the *alte heim*, perhaps he would experience it again.

Vienna! The plane was landing. Mr. Schwartz collected his luggage, passed the various checkpoints and registered at the Hotel Kontinental on the Käerntnerstrasse. He planned to stay three days — one to orient himself and make arrangements, and two for the trips to the cemeteries. He would take the train to Bratislava, formerly Pressburg, and look for a local taxi driver who knew the old Jewish places. Pressburg, Tirnau, Nitra, Topolcany, Szerdahely — the list of Jewish communities lost forever was enough to bring tears to his eyes. But he couldn't dwell on that now; he had a purpose in coming here. So — almost two days to visit the graves, and then he would be back in Vienna for just a few hours to pick up his luggage and get to the airport.

Eizik Schwartz passed through the towns and villages of his youth. Some of the cemeteries had been restored, like Nove Mesta and Pressburg; others lay in desolation and decay. Wherever he found the stones of his forebears, or of holy ancient rabbis, he threw himself on their graves, recalling their great deeds and begging them to intercede for his son before the throne of *HaKadosh Baruch Hu*, the Holy Blessed One.

And, thinking of the martyrs, those *korbanos* whose graves were earthen pits and heaps of ashes, he recalled phrases from the Memorial Service: "May the merciful Father Who dwells on high remember those saintly, upright and blameless souls ... who offered their lives for the sanctification of the Divine Name. They were beloved and pleasant in their lives, and were not parted in their death. They were swifter than eagles and stronger than lions to do the will of their Master ... May He remember them with favor; may He avenge the blood of His servants which has been shed."

Always, always he hoped to recapture that feeling of perfect and confident faith, but it eluded him. His heart was heavy, filled with an ache that was an actual physical pain. His footsteps dragged, but he kept on — another village, another desolate resting place, and the hundreds and hundreds of names! Names of men, women, children who had no one left to remember them, and whose *yahrtzeit* would be forgotten.

He was depressed and sorry that he had come. His last stop was the underground *kever* of the Chasam Sofer, Rabbi Moshe Schreiber, the great leader and advocate of Torah-true Jewry. The grave was deep beneath a road that had been built over it, a dark and awe-inspiring place, like an ancient catacomb. There, Eizik Schwartz poured out all his fears, all his pain of the past, all his doubts for the future.

And there, for the second time in his life, he felt a stirring of hope creeping into his heart. "Yitzchak Eizik, it will be good; you'll see; everything will be good."

In better spirits, Mr. Schwartz returned to Vienna, bought some gifts for his wife, children, and grandchildren, and ordered a cab to the airport. There was a pleasant-looking elderly man sharing the taxi, and of course they immediately started a conversation.

"*Fun vannet kimt a Yid*? Where do you come from?"

"From Cleveland. And you?"

"Boro Park. And what brings you to Vienna?"

"Business — but I didn't do so well. And you?"

Mr. Schwartz told Hershel Silverbaum the reason for his trip.

"Hm — I think I have somebody for your son. My granddaughter Devorah is a lovely girl"

Shimon Tzvi and Devorah are a very happy couple living in Bnei Brak. They named their firstborn Moshe, in memory and in honor of the great and holy Chasam Sofer.

The Miraculous
Succah

T HE MILLERS WERE A YOUNG FAMILY WITH THREE
children when they bought their big old house in
Monsey in the winter of 1953. Money was short, piles
of bills were tall, but when Succos approached, they realized
they must have their own succah at last. They had been
guests in other people's succahs up to that time, and they were
determined that theirs would be large enough to accommodate some who were not fortunate enough to have their own.

Soon the materials began to arrive: fresh, sweet-smelling
lumber, thick sturdy plywood panels, a small barrel of nails,
bolts and nuts from Modern Builders and long bamboo sticks
of *s'chach* imported from Williamsburg, Brooklyn, which was
then the main source for religious items. The plans were discussed at great length. Where should the succah stand? And
how should it be attached to the house? Three walls are less
costly than four, and a succah with one side consisting of the
house wall would have the advantage of being larger and stur-
dier for the same cost, or less.

The carpenter, Mr. Tischler, approved. He pointed out,

"You can climb through that low bedroom window; it opens right into the succah and you can use it for a pass-through also. No sense carrying hot pots outside." His estimate, added to the price of the materials, brought the cost way above what they had thought it would be, but — their very own succah was worth any price!

Mr. Tischler was very busy that season, and the Millers were getting a little nervous, but he assured them that their succah would be ready in good time; if necessary, he would get his brother-in-law to help. He came, two days before Succos, and began to work with a will. The panels were thick, the lumber frames heavy. It took an entire day just to prepare them. The next day, the brother-in-law also appeared. The two worked frantically, drilling, bolting, nailing. The ground was uneven, and had to be leveled; the *pater familias* took over that job. It was getting dark — the night before Succos! — and the carpenters announced they would have to break for supper, assuring the frantic Millers that they would return and finish no matter how late it became.

That supper seemed the longest in history. It seemed to be hours later that the men reappeared and went to work, full speed ahead; the yard was illuminated by flashlights and floodlights plugged into extension cords. It was after midnight when they finished at last! Now, finally, the Millers could relax; their children, too, had been awake and crying, infected by the parents' anxiety.

Erev Succos! A bright, sunny autumn day, and there stood the succah in all its glory: eight feet wide by 12 feet long, strong and sturdy, securely bolted to the house. It was surely the best succah in all of Monsey, if not in the whole world!

Mrs. Miller had prepared colorful handmade succah stars, a craft taught by their Vienna-born *Shabbos bachur*, Yankel Landau; and the two older children had made lopsided chains from the scraps — mustn't waste! Father hung the upper decorations while mother and children did the lower parts of the walls. The *s'chach* was reverently placed on top, and the succah was complete, ready for any number of family guests.

Rabbi Berel Greenbaum, *z"l*, was then the principal of the yeshivah where Hershel Miller was a teacher. The two met while attending to last-minute Yom Tov errands, and Hershel proudly invited Rabbi Greenbaum to see his brand-new succah.

Rabbi Greenbaum duly admired it: its size, its strength, its beautiful decorations. Then he glanced upwards, and became very quiet.

"I hate to tell you this, Heshy, but your succah is not kosher."

"What do you mean? Of course it's kosher!"

"Look up here," Rebbi Greenbaum patiently explained. "Don't you see that big branch of the maple tree overhanging the succah? You'd better do something — fast!" And Rabbi Greenbaum departed to see to his own succah.

The branch was an appendage of the huge tree belonging to the Millers' gentile neighbor, Mr. Jones. In a moment, Hershel was there, knocking and ringing the bell. Mrs. Jones came out, not too happy about being disturbed.

"Yes? What's the matter? You're knocking so loud!"

"Well — um — it's sort of hard to explain, but a branch from your tree is hanging over my — er — my little building there, and it has to come off — now!" How could he possibly explain what this meant to him?

"Oh, no, my husband just *loves* his trees! He wouldn't let anybody even touch a leaf of them!" And Mrs. Jones slammed the door with an emphatic bang.

Again he had to ring the bell.

"What time does Mr. Jones come home? Maybe I could speak to him?"

"Listen, he works hard all day. He doesn't come home before 5, 5:30. But don't bother, it's a waste of time." And the door slammed again, even louder than before.

What to do? What to do? But there was nothing to be

done but wait, and try to find someone to do the work, just in case. The kids were stationed at the window to watch for their neighbor's small truck, and at last he pulled in.

Time: 5:30. Before Mr. Jones even had a chance to climb out, Hershel was there. How slowly the man got down, how long it took him to light his cigarette!

"Er — Mr. Jones — we have a little problem (Ha! *Little!*). You see, we built this room especially for our holiday, and, well, there's a branch from your tree hanging over it, and that means that we can't use the room, so maybe ...?" He was perspiring, although the day had turned cool and windy.

"You mean you want to cut this branch off my beautiful maple tree? Is that what you want?" Did Mr. Jones sound threatening, or was it only imagination?

"Yes, I guess that *is* what I mean. There's just no other way."

Mr. Jones smiled. "Why, that's all right — no problem. I'll do it for you in a jiffy."

Hershel couldn't believe his ears. "What do you mean? How can you do it?"

"Why, didn't you know I'm a tree surgeon in my spare time?" And Mr. Jones pulled out a tall ladder and assorted saws, hooks, and pruning tools, and in no time at all he had the huge branch on the ground.

Now the *s'chach* only had to be lifted and replaced, and that night the Millers and their guests celebrated the most beautiful Yom Tov in their glatt kosher succah!

But the story does not end there. For years afterwards Mr. Jones cut down the overhanging branches. The Millers had many guests: the Adlers, the Breslauers, the Rosenbaums, the Kaplinskys, the Landmans, the Schorrs, the Weisbergers. The *bris* of Ephraim, son of Rabbi Nosson and Chanah Scherman, was held there. The Mattersdorfer Rav was the *sandek* and Mr. and Mrs. Krane were *kvaters*. And many other *simchahs* followed.

Every year the tree grew taller and taller. Then Mr. Jones moved away. One of the guests volunteered to trim the branch that year. When it was noticed that he was sitting on the very branch he was cutting, the Millers realized that it was time to set up their succah somewhere else, and they found a perfect spot, a concrete porch off the kitchen. It had a small roof, which was removed, and the same panels were used for only two sides, making the succah still larger — a good thing, since there were now six children, plus guests, who filled it up very nicely.

A *Simchas Bais HaSho'eva* was held every year, with beautiful singing. *"A Succah'le a klayne"* was the specialty, and this party was never rained out.

But one year — just in case — it was decided to make a *shlak*, a cover to ward off possible rain. Mr. Ralph worked diligently, constructing a wood-framed plastic panel extending upward from the succah.

The Millers were all in the succah, waiting for *Kiddush*, when the roof fell in — literally.

A tremendous hurricane blew over Monsey, destroying dozens of the temporary dwellings. That *shlak* was a real *shlak*. It acted as a sail in the wind, ripping the succah apart and causing the beams to rain down on the occupants. Daughter Rivkah was a *kallah*; her *chasan* and his parents were coming the next day, and here she was with a black eye and a bruise on her nose, and worst of all — no succah!

Another miracle — Mr. Ralph came, and with the advice and assistance of Uncle Shamshon Moller, *z"l*, the succah was quickly rebuilt. The bruises faded, and all was beauty and harmony that year.

Every year the panels seemed bigger and heavier. The sons were now in charge of putting them together. One by one the boys got married, until it was entirely up to Yossi, the youngest. One Pesach, he stole the afikoman, and asked for his prize: "Ta, Ma, I want a built-in succah! I'm old enough to get married, and then I'll be building my own, so make sure you have it ready by then!"

Sure enough, that summer Yossi became engaged, and the walls of the permanent succah rose on the porch. However, the family felt a great attachment to the old boards, which has been painted over the years — once with aquamarine ocean waves, once in harvest gold — and were thrilled when a nephew requested them. They continued to serve faithfully, and when the nephew moved to a house with a succah, he passed them on to a neighbor.

There, it seemed, the story came to an end. But last year, while visiting the succah of the Stoliner *shul*, the Millers discovered the panels of the old succah with their faded ocean waves and gold paint intact, back on Orchard Street, standing firm and strong as ever. Indeed, a miraculous succah!

Surprise! Surprise!

MINNA HARRIS WANTED TO SURPRISE HER HUS-band. It was Monday morning, the last day of his Chanukah vacation, and Meir had gone to Brooklyn the day before to visit his elderly parents — a rare occasion, since he worked a six-day week as a teacher in the Monsey Yeshivah. The children had been cranky in their father's absence — Danny, 7, the oldest, complained about being bored; the 4-year-old twins, Esti and Suri, squabbled constantly; Shragie, one-and-a-half, who had just started walking, had cut his foot on a toy and had to be carried around all day.

"Yes, we'll make Daddy a surprise, and your two *Bobbes* and *Zeides* too," announced Minna. "We'll come to them in Williamsburg — I won't call first; I know they're home in this bad weather, and we'll have a really great get-together. What do you say, kids?"

"Yay!" Danny, as usual, was the spokesman for the younger ones. "Do you think *Zeide* will give us silver dollars like he did last year? Remember, Ma?"

"Don't you dare talk about presents, Danny. We're just going to visit and maybe get to see the cousins."

The children were excited and happy. They immediately

started to pack their favorite toys to take on the trip. "Ma, can I take this? Ma, I can't find my dolly's shoes! Ma, she took my hairband! Ma, Ma, Ma …. Minna was getting a headache, along with some feelings of regret.

The trip from Monsey to Williamsburg in those days required advance planning and complicated arrangements. The Harris family, like most at that time, did not own a car; the only way to get to Brooklyn was to take a taxi to the bus depot in Spring Valley, and from there catch an hourly bus to New York, which stopped every few minutes in every little town along the route. It took an hour-and-a-half to reach Washington Heights. From there, one took an A train to 59th Street, then a D, changed to the F train at West 4th, changed again at Essex, and finally, over the bridge to Williamsburg. Minna knew the route well, and was getting cold feet — not only because it was 10 degrees outside, but because she realized that making this trip with four children would be a major, major undertaking. But — she had promised, and it was too late to back out.

Maybe one of the Monsey residents who worked in the city hadn't left yet. It was only 8:30. Minna started a chain call, alerting her friends to her need for a ride. Lo and behold! Rina from next door called to say that Mr. Korn was still home and would gladly pick her up in 10 minutes.

Minna burst into action. "Let's see — 10 diapers, rubber pants, two baby bottles, one with milk, one with water, one baby fruit, pretzels, pacifier, lollipops, etc. etc."

"Hurry, Danny, find the girls' shoes and put them on — I'll tie them. Put the hairbrush in my bag; I'll do their hair in the car. No, you can't take your red truck. Yes, Esti, you can have your dolly. I know it's not fair, but lots of things are not fair. Don't forget the pacifier — the yellow one is the only one that Shragie likes."

Minna flew about the house, opening and closing doors and drawers, making instant decisions, trying to remember every single item needed for this impulsive excursion. And, 10 minutes later, when Mr. Korn's car stood in front of the house, she was ready — breathless, disheveled, but ready!

They piled into the car — Danny in the front with Mr. Korn, the girls and Minna in the back with Shragie on her lap. (This was long before car seats and seat belts were required, or even existed.) Ahh ... at last she could relax, maybe even close her eyes for a few minutes. But it was not to be. Danny, in the front, was trying out all the handles and knobs within reach of his short arms, and Mr. Korn was getting upset.

"Little boy — just sit straight in your seat and don't touch anything, okay?"

"Okay — but can I talk?"

"Sure, but don't yell — it makes me nervous."

In a piercing whisper, Danny asked, "Mister, how come your head is so shiny? You polish it? And how come —"

Minna knew, she just *knew* that the next question would be about Mr. Korn's nose, which was blue-veined and prominent. Danny had been fascinated by noses lately.

"Danny, Mommy and Baby are both very tired. Let's all close our eyes and go to sleep. Shh, shh, shh ...."

"But the mister said I could talk."

"But I say you can't. Shh, shh, everybody. Close your eyes now ... shh ... shh."

A miracle! It worked! Only Minna could not sleep — she sat, tense as a coiled spring, waiting for the next remark ... but it didn't come. Lulled by the sound of the car and the children's breathing, she too drifted off.

"We're here, Mrs. Harris. It's time to get out. Here — let me help you with the packages." Mr. Korn had already opened the back door. Danny was on the sidewalk, staring with great interest at the multitudes of people passing by. The area was absolutely unfamiliar to Minna.

"Where are we? Isn't this Washington Heights?"

"No — it's the Bronx."

The Bronx! That word, to Minna, carried the sound of doom. Many years ago, she had been lost there, and she was frightened now, just as she had been then at age 12.

"But I don't know my way around here at all — I thought we were going to Washington Heights!"

"Oh, don't worry — I brought you to the subway. Just go straight with the D train till you catch the F train," advised Mr. Korn as he drove away.

Minna went down the dark stairs into an underworld her children had never encountered before. She gave them strict orders: "Hold on to each other; try to find a seat — stay by Mommy — don't talk to strangers." She had never realized in all her years of subway travel how many dangers it presented.

Fortunately, she found a seat near a map which she scanned desperately, trying to find out just where she was. The children were playing tag, dodging between the poles and the other passengers.

"Danny! Get the girls to sit down. Even if it's not next to me — just sit!"

By the time they were ready to obey, every seat had been taken, so Minna put Esti on her lap, next to Shragie. Danny and Suri ran to the doors at every station. "Lucky it's an express train," Minna thought. "In a local it would be much worse."

Then it was time to change trains. Minna gathered up the children. With Shragie, who seemed to weigh a ton by now, and the bags (two tons), she successfully negotiated the platform, the steps up, the steps down.

Ah, at last! The dear, familiar F train! She found seats for all quite close to her, and gave whimpering Shragie his milk bottle. A jolt of the train sent it to the floor, and there she sat, her good black coat and the floor splattered with milk, and broken glass all around her feet.

Everybody was looking at her. Everyone was laughing, sneering, or making nasty remarks. She felt her face get hot and red as a beet. "Oh — let me just get out of here — it can't get any worse than this!"

But it did.

When they got off the train at Marcy Avenue, she found that the steep metal stairs leading to Broadway were covered with a layer of ice as slick and slippery as glass. She stood for a long moment, paralyzed. How would she ever make it down these steps? But she couldn't just keep standing there. She had to *do* something!

Minna gave one bag to Danny, with orders to hold on to the railing, but he didn't want to because he had lost his mittens on the way and the railing was freezing cold. She took Shragie in an iron grip and made the twins hold on to her coat. Cautiously — one step, another step — they crawled down the icy staircase. It seemed to take forever, but they made it! They were down on Broadway, and now she just had to reach Havemeyer and then Division, and then … home! Home! Mama!

The streets were bad, but felt like the softest velvet compared to the slippery elevated steps. Down Broadway — slowly, slowly — up Havemeyer, and at last, Division! Minna felt like she had reached the top of Mt. Everest! The North Pole! The Promised Land!

With her last bit of strength, she staggered up the two flights of steps and rang the bell. When her mother answered, Minna fell into her arms.

"Minnale! What's the matter? You didn't even say you're coming … and what happened to you? You look like a ghost!"

"Ma, I can't talk now. Just give the kids something to eat, and let me lie down. Anybody in my old room? No? Good!"

With her coat still on, Minna flopped on the bed and started to cry — from fear, from tension, from relief; the tears ran down her face, and she couldn't stop them.

After a few minutes she sat up — mustn't frighten Mama like this! She took off her coat and her soggy boots, fixed her face, and tried to make herself look presentable. When she came into the kitchen, she saw the three older children at the table, happily consuming Mama's famous, slightly burned, hot chocolate pudding. Shragie was on the floor, banging pots and pans.

"Mama, could you do me a big favor? Call Meir at his parents' house and tell him to come over here, and to please call Mr. Berger to find out when he's leaving, and if he has room to take us home."

"You mean Avrum Berger from the bakery? You're not even going to your in-laws as long as you're here already? Minnale, what's the matter? Tell me —"

"Ma, just call Meir, please. I'll tell you later. I have to lie down again ... can't stand on my feet." Minna retreated to the bedroom.

After she had made the call and settled the children, her mother came in and sat next to her on the bed. "Nu, Minnale?"

The whole story of her daughter's ordeal poured out — the children's pestering, the hasty decision, the awful subway ride, the broken bottle, the frozen steps. Her mother patted her shoulder as if she were a baby, and crooned gently. "There, there, Minnale — it's all right, it's all right now."

After a while, it was quiet in the room. Minna's tears were spent, and she began to worry about getting home. Had Mama reached Meir, and had he called Avrum Berger?

"Yes, he did. And by the way, that reminds me — I wanted to ask you about the Bergers. You know them pretty well, don't you?"

This change of subject was just what Minna needed. "Oh, they're just wonderful! He's the sweetest, kindest man! You know we have a lot of *kollel* people in Monsey, and he waits and waits to get paid for his merchandise, without ever nudging. Hilda Berger — she's not that much older than most of us, but she's so good and kind, almost like a mother. Like — hardly anyone drives, so when she picks up her kids from school on Sunday, she fills up her car, and she'll even make extra trips when there's somebody left over. And she brought a big pot of soup when I was sick, and — "

"So listen, Minna. Don't they have a daughter? And how old is she?"

"Yes, they do, but if you're asking because of a *shidduch*, she's just a kid. She certainly looks like one ... but ... maybe she *is* 18, 19 already. Why are you asking?"

"I know of a wonderful boy for her — Chaim Goldenberg. He's so fine, a real *talmid chacham*, so intelligent. I think he'll be just right for her, and the families also fit together perfectly. You're friendly with them — why don't you suggest it?"

"Oh, Ma, I can't — they wouldn't listen to me, and ... and ...."

"Minnale, why shouldn't they listen? Aren't you a friend?"

"Well, first of all, I don't even know this boy. How can I say, 'He's this, he's that,' if I never met him in my life? And anyway, you need somebody more *choshuv*, more — well, more grown-up to talk a *shidduch*. I'm just not the type!"

"Type, shmipe! I'll tell you all about him. He's the oldest, he's got three younger brothers, he's got a good position with a school, very nice parents ... and I noticed after *shul* last Shabbos that he's got the most beautiful blue eyes! So talk to the Bergers."

"Ma, I just can't do it! I'll feel like a fool — and what if they say no?"

"They won't — I'm telling you they won't! So do it."

Minna was in a dilemma. How could she refuse her mother? But she just felt it wasn't the right thing for her to do; she had never suggested a *shidduch* in her life, and yet ....

Suddenly, the doorbell rang. Ah! Saved by the bell! It was Meir, very distressed at seeing her so exhausted and upset.

"Minna — I'm so sorry about this whole ordeal. You should have let me know. Are you feeling any better? Maybe we can still go over to my parents. And we could sleep over — it'll be a little crowded, but so what? You're here already."

"Did you call Mr. Berger?"

"Yes, I did, and he said he's leaving the store soon — 10, 15 minutes. Are you sure you want to go home with him?"

"Yes, yes, please! Even if he's leaving this minute! Just pack up the kids, and get another bottle — Ma usually has a spare — and let's get home right now."

"Well, you got your wish, Minna. I think I hear him honking downstairs. Yes," after a look out the window, "that's him in front of the house."

Minna jumped up, all her exhaustion forgotten, and together with Meir packed the bags, dressed the four tearful children (who resisted fiercely), accepted a hug and a big *kokosh* cake from her mother, and was downstairs in less than three minutes. Meir somehow got the children settled in the station wagon with extravagant promises of treats, outings, and silver dollars from *Zeide*. Minna was quiet in the back, thinking about what her mother had said.

"No! I can't do it! I'm just not old enough or experienced enough for such a thing! And I don't even know him. No! But Ma practically begged me to do it. When does she ever ask for anything? And this one time I shouldn't listen? But how do I know if Chanie Berger is even up to that? She looks like she's about 14. No — I'll tell Ma to find somebody else."

At home in Monsey, Meir served the children their favorite sugar-coated cereal, peanut-butter sandwiches with raisins (the only kind he knew how to make), black-and-white cookies, and lime soda — forget about cavities! — and got them to bed with visions of a trip to the candy store tomorrow. Minna fell into a deep sleep on the living-room couch.

She awoke to the ringing of the telephone and complete confusion. The house was dark and silent. Where were the children? And where was Meir? He must have gone to *Maariv*. She staggered into the kitchen to answer the phone.

"Minna? This is Hilda Berger. You sound a little funny — are you okay? Sure? Well, I wanted to ask you about a boy for our Chanie. The *shadchan* said you could give us information — they live in Williamsburg near your parents. His name is Chaim Goldberg."

This was fate indeed! Here her mother had begged her to suggest the *shidduch*, and she had absolutely decided not to, and now — now Hilda was calling *her*!

"Oh, Chaim is a super-duper terrific boy! My mother was just raving about him. She said he's really great — a *talmid chacham*, and so brilliant and a fine family and just right for your Chanie. And he also has beautiful blue eyes."

She heard Hilda laughing. "It sounds good. I'll talk it over with Avrum and I'll call you again tomorrow. You sound much better than before, Minna. Feel good! And good night now." She hung up, and Minna went back to sleep — in her own bed this time.

In the morning, the whole thing seemed like a dream — the horrible ride, the icy steps, the *shidduch* her mother had asked her to suggest. Meir had left for teaching already, and it was back to school for Danny. She was busy fixing breakfast and packing lunch, finding the mittens, pulling on the boots. Finally her son left. Now she only had to bathe the baby, dress the twins, and feed them all — terrible eaters they were — and restore the house to order after yesterday's hurricane.

The phone rang. It was Hilda Berger. She did not waste words

"Minna? We're interested. Give me their number. Avrum will call them, and if it's okay with them, he'll bring the boy back with him tonight to meet Chanie."

"Wow! You sure act fast! Just a minute — I'll look up the number. Oh, here it is — Evergreen 7-7917. Oh, I'm so excited."

"Me, too. I really appreciate your help! Bye now!"

The rest of Minna's day passed in a busy, dizzy rush: the house, the children, the laundry — before dryers, that was a big problem in wintertime; supper — no freezers or take-out stores, then! She was hanging diapers on the radiator when the phone rang. It was her mother, who inquired about her trip home, and then asked, "Maybe you changed your mind about speaking the *shidduch*? He's such a fine boy."

"Ma, you'll never believe this! That same night, Mrs. Berger called me and asked me about him, and they're ready to go ahead with it!"

"See how everything is *bashert*, Minnale? Mrs. Goldenberg will be so happy."

Minna snapped to attention. "Ma, did you say Goldenberg? Isn't his name Goldberg — Chaim Goldberg?"

"No, of course not. That Goldberg boy is the exact opposite of Chaim Goldenberg; he left school a long time ago, and — well, he hasn't done much since."

A terrible sinking feeling swept over Minna.

"Ma — I have to hang up — it's an emergency. No, no, the kids are fine. I'll call you back later."

Chaim Goldberg ... Chaim Goldenberg ... how could she have made such a mistake? Maybe, maybe Hilda Berger had not called her husband yet....

Frantically she dialed Elmwood 0321. "Bzz, bzz, bzz — busy, busy!" She tried again and again. "Oh, I bet she's calling him right now, and he'll bring home this Goldberg boy, and it will all be my fault. I'll try the store in Brooklyn."

"Bzz, bzz — busy too! They're talking to each other — or maybe *he's* calling the Goldbergs right now!"

There was only one thing to do. It was freezing outside, but Minna dressed Esti, Suri, and the baby and dragged the carriage out of the garage. She would have to walk over to the Bergers and tell them about her error. The walk would take about 15 minutes in good weather, but with this snow, and with the children along — well, she'd try the phone once more.

Rrring! Rrring! And — oh, blessed heaven — Hilda answered!

"It's me, Minna ... Hilda, I made a terrible mistake — you asked me about Chaim Goldberg, but I told you about Chaim Goldenberg. *That* Chaim is altogether different. Did you reach your husband yet? Oh, I hope ...."

"Hey, calm down, Minna. No, I didn't reach Avrum yet. Today he gets the orders for Shabbos, so the phone is always busy. Now please explain — what's all this about Chaim Goldberg or Goldenberg?"

Minna explained while Hilda listened. There was a long silence, enabling Minna to catch her breath. Now Hilda was talking. "You know what? Your mother is right — Chaim Goldenberg sounds just right for Chanie. Why don't you ask your mother to call the Goldenbergs? And if it's okay with them, Avrum can bring the boy tonight to meet Chanie — if he's available." Life was so simple in those days ....

That same evening, Chaim Goldenberg met Chanie, and not only Chanie, but the whole Berger family. Sister Bassie with her husband and children decided to visit that night, big brother Yankel was home from yeshivah, nephew Shloimie was there with his crew, plus a few kids from down the street who liked Mrs. Berger's potato latkes. The small house was crowded and overflowing with talk and laughter. Chaim came from a more sedate family. There was so much going on here that he was overwhelmed.

"Miss — I mean Chanie — is there any place we can talk — er — privately?"

Chanie thought for a moment. "I guess the only place is outdoors." The young people went outside into the snow. Then and there, by the light of the porch lamp in front of the house, they realized that they were meant for each other. When they came back in, they realized that no one had even missed them.

Chaim and Chanie married, and all their children have beautiful blue eyes.

Tales of Chesed

⤳ "Meter Keneged Meter"

ARIELLA COHEN, FORMERLY OF FLATBUSH, NOW OF Kiryat Sefer, Israel, tells the following story:

She was walking along 13th Avenue with a friend — let's call her Eva — chatting and window shopping, when she noticed an expired parking meter. The vehicle parked next to it was easily identified as a real *yeshivishe* car — *sefer* on the dashboard, an infant car seat, a toddler-size seat, toys, and a baby bottle in the back.

Ariella has a vivid imagination. She could picture the policeman sauntering along, checking the meters — "Hey, here's one!" — writing out the ticket, sticking it under the windshield wiper and going whistling on his way.

The car's owner comes out of the store. She's a frazzled lady pushing a baby in a stroller laden with packages, with an older child holding on.

"Oh, no! Another ticket! What will Daddy say?" And all the way home, she's nervous and upset with the children, although she knows it's not their fault.

Usually she looks forward to her husband's homecoming, but tonight she dreads it and decides to say nothing until the children are asleep.

Finally she can't put it off any longer.

"Yankel, I — um — I got a parking ticket today. It really wasn't my fault."

"What do you mean, it wasn't your fault? And it's the second one since Pesach! Another $50 out the window ... and we still owe tuition. How could you be so careless? You'll just have to stop using the car, that's all!"

"What am I supposed to do, *shlep* the kids and the packages on foot and wait for the bus for an hour! Just because I happened to get a ticket! And is it my fault the tuition isn't paid? You're supposed to take care of these things, not me, and besides, who got a big moving violation this summer, with a $100 fine and a day in court? About that you forgot already!"

And so the battle escalates until the baby wakes up ....

All this takes only seconds to flash through Ariella's mind. She drops a quarter in the meter and the indicator moves to 60 minutes of parking time.

Her friend looks at her but says nothing.

They continue walking, and pretty soon they come to another car with that familiar well-used look, parked next to an expired meter.

Ariella puts in a quarter.

Eva says, "Tell me, are you planning to put money in every expired meter on 13th Avenue? One I could understand, but if you keep on doing this, where will it end?"

"These couple of quarters mean nothing in my life," says Ariella, "but think what a difference they can make in someone else's life!"

That afternoon Ariella goes shopping in Waldbaum's. A woman she has never seen before comes over at the checkout counter and looks into her basket.

"Oh, I have coupons for these items that I don't need. Here — please take them!"

The favor Ariella did for a complete stranger was soon rewarded by a favor done to her — by a complete stranger! We seldom see such an immediate return, *middah keneged middah*; it might take years and is often not obvious — but the credit remains there, in the Great Book of Records, for eternity.

~ Drive-by Chesed

A wealthy and kindhearted Jew came to consult the Chofetz Chaim during the Knessiah Gedolah in Vienna. His problem? His family was complaining about the great amount of time and money he spent helping the needy.

"You're always busy helping poor people and listening to their troubles. And what about your responsibilities to your family? The little that you're home, you're still busy with *shnorrers*. Why can't you just say 'no' sometimes?" his wife had asked.

When the man entered the room, the Chofetz Chaim was expounding on the *pasuk, "Ach tov vachesed yirdefuni kol yemei chayoy* — Surely goodness and mercy will follow me all the days of my life."

"This was the prayer of David HaMelech, who was so often pursued by trouble and danger," said the venerable sage. "If one must be pursued, let it be by opportunities to do good and to demonstrate *chesed*. Isn't it much better than being pursued by creditors and police?"

The rich man had his answer without ever asking the question.

Those who extend themselves for others are like Pharaoh's daughter, who stretched out her arm to save Moshe. Even though the child was far away, her arm lengthened until she was able to reach him. Although a task may seem impossible, *az men tut vert getun* — when an effort is made, help is given from Above, as in the following stories:

Ariella Cohen was on her way home, thinking about what to make for supper, when she came upon the scene of an accident, with policemen, ambulances, curious bystanders, lots of noise and excitement — an all too familiar sight on the busy streets of Flatbush. Mrs. Cohen stopped to see if she could help.

An elderly couple had been hit by a car. The wife was unconscious; her husband was moaning and groaning, but refused to be taken to the hospital. When Ariella asked if she could be of assistance, he answered with what sounded like "Isabella."

"Isabella?" What could that mean? With much coaxing, she elicited the story. The husband and wife were on their way to visit someone in the neighborhood when the accident occurred. He couldn't remember the address or even the last name, only the word *Isabella*, which he kept repeating. How could he go to the hospital? Isabella would be waiting for them and wouldn't know what happened!

Ariella assured him that she would find Isabella and deliver the message, although she had no idea as to how she could accomplish this. The accident happened on a block that had multi-storied apartment houses on both sides of the street, containing hundreds of families. And the elusive Isabella might live on another block altogether.

A promise is a promise. Ariella chose a building at random. Someone was just leaving, and admitted her to the lobby. She rang the bell of the first apartment. No answer. She rang the next bell.

"You're looking for Isabella? On the sixth floor."

With wings on her feet and a song in her heart, Ariella took the elevator upstairs and notified the family about the accident. Isabella came down to the street with her. She calmed and comforted the couple and accompanied them to the emergency room.

Ariella noticed that a woman had come out of her house to offer cake and coffee to the rescuers. "What a nice thing to do!" she thought and made another mental entry in her *chesed* notebook.

The odds of finding Isabella so quickly were several hundred to one — but those seeking to do *chesed* find that their footsteps are guided by the One Above.

Certain people seem to be pursued by chances to do *mitzvos* more than others, or is it that they are more attuned, more aware of opportunities to do *chesed*? It probably works both ways.

On a short Friday afternoon in the winter, Ariella Cohen had done some last-minute shopping at G and Sons, a popular Boro Park store in those days. She was on her way home when it occurred to her that she was only several blocks from Maimonides Hospital, where people would be waiting for the bus — a bus that takes its time in coming and is usually full.

When she came to the bus-stop near the hospital, she saw a big crowd waiting impatiently. It was getting late, and there was no way she could possibly take all these people into her car. And how did she know that they wanted to go in her direction anyway?

She drove on.

After passing a few streets, she thought: "Well, I went so many blocks out of my way already, and just like it's late for me, it's late for somebody else too." She went back and picked up a young woman whose face was tense with anxiety; she dropped into the seat with a sigh of relief.

"You came back, didn't you?" she said in a soft voice.

She had seen Ariella pause in passing the first time and had hoped desperately for a ride, and when she saw the car going on without stopping ….

And how did the author, who's been living a quiet, almost secluded life in Monsey, N.Y. for the past 50 years, meet that fountain of fascinating stories, Ariella Cohen, formerly of Flatbush and now of Kiryat Sefer?

The first time, it was at a *berachos* party in Chavie's English-speaking *gan* in Jerusalem, to which the grandmothers of the toddlers had been invited. Ariella and the author occupied adjoining seats and soon found that they had much in common, besides having the cutest, smartest little grandkids in the whole world.

Ariella told me the story of the parking meters and gave me her telephone number — she had many other interesting tales, she said. But a couple of days later, when there was time for a long phone call to get all the details, the number had disappeared. Go find someone by the name of Cohen somewhere on the outskirts of Jerusalem!

Maybe Chavie from the *gan* would know? No. She had no Cohens in her group, and had no idea which child this grandmother belonged to.

Too bad! I should have been more careful. I resigned myself to the loss of some potentially terrific stories, and after a while, I forgot about Ariella.

Weeks later was the date of the annual *Yom Iyun* promoting *Shmiras HaLashon,* guarding one's tongue. It was an exceptionally hot day, even for August, but this is an event not to be missed, especially the speech by the renowned Ruchama Shain; so I came extra early and carefully chose a seat in the back, near an open window, near a fan, near an exit, so I could leave before the crush at the end.

I had just settled down when I saw Mrs. Shain entering at the front. I knew I had something to tell her which would be of great interest, so I made my way to her seat and told her about my "chance" encounter — with a packing case! Off

Rechov Sorotzkin, there is a little shoemaker's booth next to the steps leading down to a fruit store. I had passed it dozens of times, but just the day before, I had noticed the black lettering on the back — RUCHAMA SHA1N, HAIFA, ISRAEL. This must be the famous lift she writes about in her book, I thought.

When I told Mrs. Shain about it, she was thrilled. "Yes, that must be the same crate which brought our things to Israel 30 years ago! And imagine, it's still coming to use! I must go pay it a visit."

"No problem — it's only a couple of blocks away." I, too, was thrilled to find that it was indeed her original packing crate, inside of which a cobbler now sat every afternoon mending shoes. It seems that even the castoffs of the righteous continue to serve a good purpose.

It was time for the lecture to begin. I returned to my seat near the exit, but too late — the hall was filled and my seat was taken. I was lucky enough to find another place at the opposite end of the hall, not near a window, fan, or exit, but next to a nice lady in a hat who looked vaguely familiar.

Where had I seen her before?

We stared at each other for a few moments. It was Ariella Cohen, of course, and it had taken a whole long series of "coincidences" to bring us together again.

Steps

Miriam Stern, the landlady, lived downstairs in a two-family house. The upstairs tenant, Rachel Yaffason, was the mother of a lively one-year-old, born after years of waiting. One afternoon, while the two ladies were having a comfortable chat in the hall, little Yossi opened the latch of the safety gate and tumbled down all 15 of the steep wooden stairs, his head seeming to bounce on every step.

Panic! Yossi howled, and his mother cried hysterically, blaming herself and everyone else for the accident. The Stern children came rushing out of the downstairs apartment to see what was causing the excitement, adding to the noise and confusion.

Together, Yossi's mother and Miriam carefully picked up Yossi and checked him from head to foot. He had plenty of scratches from the splintery wood, and a purple bruise on his forehead, but was otherwise unhurt.

With a cold compress wrapped around his head and a cherry lollipop in his mouth, Yossi was put in his playpen. Soon he was busy playing with his toys, and after a while he fell asleep.

But Miriam could not sleep that night. She kept thinking of what might have happened — a concussion, a broken arm or leg, or worse ….

She woke up her husband. "Sam, we must do something about those steps!"

"What — mmf — what are you talking about?"

"The steps — when I heard that little Yossi's head come bumping down, I was terrified. We've got to put a carpet on them right away — tomorrow!"

"That's too expensive" — he was wide awake now — "and it's not practical; it'll always be dusty with the kids going up and down. Anyway, we can't afford it right now. I'm sure his mother will be more careful after this and it will never happen again."

"If you would have been there, Sam, you'd think differently! Please, let's call the carpet man tomorrow."

"Okay, okay! Just let me go back to sleep."

The next day, Mr. Jalbe came and put a remnant of olive green carpet — last year's color because it was cheaper — on the steps. But Miriam was not satisfied. It didn't look right, somehow. Then she realized — the landing downstairs should also be carpeted. If G-d forbid, the kid should fall again and land on the hard floor of the hall — she didn't even want to think about it!

So Mr. Jalbe came back with another remnant for the hall that didn't quite match the one on the steps. Miriam paid him what she felt was a king's ransom, but no regrets — they had done the right thing!

Many years passed. Yossi and his parents moved away and other tenants took their place. The old green carpet and its padding, too, had been replaced — burnt orange this time.

One day Miriam carried an armload of books down from the attic. She did everything wrong — trailing robe, backless slippers, both hands full, not holding on to the railing. It was an accident waiting to happen, and it did. She fell headfirst from the top to the bottom of the steps. For a few moments she lay there, stunned and shaken. Then she got up and walked away without a scratch.

When Yossi had fallen down the stairs 20 years earlier, the Sterns were hard-pressed financially, and the carpet was an extra unnecessary expense. But, as it turned out, Yossi didn't need the cushioned steps and hall — it was Miriam Stern who did.

What you do for others ….

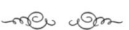

And sometimes the action of one person can benefit hundreds of thousands, as in the story of "Queen Victoria and the Rabbi" (see page 41).

❧ Mix-and-Match

It had been a hectic week of packing, of frantic telephone calls, of last-minute changes, of tearful farewells — but finally, finally the Millers were safely ensconced in their assigned seats, luggage stowed overhead, seat belts fastened, on their way to Eretz Yisrael, where they had rented an apartment, sight unseen, for their annual summer vacation.

"Did you remember to take your glasses? And film and batteries for the camera?" asked Tzvi.

"Yes — they're in my handbag," answered Molly, with a weary sigh. "But what about the new camera? You were supposed to put it in your carry-on, together with the tape recorder. You can't remember? Well, we can always borrow one from the *eineklach* — they're all camera bugs."

At the thought of the grandchildren, the faces of Tzvi and Molly Miller were wreathed in smiles. The annual reunion with their daughter, son-in-law, and grandchildren was the chief reason for the arduous packing and the long plane trip.

After a few moments of silence, Molly said, "I wonder what kind of kitchen the apartment has? That summer we spent in Geulah, it was even smaller than the galley in this plane. And that tiny washing machine ...."

"Stop worrying so much." Tzvi was getting ready to go to sleep. "You know what Carrie said, that the kitchen is big enough to eat in comfortably, with kosher sinks and an American washer and dryer. And it's a great location, right near the children and the *shul* and the bus and the stores. What more could you want?"

"But Tzvi — remember that place in Meah Shearim, where we had to keep the windows closed all the time because of the noise? We almost roasted there. And the broken steps ... I just can't help worrying."

"Well, this place is in a quiet residential neighborhood, and it's on the ground floor. So relax and let's both go to sleep, okay?"

Tzvi adjusted his pillow, wrapped himself in his blanket, and was instantly asleep. After a few minutes of fidgeting, Molly followed suit. She dreamt of broken windows, leaking roofs, mountains of garbage .....

When they arrived in Jerusalem they were pleasantly surprised at the apartment that their daughter had rented for them. It was spacious, well-equipped with modern appliances, and nicely furnished. Carrie and the children had made the beds and stocked the kitchen with all the essentials. After unpacking, the Millers felt quite settled and comfortable. Tzvi said, "You see, Molly, there was nothing to worry about. This will be a great summer!"

"You're right, Tzvi, as usual. I'm really going to enjoy it here!" Molly yawned. Jet lag told her that it was time to go to sleep — though it was bright daylight — so she did.

When she awoke a couple of hours later, planning to call her children in America to tell of their safe arrival and the nice apartment, she found that the number four on the telephone did not work. No problem — she called her daughter in Boro Park, whose number fortunately contained no fours, and asked her to notify the others. Now for a refreshing shower — she'd been looking forward to it the entire trip — but there was no shower curtain. Molly awkwardly tried to do without, but flooded the floor. There was no mop, so she used three towels to dry it.

When Tzvi returned from *shul*, she served a simple meal. Washing up afterwards, she discovered that one sink had no hot water, the other no cold, and both faucets sprayed atrociously, soaking the front of her dress as well as the floor tiles.

"What should I do, Tzvi? We can't live like this all summer!" Molly was almost in tears.

"Let's call Carrie," suggested Tzvi, "Maybe she has some ideas."

And of course she did.

"Ma, you have great neighbors across the hall, the Traubmans. He knows how to fix almost anything, and she knows whom to ask, just in case he can't. I'll call them and tell them about you."

A few minutes later, a chassidic young man was at their

door, carrying a tool kit and a large wrench. After a hearty welcome, he cast a quick professional glance at the sinks. With a few twists of the wrench he got the hot and cold water flowing. "And the faucets only need new strainers — you can buy them at the store around the corner. The shower? My Etty always has a spare curtain with hooks. Just use it *gezunterheit!*"

Well, as the old saying goes, *"Afilu tzum shlemazel muz men hubben mazel* — Even with bad luck you've got to have luck."* Almost every day there was a new emergency — the washing machine that flooded the whole apartment, the light in the windowless bathroom that didn't work, the defective front-door lock that kept them prisoner for half a day — but Mayer and Etty Traubman were always ready, willing, and able to solve any problem. So when they told the Millers that they would be going away on vacation for a couple of weeks, Molly felt a rising sense of panic — who would help them through the next exciting event in what had become a long list of almost daily disasters?

The Traubmans left on Thursday in an overloaded vehicle with a crib, bicycles, tricycles, pillows, blankets, a swing set, and, of course, the tool chest roped to the roof.

"It looks like they'll be away for a year," Molly agonized, "and what'll we do in case ...."

"Here you go, worrying again! What more could happen? The phone is fixed, so is the door, and the bathroom, and the washing machine. So relax already!" Tzvi had always been the optimistic type.

"Okay, but still ... I guess you're right. So help me with the shopping list — tomorrow is Shabbos already."

The next day, minutes before candlelighting time, there was a knock at the door. A pleasant young woman requested two items urgently needed before Shabbos. When she returned them after *Havdalah* the next night, she revealed that she and her family had exchanged apartments with the Traubmans for a while, and had neglected to bring the shoe-brush and polish from their home in Moshav Yesodot.

"Oh, is that where you live?" The Millers were excited. They had been in that area several times and had friends there, "Do you know Label and Baila Deutsch? They're from Monsey, our home town."

"Of course we know them! They've been living there even longer than us. And do you know my aunt Rivky Kaufman in Monsey?"

The Millers had known the Kaufmans for ages. Soon a lively game of "Jewish Geography" was in progress, leading (again!) to the realization of how closely knit the observant community really is. There are invisible links joining Jews from anywhere and everywhere, links of "relativity" or friendship, or at least of being the friend of a friend. *Chaverim kol Yisrael!*

The new temporary neighbors, Avraham and Leili Ellis, turned out to be a friendly and fascinating pair, with charming little children. The two couples, although years apart in age, found they had much in common. When Molly told the Ellises about her efforts to find suitable *shidduchim* for two difficult cases, they offered some good suggestions, followed by stories of their own successes in this field, several of which had occurred even before they made their own match. Again and again we are reminded that finding the destined mate requires a certain amount of human effort and tremendous *siyata d'Shmaya,* as openly revealed in the stories that follow.

⮡ The Case of the Reluctant Roommate

Avraham and Shimon were two Americans learning in Jerusalem. Outwardly they couldn't have been more differ-ent. Avraham was tall, gangly, outgoing, and cheerful, while

Shimon was short and of a serious nature. Despite their differences, they got along very well and, being roommates, became quite close. At the time, they were 24 and 25 respectively, seriously into the business of seeking their *basherte,* but not finding it easy at all.

Late one night as Avraham was learning in the *beis midrash,* trying to forget his worries about his single state, Shimon entered and poured out his woes. Avraham commiserated and felt an intense desire to help his friend. "But what can I do?" he recalls thinking, "I'm just a *bachur* myself."

The next day, Avraham went to see Rebbetzin Heiman, a successful *shadchanis.* She had a suggestion for him. Then the rebbetzin talked about several young ladies who had consulted her, and at one point, lights began to flash in Avraham's mind.

"Wait a minute," he said to Rebbetzin Heiman, "Is this girl short?"

The rebbetzin was taken aback, but answered, "Yes, Chanah *is* quite short."

"Then I have a *shidduch* for her!" Avraham declared. He described his friend Shimon and the rebbetzin thought that they might be compatible. Avraham left, with Chanah's name and Rebbetzin Heiman's phone number jotted on a piece of paper.

The following morning, after *davening*, Avraham went to tell Shimon to call Rebbetzin Heiman. When he knocked on the door, Shimon invited him in, but suddenly the whole idea seemed crazy to Avraham.

"How in the world can I suggest a *shidduch* if I don't know the girl at all, just a few words about her?" he asked himself, "Forget it!"

Shimon looked up at his friend expectantly. Flustered and at a loss for words, Avraham began talking about the weather. But Shimon was smarter than that.

"All right, Avraham, what did you *really* want to tell me?" he asked.

Put on the spot, Avraham told about his meeting with Rebbetzin Heiman, and the idea that had occurred to him while he was there, but, "I'm sure it's nothing," he said, "I really don't know a thing about her."

"I'll take this paper anyway. You never know." Shimon pocketed the note with the name and telephone number.

That was the end of it, or so it seemed. Shimon was seeing someone else at the time and forgot about it. The suggestion that the rebbetzin had made for Avraham was not suitable either.

A couple of months later, Shimon stuck his hand in the pocket of his old jacket and found the crumpled note there. Since he was still spectacularly single, he decided to give Rebbetzin Heiman a try. Avraham tried to dissuade him. "How can I shoulder the responsibility of putting together two people without knowing one of them at all? Please, Shimon, just forget about it!" he pleaded.

But Shimon called Rebbetzin Heiman, despite his friend's misgivings. She told him that Chanah had scheduled a flight back to the States, but she would speak to her anyway. Chanah decided to push off her return trip in order to meet Shimon. They continued seeing each other, while Avraham prayed that the two would break up — he was afraid, in fact terrified, of the responsibility.

Late one night, when Avraham was fast asleep, he suddenly felt the earth shake.

"C'mon, Avraham, wake up!" he heard a voice from afar, and when he forced his eyelids half open, he saw Shimon's smiling face in the dim light. He sat up and Shimon told him to get dressed, but fast! Shimon dragged him to the door of their apartment, and there in the hall was a very short young lady who said in a sweet little voice, "Thank you!"

Avraham snapped to it, got out his musical instruments, and entertained the crowd at the very joyous engagement of Shimon and Chanah.

~~ The Case of the Proper Miss

While Shimon's success was behind him, Avraham was still single, and becoming quite desperate. Someone suggested Mindy, and the two were introduced. In retrospect, Avraham wonders what compelled them to meet so many times, since they were different as can be. Avraham was very laid back, completely the opposite of the "veddy propah" British Mindy. After a while, they both realized that they had no common interests or future together, and they broke up.

But Avraham had gotten to know Mindy quite well, and tried to think of someone suitable for her. He spoke to Chaim, an English friend, but Chaim was hesitant. How could it work? Would she even agree to meet him? She came from a prominent Torah family, while he had only recently tasted intensive Torah learning.

Avraham begged Chaim, "Don't make that the most important factor! I think you have a lot in common — you should meet at least once, and judge her on her own merits."

Chaim refused.

Meanwhile, Avraham tried to contact Mindy, but the only address he had was that of her workplace, so he sent a letter suggesting that she meet Chaim. Some time passed, and the two didn't meet, so he sent a second letter. Still no progress! Avraham told Chaim that he was passing over his *basherte* by refusing to consider Mindy. The answer was still "No!"

Family matters forced Avraham to return to America, but he felt so strongly about Chaim and Mindy that he mailed a *third* letter to Mindy on his way to the airport and told her bluntly that she *must* meet Chaim. No response from either one .... Avraham was quite busy searching for his own *zivug,* yet the problem of Chaim and Mindy kept turning up in his thoughts. "They're so suited to one another! How can I force them to meet?"

But a Higher Power had already intervened. Mindy later reported how embarrassed she had been to find letters in a masculine handwriting hanging on the bulletin board at work; but Avraham's conviction and sincerity struck a chord, and she asked her brother for advice. He promised her that he would bring it up with his rav. Chaim, meanwhile, felt guilty, and with Avraham's words ringing in his ears, decided to turn to *his* rav.

Who would believe that in the entire city of Jerusalem, the two men chose to consult the very same rav? He warmly recommended that Chaim and Mindy meet. It didn't take them long to realize that Avraham was right.

A few weeks later, he received the invitation to their wedding — which was the same night as his own — but that's another story.

⤳ The Blessing and the Bet

(as told by Leili Ellis)

When I started to work, I felt like a little girl dressing up in my Mommy's old finery. I usually wore casual clothing and sneakers, and when I discovered that it was permitted to dress that way on the job, I was thrilled!

Simie, a wise 14-year-old neighbor, scolded me, "You're a *kallah meidel,* Leili. You can't wear sneakers to work!" All my talk of "new fashions" didn't convince Simie one bit.

One evening, I found my father in the living room with an impressive looking rav from Eretz Yisrael, who told us that he has a special *koach* to give *berochos,* and that he feels that this one will come true. He blessed me that I would find my mate within the year. I was then 22, and I felt that was the best *berachah* he could give me. The next time Simie made fun of my footwear, I said, "Never mind — I got a *berachah* from Rav C. that I'd be a *kallah* within a year."

Simie checked the date and we made a $10 bet. I am not

a gambler, but I felt so strongly that the *tzaddik's berachah* would be fulfilled, that I agreed to the wager!

When Avraham left Jerusalem after working on Chaim and Mindy's consciences so intensely, he felt ready to give up for himself. At age 25, he felt burned out, and had relinquished his dream of living in Eretz Yisrael after his marriage. After all, hadn't he met all the girls there? When he made plans for his return ticket, his father told him about a girl in New York that had been suggested, while Mrs. Stern, a family friend, had mentioned someone in his hometown — me. Avraham decided to fly to New York first, "because that's where the action is," and if that wouldn't work out — like all the others before her, and who knows how many more after her — he would return home to meet me. In his mind's eye, he had been in this *parshah* forever, and would continue forever.

Man toils and the A-mighty foils .... The travel agent simply could not get a seat on a New York-bound flight. Avraham started to think about where he would stay in New York, since he had no relatives there, and about shlepping his luggage twice, once to New York and then home. Not too appealing!

"Do you have any direct flights to Toronto?" he asked.

A look at the computer screen confirmed that he could indeed go directly to Toronto. Avraham booked the flight, relieved that he wouldn't have to drag his suitcases all over the continent.

Back home, he called up Mrs. Stern. With her customary cheer, she said, "I've been working on something for you for a whole year!" It seems that two years earlier, Avraham had made a comment that struck Mrs. Stern and remained with her. When, a year later, I made a similar remark, sirens went off in Mrs. Stern's mind. She let the idea incubate for a while, and when she saw still more similarities, she approached Avraham's parents, who agreed in theory — but what could they do? Avraham was in Jerusalem and wanted only to stay there. And I just wasn't interested in him. Then another neighbor suggested

Avraham's younger brother for me, and I saw possibilities … So when Mrs. Stern pressured me about Avraham, I agreed; I even found myself eagerly awaiting his arrival.

I figured that Avraham must certainly be very tall, so the first time we met, I wore my highest heels. From that perspective, he wasn't so tall. On the second date, we did a lot of walking; when we finally sat down, I asked him if he would mind if I took off my shoes. That's when Avraham decided that I was for him.

Despite the fact that he truly hoped to live in Eretz Yisrael, he didn't bring this topic up, since he had given up on it. I didn't bring it up either — Mrs. Stern had told me how much Avraham wanted it, no less than I myself did.

One morning, a few weeks after Avraham and I had met for the first time, Simie opened her eyes, looked at her calendar, and told her sister, "Today is the last day of May. I had a bet that Leili would be engaged by June, and she's not. I won the bet!"

Sorry, Simie — the rebbe said one year from when he gave the *berachah,* and that was at the end of June!

Right before Avraham and I were scheduled to meet that day, he called me and asked me not to wear my much-maligned sneakers. When we got back from this last date, Simie was one of the first people I told. Graciously, I forgave Simie the $10. Today, Avraham and I live in Eretz Yisrael with our family. Our mutual dream has come true.

~⊙~ Higher Education
(as told by Leili Ellis)

When I was five, a boy named Yitzchak Green used to come over to learn with my father on Shabbos afternoons. His parents wanted him to get more learning than he could just at school.

Years passed. I was an eligible young lady, and among the *shidduch* suggestions was — Yitzchak Green. I debated whether or not to meet him, since he worked part-time and I wanted someone who would learn full-time before facing the burden of supporting a family. While working this out, I popped by to visit Mrs. Stern, a neighbor whom I had often consulted, especially on *shidduch* issues. In the course of the conversation, she said, "Oh, you should meet Yitzchak Green."

I stared at her in surprise. "How did you know?" I stammered.

"How did I know what?"

"Someone suggested Yitzy Green — you know — from that big family, but I'm still debating," I said.

"Oh, I don't mean *that* family," Mrs. Stern smiled, "I meant a different family, Rabbi D.'s *mishpachah*. By the way, someone suggested as a *shidduch* for Leah Ratner the Yitzy Green you mentioned."

Leah, a girl in my circle of acquaintances, also often turned to Mrs. Stern for advice. We were quite friendly and the fact that Yitz had been suggested for Leah raised my opinion of him. "They never met, though," Mrs. Stern added, "Yitzchak wasn't interested."

I had been seeking a husband totally involved in learning, and except for this point, Yitzy looked like an excellent *shidduch*, so I asked a rav for advice. He told me that if the boy is sincerely learning, there is no reason to turn him down if he works part time. "There's no *mitzvah* to be poor if you don't have to be," was his wise advice.

So we met. I recognized him, but we never discussed the fact that he had come to learn with my father at age seven. We *did*, however, discuss why such a sterling *bachur* had a college degree and a part-time job. It seems that his parents insisted that he get a good degree, and he complied out of respect for them. Then they demanded that he get a suitable job. Not wanting to leave the yeshivah environment, he called his *rebbe muvhok* and described his dilemma.

His rebbe consulted with one of the *gedolei hador,* who, to Yitzchak's complete surprise, advised him to get a part-time job. Yitzchak found a position where he finished work at three. By 3:15 he was in the yeshivah for *minchah.* "They built that highway just for me," he said, and he was probably right!

For all of Yitzchak's fine qualities, I sensed that he wasn't for me. I mentioned to a *shadchanta* that Leah Ratner was highly intellectual, and that her parents insisted that *she* get a degree. She had given in and was working on her Master's at that point.

Two weeks later, I met Leah in the street. She told me that she would be meeting Yitzchak for the fourth time. A few weeks later, I sent her a *mishloach manos* in a container disguised as a *kallah.* I made sure to wrap it well so that no one else would see it.

They got engaged after Purim, and only then did I find out that when Leah was first suggested, Yitzchak's reply was, "So why are you calling me? You know I don't want someone who goes to college!"

Well, neither did she, so the match was made between two very fine, very *frum* young people with a higher education. Leah Green never did finish her Master's, and has no regrets.

ᲐᲘ Telegemach

As well as being an interesting and kindhearted couple, the Ellises are very modest. It came out only after many conversations that Avraham is the originator, founder, and head of Telegemach, the unique organization that tries to provide answers to all sorts of questions and requests in countless locations all over the world.

Telegemach is the result of inspiration — and perspiration — on the part of Avraham Ellis. He was in charge of the dairy farm on Moshav Yesodot. Learning, *davening,* doing his part as a good husband and father — yet he felt there was something missing. *Chesed!* From his early youth, he had a deep yearning to help others, a yearning which had found expression in action: As a teenager, he drove fundraisers all over town, tutored needy children, played at *mitzvah* weddings — an impressive list. But what could he accomplish from his post at this isolated *moshav?*

Avraham called several organizations that had advertised for volunteers. Some wanted him to go collecting for them, or to come to Tel Aviv and run their computers, or to set up an office in Beersheva. None of these offers appealed to his deep desire to give of himself. He decided to take a day off from the dairy to recite *Tehillim,* asking the A-mighty to show him the way.

"I thought of a ge*mach* — a self-perpetuating kind of thing," says Avraham, "but what could I offer? I had no money or furniture or books. Then it hit me — a ge*mach* of information! I had an old answering machine. With it I could be in contact with the entire world!"

He made a few posters advertising the new service and hung them up in Tel Aviv. The response was almost immediate: Parents of a handicapped child living in the sticks left a message on his machine asking for assistance in educating their son. Soon, they had replies offering the help they had sought in vain, until they contacted Telegemach.

And the telephones have not stopped ringing since! An impoverished mother was terribly injured in an accident. The insurance company refused to pay. She told a friend her plan for committing suicide. When she arrived at the place she had selected as the scene of her departure from this world, police officers were waiting, and one of them provided her with an article about Telegemach, assuring her that someone cared. Avraham Ellis connected her to his Ashkelon branch, which provided for her needs, including volunteer lawyers.

So, if there's a need for an attorney, a bed, a chiropractor, a driver, any kind of expert, a farmer, a gynecologist, a hairdresser, information, a job, a musical or computer keyboard, laboratory tests, a mortgage, a name, an optometrist, a pediatrician, quilts, recipes, *shidduchim*, teachers, an underwriter, vegetables, a washing machine, x-rays, yams, or zoos — someone will soon be calling back with the required information or help. Telegemach quickly matches the request with the response. Only phone numbers are used for identification so that privacy is maintained.

Telegemach is for everyone: those who have items to donate or sell, for lost-and-found, for employment, matchmaking, house rentals or purchases, financial help — you name it, and Telegemach calls upon its many sources to supply it.

From the Chief Rabbi in Moscow to children around the world, Telegemach sparks interest and receives assistance from its members and from the One Above, often in a miraculous way. A call came from a woman who needed several kinds of help, but most of all, contact with others, warmth, and friendship. Soon after, there was a call from someone who wanted to volunteer to help another woman. Not only were the two living in the same town, but they worked in the same office! They might never have known of the other's needs.

A letter from the Rav of Yesodot states: "Many who have nowhere to turn receive help from Avraham Ellis. As our Sages have taught: 'The whole world is built on lovingkindness.' May Hashem grant him success in his efforts." Signed, Rabbi David Bentzion Klein

Avraham and Leili had worked diligently, against great odds, to bring about a *shidduch* between two people who were having a hard time; both were older, a bit set in their ways, hard to please. Now, *baruch Hashem,* they were getting engaged!

The bride, Miriam, had several close friends who were eager to attend the *simchah* but they lived on scattered *moshavim* with no transportation available at night. Avraham Ellis decided to pick them up in a van after work and bring them to the party. This involved several hours of driving, but would add immeasurably to Miriam's happiness. The engagement party was lovely, with a beaming *chasan,* a joyous *kallah,* and all her happy friends.

However, after a few weeks, it appeared that the engaged couple had differences too great to surmount, and the *shidduch* broke up. The Ellises were heartsick — all their work, all the phoning and explaining, encouraging and arranging had been in vain. But what can you do? It's all in Hashem's hands!

Some months later, a young woman came up to Avraham in the street. "Thank you! Thank you!" she beamed, "Don't you remember me?"

"Can't say I do," Avraham was puzzled — he had no idea who this could be.

"Well, my name is now Abby Gold. It used to be Maimon; I just got married last week and I owe it all to you!"

Avraham racked his brains. Who was this stranger?

She bubbled on, "Don't you remember when you brought a bunch of Miriam's friends to her engagement? Yes, I know they broke up — but that's where I met my wonderful husband! Thank you again and again!"

In the words of Rabbi Tarfon in *Pirkei Avos*: "It is not incumbent upon you to complete the work, yet you are not free to desist from it." We do not know where our actions may lead; sometimes it takes years to see the outcome. Abby met her husband as a result of Avraham's dedication to promoting someone else's happiness.

The Millers spent enjoyable hours in the company of Avraham and Leili, and were truly sorry when the time came for them to return to Yesodot. With fond farewells and promises to keep in touch, they watched the Ellises' departure.

"Do you realize that not a single thing broke in this house as long as Avraham and Leili were next door?" asked Molly.

"You know, you're right. But I guess that everything that could possibly happen here already did," said Tzvi.

That night, a cat jumped through the grate on the kitchen window and escaped with a quarter of a chicken intended for the Millers' supper. The next morning, the solar heater on the roof started leaking — no hot water for a shower. While Molly was trying to wash up at the sink, the mirror fell off the wall. But by then the Traubmans and their tool chest were back home again.

Esther Adams — A Cautionary Tale

ESTHER ADAMS' LIFE WAS IN SHAMBLES.

She had been married for 13 years to Yaron Adams, a wealthy and respected businessman, and had borne a son and a daughter. She came from a religious background; his family, wealthy and highly cultured, was strictly secular, strongly committed to a worldly lifestyle.

What had brought this odd couple together? Perhaps it was simple proximity — he had been a rising young professor at a great university; she had been a highly intelligent and impressionable graduate student. Perhaps it was because he spouted high-flown idealistic sentiments about improving the lot of humanity — most appealing to one brought up in an observant home, where the commandments to assist the stranger, to give charity, to seek social justice were part of the very air she breathed. Perhaps it was simply a case of an insecure girl flattered by the attention of a charismatic figure who had already made a place for himself in a sphere toward which she was still struggling. Perhaps it was for all of these reasons, or for none of them; no one, even Esther herself, really knew.

In any case, they married and settled in a small apartment on campus. Esther continued her studies while keeping house and entertaining Yaron's many professional acquaintances. Then the children came, Joshua and Sharon, close in age, bright and high-spirited, and very demanding of their mother's time and energy.

Esther's studies had to take second place. She still attended most of her classes, but found the burden of research and constant writing quite overwhelming. She tried to make time by getting up extra early and by staying up late at night, but found herself always tired, even irritable. She cut down the number of her courses, and that helped a bit, but combined with the social demands — the entertaining, the going out with friends — it was still too much. She came to a decision: The children came first! Yaron agreed: Yes, the children came first.

So Esther stayed home, only occasionally reading the latest publications so as not to fall too far behind in her field. She found the children better behaved and calmer as the stress at home was reduced. Esther firmly decreed that the television had to go, and found the home environment much improved, after the initial resentment had passed. She, too, began to enjoy life more. She had time to play her violin, to take long walks in the countryside, to live!

But after a while — was it her imagination, or was it fact? — it seemed that Yaron was growing distant from her, cold, critical. In public, he was still the same interesting, affable fellow she had first met, but at home, he often ignored her completely and at times was almost hostile to the children. He was embarking on a new career in the import-export business; he had great financial ambitions and life in academe could never furnish the money he needed to pursue his ideal lifestyle. "Maybe it's the stress of trying to establish himself, starting from scratch," she told herself.

Esther started to think back to her early years; had it been like that at home? No, even in the worst of times, her parents had always been a team, working together, tackling problems together, deeply devoted to their child and to each other.

"Why can't my life be like that? It must be my fault. I'll do my best to please Yaron, and maybe try to live the same kind of life my parents did."

Esther now became solicitous of her husband. His slightest whim became her command. She cooked only the foods he preferred, invited only his closest friends, tried in every possible way to please him. At the same time, she returned to the life she had experienced as a child — lighting candles on Friday night, avoiding work or driving on Shabbos, using only kosher food.

At first Yaron quite enjoyed the extra, almost slavish attention she gave him, but soon he began criticizing again, and worse: He berated her for her observance of those silly, medieval outdated laws; for being so *out* of it; for being so … *dumb*, the worst adjective he could possibly find.

For the first few weeks, the children had enjoyed the festive atmosphere, the candlelight, and the Shabbos songs she taught them, but soon the day of rest became a day of quarrels and anger.

This was not what Esther had intended. She though she was doing everything possible to save, even to improve her marriage, but her plan seemed to be backfiring. Yaron was perpetually angry and silent and the children were increasingly nervous, not wanting to go to school or even to play with their friends. Tantrums and crying spells became the order of the day.

Esther found excuses for Yaron's behavior: He had a great need for the respect he had received from his colleagues, and for the uncritical admiration of his students. The world of business was quite different; education and reputation didn't count, only results, and these, despite his workaholic habits, were slow in coming. Esther constantly tried to build him up, flattering him outrageously, but she felt she was being untrue to her husband and to herself. And she saw that the children sensed the falseness that permeated their lives.

So the couple drifted along — not happy — but not absolutely miserable either. As the children grew, decisions had to be made about their education. Esther timidly suggested removing Josh from his progressive school, where at the age of 8, he majored in finger painting and "creative mathematics," where one and one *could* add up to two occasionally, but many other choices were available. A Hebrew Day School had opened not far away, and she liked the way the children there looked and acted — clean, neat, polite — the way children had been in her own youth, which seemed ages ago. And the few friends that Josh and Sharon had made weren't at all like those she saw in the new school's playground. No — they were noisy, demanding, often rude, as were her own children, she realized.

When she broached the subject of enrolling Josh in the Hebrew Day School, Yaron went berserk.

"You want to ruin my son! The best minds in the university send their children to the same school, but it's not good enough for Her Highness! You want Josh to be a fanatic, an ignorant fool like your father? Over my dead body! He'll stay where he is or …."

Esther left the room before he had a chance to finish his threat. What should she do? What *could* she do? Her orderly study habits now came to her aid. She would investigate the "Cali Progressive Academy" thoroughly in all its aspects, and compare it with the Hebrew school. Surely Yaron, with his scientific mind, would accept the results, whatever they might turn out to be.

The next morning found her at the children's school. She watched the students get off the bus, pushing and shoving, with little regard for the smaller ones. In the hall, it was pandemonium — teachers scurrying around, trying to beat the bell, students with their heavy backpacks playing a "game" of trying to knock others off their feet. Bypassing the secretary, who was engaged in an intense telephone conversation, Esther entered the principal's office.

Dr. Gerbow, too, was busy on the telephone. "Yes, Mrs. Bloom, I'm really sorry, I didn't realize that your Gregory is that sensitive. Yes, I will give Miss Smith a very strong warning about punishing your son. Well, no — I wouldn't call it child abuse — she only took away his water gun, and only because it was filled with ink — I'll make sure it doesn't happen again, and thank you so much for calling."

With a sigh, the principal turned toward Esther. His face brightened. She was one of his "good" mothers, helping the school in various ways, and seldom, if ever, complaining or demanding. "What can I do for you today, Mrs. Adams? It's a pleasure to see you."

"Dr. Gerbow, I hope you can answer some questions for me, about the school."

"Gladly. Now, what did you have in mind?"

"Well, it's about my children's behavior. I hear them using language that is absolutely shocking, and they're constantly fighting with each other, and even with their friends. They have no respect for my husband and me. And Josh seems to be way behind in his schoolwork; it seems to me I knew much more at his age."

Dr. Gerbow steepled his fingers, removed his glasses, and gave Esther his most sincere, practiced smile. He cleared his throat several times and began: "Perhaps, Mrs. Adams, you are over-reacting. Children must be allowed to express themselves without the artificial restraints imposed by old-fashioned mores. The language which is considered offensive today will eventually become the norm — youth is always somewhat in advance of its elders. As far as what you call "fighting" is concerned, this is simply part of the normal interaction between children. It is a way for them to learn the assertiveness and self-confidence that are so necessary for their future success. I consider your children well-balanced and well within the median range."

"But Doctor" — Esther had quickly realized that respect for elders was not even an issue — "what about learning the basics: reading, writing, spelling, arithmetic? Josh seems to have no idea of these subjects. He's in third grade; shouldn't he at least know how to add, subtract, multiply? And how to read easy books? It seems to me he's still stuck at the *cat, hat, rat* stage."

"Dear Mrs. Adams, our methodology is the latest, most up-to-date product of educational philosophy. Let each child advance at his own pace, without adult interference, without inhibiting the child's creative processes. That is the only way to produce the man — uh, pardon me — the man or *woman* — who will fit into our future society. I hope this discussion has been of help to you — it has certainly been most interesting to me."

Esther knew when she was being dismissed. She took her leave graciously, smiling at the secretary, who was filing her nails. As she passed by the glass-doored classrooms, she could see a little girl sprawling on the teacher's desk, and in another room, three children smearing each other with what looked like peanut butter. She had seen and heard enough, and she was exhausted. "Home ... home and a cup of coffee," was all that she could think about.

Esther was well prepared for Yaron's arrival that night and served him an elaborate meal, with all the foods he loved. Afterward, over drinks in the living room, she started to tell him what she had seen that day. Yaron's reaction was cold anger. "We've been over all that before. You think you know more that the world's greatest educators? You're dumb, dumb, dumb!" and he rushed out of the room, knocking over her drink on the way.

After that, Esther did not bring up the subject again. She spent as much time as possible with Josh and Sharon, supervising them closely, and trying to keep them away from the most difficult and disruptive of their friends. One especially beautiful afternoon she decided to take them to the playground. She sat on a bench, trying to read a book, while watching them from a distance. Suddenly she became aware of furious screaming, and the voices were her children's!

Sharon had grabbed her brother's new ball and scampered away with it. Josh ran after her, yelling like a banshee, "You rotten stupid idiot! You're just as dumb as your mother! You give that ball back to me or else!"

He caught Sharon by her hair and slammed the hand holding the ball against the stone water fountain.

Esther heard Sharon's screams from across the park. She flew to her children and broke up the unequal fight by forcing her son's hand open. When he finally released Sharon's hair, he turned all his anger against his mother, pummeling her with both fists.

This was too much. All her fears, all her frustration at the home situation rose in her throat. She literally saw red. She grabbed Joshua by the neck and pushed him away with a strength she never knew she possessed.

"Stop — now — or I'll kill you!"

All her carefully nurtured parenting skills, all her psychological expertise had left her. She was like a wild beast, lashing out in pain and fury.

Through the red haze, she suddenly noticed Sharon trembling, her face white with terror, the ball still held tightly in her grasp. Josh had turned away.

"I'm sorry, Ma — she just makes me so mad. Everything and everybody is making me crazy. I'm sorry."

Esther took his hand. "I'm sorry, too. I shouldn't have gotten so upset. Let's go home now."

Usually the children protested vociferously whenever it was time to leave the playground, but now they took her hands and set out for home. No one said a word.

Esther gave them their suppers, bathed them, and put them to bed, moving like an automaton. Sharon and Josh ignored each other, forgoing their usual squabbling. It was the quietest evening she could remember.

When Yaron came home, even later than usual, she reported the events at the playground. She tried to appear calm and objective, but could not keep her voice from trembling while telling her husband of her complete loss of control.

"I'm so ashamed, and I'm scared. I really felt like choking him, like killing him. What if it happens again? What if I … can't stop?"

Yaron seemed quite unmoved. His cool, analytical glance went over her from head to foot. "I've noticed for a long time that you overreact emotionally. Perhaps you should be under psychiatric care — the kids could go to my parents, or to my brother Peter's family until you recover. Of course, they'll be exposed to all that TV violence you're so worried about, but isn't that better than living with a violent woman who can't control her murderous impulses?"

"You really would do that?" Esther felt she couldn't breathe.

"And why not? They'll be in a normal atmosphere, without that religious drivel, without all that moralizing and analyzing. Yes, I'll speak to my good friend Dr. Harry Krakovich. I'm sure he'll lower his fee for me; and I'll call Peter right now."

"And that's all you have to say about it? It's not that school, it's not the bad friends they have, it's not the tension at home — it's just — me?"

"You said that, not me. Let's not discuss it any more." Yaron slammed the door to his den. She heard the key turn in the lock.

All that night, Esther tossed and turned. In the morning her decision was made. After Yaron had left for the office and the children for school, she packed two suitcases: one with the children's clothes and a few favorite toys, and one with her clothing and books, her Shabbos candlesticks and her personal papers. She checked the airlines for the cheapest flight east that same afternoon. She drove to the bank and closed her small account — it would be just enough to get them to her parents in Philadelphia.

She could not worry beyond that. She knew she had to act immediately, before she lost her brave resolve, and she prayed that Yaron would not come home unexpectedly early. Would he try to hinder her, to hold her back? She did not think so. But the children —

No — it would *have* to be all right.

The flight was uneventful. Josh and Sharon had been surprised, and then delighted at this unexpected adventure.

"You know, I don't even remember what Nana looks like," said Sharon. "She must be awfully old, with all those lines on her face. Do you think she's 100 yet, Josh?"

"Maybe, but who cares how old she is, as long as she's living!" Josh was ever the realist. "And last time, she baked us the best chocolate cookies ever. I hope she still remembers how to make them."

Esther barely heard them — she was too busy thinking, planning. She would probably move into her old room, pink, frilly, unchanged from her teenage years, and somehow manage to crowd in with her two children. Should she tell her parents about her decision to leave her husband? Better not. She'd just pretend it was a visit made on impulse — why worry them? And maybe — it was a very faint hope — maybe Yaron would miss them, would plead with her to return, would change back to the affable, charming husband of their early days together.

Absence does make the heart grow fonder, and already Esther felt an impulse, a yearning to turn back.

"No. Why fool myself? He won't change. I'll have to find work as soon as possible, I can't burden my parents."

Only half-hearing her children's chatter, she had to

smile. Her father was 65, her mother seven years younger. To children, any adult seems ancient, but as she grew older, her parents seemed younger. She couldn't wait to see them.

There was no one home when the little family arrived at 183 Chestnut Street. The door was locked, and there was no response to her steady knocking. She decided to try the neighboring house; Mrs. Rubin had a key, she knew.

"Oh — Esther — I hardly recognized you — you're so thin. The children are just darling. Of course I have the key. How were you able to come so fast? It just happened this morning," sighed Mrs. Rubin.

"What — what happened?"

"Didn't someone tell you? Isn't that why you came? Your father had a heart attack. They're doing everything they can, and he has the best doctors. Oh, poor thing, poor thing that I had to tell you such news," and Mrs. Rubin squeezed her eyes shut to prevent the tears from escaping.

"Where is he? Oh, at the General Hospital. Mrs. Rubin, could you possibly take the children for a little while? I must get to the hospital right away. This is Josh, he's 8, and Sharon is almost 5, and I hope they won't be too much trouble. Their clothing is in the valise."

Esther didn't even wait for Mrs. Rubin to agree; the kind look in her eyes was answer enough. The children, bewildered, clung to her skirt, but she quickly detached them and handed them over to Mrs. Rubin.

"You'll have lots of toys to play with, and Mrs. Rubin will give you ice cream, any kind you want." Esther remembered the well-stocked freezer of years ago, always open for her choice of flavors.

Mrs. Rubin gathered the frightened children to her flowered apron. "That's right, just come in and make yourselves at home. Mommy will be back soon." It was more a hope and a prayer than a statement.

Esther hailed a taxi. "To the General Hospital, please — fast!"

Arriving there a few minutes later, she dashed through the lobby to the information desk. "Samuel Feinberg — he had a heart attack this morning."

"You'll want cardiology." The receptionist pushed some buttons on the computer, then shuffled a card file. After what seemed like endless searching, she muttered, "I see you."

"I see you?" Esther thought she was going crazy. Or was this woman crazy?

"Sure. Intensive Care Unit, on the second floor, to your left. Room 200."

The elevator — couldn't she will it to go faster? Another dash down the hall. Room 200 at last! She opened the door. By the blind look on her mother's face, she knew it was all over.

Now began a period of struggle for Esther Adams. Her mother, who had survived so many troubles and challenges together with her husband, could not cope alone. She refused to leave the house, and clung to Esther like a child. Esther tried: "Mom, would you like to visit Aunt Rose? She's always calling and asking for you."

"So let her. I'm not interested."

"How about the park? It's such a gorgeous day, and we'll take the kids and feed the pigeons. You used to like that."

"The pigeons can look out for themselves. I'll just sit here and look at the old albums of when Dad and I were first married and when you were a baby. How long we had to wait for you … and what a kewpie doll you were."

Day after day, her mother resisted all Esther's efforts at comforting her, at getting her out of the house. And money was getting tight. The proceeds of her father's life insurance policy — $15,000 had seemed like a fortune over 40 years ago — were nearly used up, barely covering the hospital and funeral expenses. Her mother's small Social Security widow's benefit was not enough to support one person, much less four. Esther appealed to Yaron several times, by phone and by letter, but his answer was brief and cutting: "You made your bed .... The children are entirely your responsibility, since you removed them from my sphere of influence."

Esther went next door to Mrs. Rubin and poured out her heart.

"What you need and what your mother needs are the same thing; you both need jobs, and the sooner the better." Mrs. Rubin did not mince words.

"How can you say that, Mrs. Rubin?" Esther was shocked. "Why, Mom has been a housewife for the past 40 years. Of course, she always helped Pop in the store, but that's not like a regular job. And do you think I haven't tried to get work? Yes, I could probably get the night shift at McDonald's or something like that. I answered so many ads in the paper, and all I get is, "Sorry, the position is filled!" I'm ready to give up. And anyway, what about my kids?"

"Listen, Esther. Your mother can have the best job in the world — taking care of her grandchildren. She's not old, and she was always active until ... now. All she needs is to be needed. And I'll help you find work: I'll call the whole Ladies Auxiliary from my Emunas Tzaddikim *shul*, and I'm sure something will turn up."

Mrs. Rubin was not one to waste time. The next evening, she presented Esther with the results of her telephone calls: a list of four possible jobs, neatly written in her spidery European penmanship:

1. Bookkeeper in a 5- and 10-cent store; needs experience.

2. Lawyer's office. There's a full-time secretary, but she needs an assistant.

3. Substitute arithmetic teacher for third and fourth grade in public school; call between 3 and 5.

4. Training in sweater factory. Nice Hungarian boss; *davens* by my nephew, the rabbi.

Esther eliminated the first entry immediately. She had no bookkeeping experience, and could barely keep her own checkbook straight, but mainly it was the thought of all those millions of nickels and dimes she'd be responsible for, although she knew the cheapest item in the five-and-ten cost 69 cents. No — she marked an X next to the first line.

Teacher — well, math wasn't her strong point, but she *was* a college grad with an M.A., wasn't she? She would surely be able to handle simple third- and fourth-grade arithmetic, and she was good with children. Check!

Assistant secretary in lawyer's office — that sounded good, even rather glamorous. She was a quick learner; maybe she would work her way up to paralegal and go to law school at night. It would be a long struggle, but she would pass her boards with flying colors. Her mother would be so proud at her graduation! She would take on all the cases that no lawyer wanted to touch — the poor, the persecuted — and She would win them all! Perhaps she would enter politics. She could see herself, middle-aged and dignified, as Secretary of Labor like Frances Perkins, or Health and Education, or even Secretary of State.

With a thud, she came back to reality. Her father had often called her "*mein kleine treimerke*, my little dreamer." But this job did offer good possibilities, and it might prove helpful when the time came for a divorce. Alone and without means, she would never be able to prevail against Yaron. He could afford the most experienced and prominent divorce lawyers. And what if he insisted on custody of the children? Yes, the law office was it. Check!

Training in a sweater factory? What could that mean? Oh … trainee! Esther saw herself chained to an enormous clacking machine, madly pushing buttons and levers, while bales of fuzzy wool threatened to engulf her. No, positively not!

The job search began the next morning. Esther would not

broach the subject to her mother until she actually had a job. There was no point in getting her upset.

"Hello? Sherman and Dwight? My name is Esther Adams. I understand you have an opening for an assistant secretary — oh, sorry, assistant to the executive secretary. I'm a college graduate. (Better not mention my M.A.; they'll say I'm over-qualified.) Yes, I can work full time. (I hope, I hope!) Computer skills? I'm quite an accurate typist (hundreds of term papers, and the beginning of a thesis) and I'm sure I can catch on to computers. You'll see me at 2 tomorrow? Great! Thank you, thank you so much."

Esther hauled out her old manual Royal, grown dusty in the basement after years of storage, and tried to recapture her old speed and skill. It was hard going. The ribbon was almost worn out, and there were just so many things to do, things she never had to think about with her trusty Selectric. She should have taken it along, and also her warm coat, and boots for the children — winter was coming.

She caught herself — should have, could have .... Why was she always distracted and dreaming, out of touch with the present? "No more *narrishkeiten,*" she heard her father's voice say. No more foolishness — back to work!

After an hour at the typewriter, her back ached and her eyes were blurring, but she doggedly continued. She *had* to get a job, and this one appealed to her the most. But she would call the school anyway, just in case. It was almost 3 already!

"Hello? This is Esther Adams. (Should she have said Mrs.? It would have sounded more grown-up and teacherish.) I am applying for the job as substitute arithmetic teacher for grades three and four. My educational background? Well, I have a B.A. and an M.A. No, in languages. School of education? No, I'm sorry. You did say third or fourth grade? I'm sure I can handle it. If you'll give me an interview you may be able to waive certification requirements based on my degrees. That would be wonderful! Thank you so much. Yes, I'll be there at 3 sharp."

The next day, after sending off the children, she dressed in her business-like navy suit and a white blouse, put on pearl earrings, and took a black leather purse equipped with tissues, carfare, and her Social Security number. Her mother was surprised.

"Esther, why are you so dressed up, with your high heels and everything?"

"Oh, I thought I'd go downtown to do some shopping. I don't have a thing to wear, especially winter stuff." It sounded like a weak excuse, even to her.

"Esther, maybe you forgot — to shop, you need money! I hope we have enough to get us through the week, but I'm not sure." Her voice trailed off. Esther noticed, for the first time, the many new lines on her mother's face.

"Oh, Mom, it'll just be window shopping. I'll only be looking around." At least she hadn't told an outright lie. Yes, she'd be window shopping and looking around and hoping ....

The law office was on the fifth floor of a handsome, modern building. When Esther got off the elevator, she was overwhelmed by the rows and rows of doors that faced her. Finally she saw an engraved brass plate which read, "Sherman and Dwight, Attorneys at Law," followed by a long list of names, all masculine, and underneath, "Executive Secretary, Linda Clarkson." Esther pushed the bell, and heard a discreet buzzing, seemingly miles away. A disembodied voice from the intercom bade her enter.

She found herself in a small reception room, where several women and one man were filling out forms. No one seemed to notice her, except for a gum-chewing, brassy blonde, who gave her a wink and pointed to a door almost hidden by an ornate carved screen.

"Just go right in, kid, she won't bite!"

Kid! Esther drew herself up — she resented being called

a "kid" — and entered the room indicated. Seated at a vast desk with a single white rose in a crystal vase adorning its glossy surface was a smooth-faced, elegant woman of about her own age, who barely looked up.

"You are — ahem — Esther Adams?"

"Yes I have an appointment about the position as assistant — er — to the executive secretary."

"Did you fill out a form in the anteroom?"

"Uh — sorry — no one told me to. But —"

"You may as well try out on the word processor."

Esther was handed a paper and a sample text to follow. She was directed to a desk that held an enormous machine. Unsure of what to do, she stood for a moment, staring at the word processor, which seemed to glare back at her malevolently.

"Well?!" Ms. Clarkson's voice held volumes of disdain.

Esther sat down and with trembling hands inserted the paper and started to type, but nothing happened on the small screen. She felt the woman's eyes drilling into her back and turned toward her.

"Don't you know how to turn it on? It's the switch on the left."

Esther flipped it and was rewarded by seeing words flash on the screen. She willed her fingers to move faster, but words skipped or misspelled were the only result. For five minutes, which seemed like five hours, she kept typing.

"That's enough. Please fill out the form you'll find on the bookcase in the reception room. Don't call us, we'll call you!"

Tears welling in her eyes, Esther walked out. Only the blonde was still there; the others had left.

"Her Majesty give you a hard time, huh? They're all like that — big shots! Don't let it get ya!" Snapping her gum, she gathered up a makeup case, hobo bag, and fringed poncho. "Gotta put on my face — see ya!" With another wink, she slammed the door and was gone.

Esther did not fill out the application. She still had some

pride left. Why even ask for the position when she already knew the answer? Slowly she headed downstairs to the bus stop and sat there for a long time, trying to get up her courage for the next interview. A procession of buses passed by, but not hers.

"Hi, kid! You still here?" It was the blonde from upstairs.

Esther sat up very straight, trying to assume a dignity she did not feel.

"Listen, I'm calling you kid 'cause that's what you are! Don't you know anything ... coming in all dressed up in that fancy suit! Clarkson up there figures you're angling for her job! Besides, I already got the *yes* from her."

Esther was puzzled. "Then why did she give me an interview? And what about all the others who were filling out applications?"

"That was just for looks, to show they're not prejudiced, like they're giving everybody a chance. Those forms they filled out are going straight in the round file."

"In the garbage? Then how does anyone get a job? And what kind of training ...."

"Look, kid, wake up and smell the coffee! I can get a job anytime, anywhere. I can type in my sleep, I never ask any questions and just act dumb, like I don't know what's going on. I keep my mouth shut and find out who the big shots are, and when I get bored I quit. I can always get another job!"

Esther stared, wide-eyed, as the girl proceeded to tell her how she should dress, look, and act.

"Don't call it a 'position'; it's a job. The main thing is, don't come on like you're too smart or too educated, and learn to type real fast. Just remember: A job is a job and a paycheck is money!"

Esther's bus was approaching. She sincerely thanked the blonde for her unsolicited advice and boarded the bus for her next appointment, the school.

P.S. Woodrow Wilson was in an enormous red-brick building, adjoined by a narrow cement yard where hundreds of children pushed and shoved each other, trying to play games or maybe just grab a bit of outside air. Yellow school buses were lined up at the curb; some frazzled teachers were herding the children into a semblance of a double file while others checked passes as the youngsters piled into a bus.

"Principal's office? Room 101, first floor on the right." The guard outside the front door gave her a friendly smile; a good sign, Esther thought.

She was admitted by another guard into a large room lined with bookshelves, with more books piled on every available surface. The principal, dressed in sweatshirt and jeans, and identified as Dr. Jack Samers by the plaque on his desk, gave Esther an automatic smile.

"Welcome to Woodrow Wilson, Ms. — er — Mrs. Adams. We're happy to have you join our family, 'cause that's what we are here, just one big happy family."

"But, Dr. Samers, you haven't even told me what the position — I mean the job — is all about. Please —"

"It's a *position*, and a very important position, I may say. You will be using the latest program, called Math Slant. Each class of 30 or so is divided into four homogeneous groups with two subsets in each. Your job — I mean assignment — is to guide the students to the discovery of mathematical principles, enabling them to draw their own conclusions. Each of the groups represents a different level of achievement. You will be constantly aware of each student's progress, placing them in different groups accordingly. You may have a bit of a problem adapting to the latest techniques, but —"

"Uh, Dr. Samers, may I see the third- and fourth-grade math books?"

"Certainly." The principal seemed surprised at her question. After some searching, he came up with two thick, brand-new books with bright covers.

"Yes, here they are, Math Slant 3 and 4. We are among the first to use these new techniques."

Esther reached for the books and started to turn the pages. Charming, colorful illustrations, but the text seemed completely unfamiliar. Symbols she had never seen before, problems in abstruse language, and these groups — how could she ever manage all that?

"Dr. Samers, would I have any help from the previous teacher? All this is so unfamiliar."

"I'm sorry, Mrs. Adams — may I call you Esther? We're a big happy family here — but she left some time ago, and we haven't been able to replace her. She suffered a slight — um — crisis. I see you're a language major — *crise de nerfs*."

"You mean a breakdown? Well, what about the regular teacher? Can I speak to her?"

"It's a him." Looking at his watch, Dr. Samers calculated. "Bob Jackson is probably in the teachers' lounge — let's go down."

After walking down two flights to the basement, they entered a dark, low-ceilinged room littered with coffee cups, cigarette butts, and old newspapers. A stocky, bearded young man wearing a "Dodger" T-shirt and frayed jeans rose from an ancient recliner to greet them. Dr. Samers introduced Esther as the future permanent substitute for Math 3 and 4, and she was too startled to protest.

"Esther, meet Bob. We all use first names here — big, happy family, you know. I'm sure you'll be good friends in no time." He smiled graciously and hurried up the stairs.

"Mr. Jackson," she just couldn't bring herself to call this complete stranger by his first name, "I have lots of questions."

"Okay, Esther, here's the score. You're on call whenever there's someone sick, for any math class, and the rest of the time you'll be my assistant. Just one thing: Don't ever turn your back on the class; you never know what these kids'll do."

"What do you mean?" Esther didn't want to show her

ignorance. Maybe this man was talking in metaphors?

"Well, if you don't watch 'em every minute, they might start a fight and really hurt each other, or you. Of course the guards check for metal, but you never know."

Esther had heard enough. "Excuse me, I think I'd better leave now. Please give my regards to Dr. Samers." She hurried upstairs and out. The guard smiled at her again, but now it seemed to her that his expression was cynical, almost a sneer.

Esther looked at her watch. She couldn't believe her eyes, it was not even 4 o'clock! She felt she had been on the job hunt forever, and her knees were buckling. She sank down on a park bench, drained, too weary for words. "Well, it's time to go home home," she thought. At least Mom wouldn't know about her humiliating experiences.

She rummaged around in her purse for the bus fare and found Mrs. Rubin's list. The sweater factory! Maybe she *should* try it. After the mysterious computer and the possibly knife-carrying students, it sounded quite tame, and it was only four blocks away. Maybe — at least it was better than nothing.

Esther pulled herself together and started walking toward Pinehurst Street. But why was she even bothering? She knew nothing about sweaters or machinery, she had a B.A. and an M.A. and the beginnings of a doctoral thesis. No! That fresh blonde was right; a job is a job, and she needed one desperately!

She was surprised when she reached the address. It was a well-kept building with a loading platform in front, entirely occupied by Admor Knit Company, as advertised by huge letters painted on the side of the building. Her heart beating wildly, she went through the side entrance marked, "Office."

"Yeah, yeah, I'm shipping it out as soon as we get your

check. It's in the mail? Okay, but not before and what can I do for you, miss?" This was said all in one breath. She had not realized the bearded young man was talking to her.

"Ah, I'm here to apply for the trainee job. Mrs. Rubin, my neighbor, told me about it."

He waved vaguely to the left. "Go see the boss ... *Yossi Batshi*," and he yelled into the intercom, "There's a lady here about the trainee job."

"Go in there and just knock ... the boss is always in," he said, and was already punching in the next phone number before she had taken a step.

In the narrow corridor, she felt, rather than heard, the thrum of heavy machinery. A small sign at the end of the hall read, "Joseph Roth, Pres., Admor Knits." The door flew open.

"Come in, come in, young lady. What can I do for you?"

Mr. Roth was somewhat portly, with a gray, neatly trimmed beard, and he wore a fuzzy dark suit and black cap that seemed strangely out of place in the cluttered office. He had a strong European accent and his voice was loud, probably from having to shout above the noise of the machinery, Esther guessed.

"I — er — I came to apply for the trainee job. Mrs. Rubin recommended me."

"Oh, yes. I'm a member by her nephew, the rabbi. Sure, sure, she called me about you," and Mr. Roth started shuffling through the piles of paper on his desk. "You're Esther Adams. Yes, here it is .... We need someone to go around the third and fourth floor every hour, make sure all the women are working good, and all the supplies are ready where they're supposed to be. Upstairs, that's where they do the sewing and the embroidery and packaging.

"It's a full-time job, 37 hours a week. In winter, Friday afternoon and *Erev Yom Tov* you leave early. Sundays you get overtime when it's the busy season. What else? Well, I got good workers, I don't want them to quit. You talk nice to them; if they make a mistake, straighten it out; no yelling in this place."

Esther thought that was rather funny, since Mr. Roth did not really talk, he yelled! But she understood.

"But how will I know if there's anything wrong? All those machines ...."

"That's okay; we'll teach you. Mrs. Rubin said you're a smart girl; anyway, mostly they can fix it themselves. If not, you call the machine shop, and anyway, I'm here all the time too, and so is Shea downstairs. Just when I'm talking to a customer, you shouldn't bother me."

"Er, what's the pay?" Esther was embarrassed to ask, but, as her blonde "mentor" had said, "A job is a job, and a paycheck is money!"

"You get minimum wage; if it works out good, you get a raise soon. Also you get paid like for 40 hours, also Yom Tov and medical insurance. You got kids?"

"Yes — two, a boy and a girl."

"So get somebody to take good care — no coming in late if they're sick. It's a full-time job!"

Esther thought quickly. The medical insurance, that was very important. If she or her children ever got sick ... and when did they have their last checkup? And the cost of the inoculations! She hoped that her mother was up to minding them.

"I'll take it, Mr. Roth, and thank you very much. When do I start?"

"You can start tomorrow. Give your Social Security number to the bookkeeper and fill out the forms; she's down the hall, left door. And *mazel ubrocheh,* good luck to you." He picked up the phone and was yelling into it as she left.

Esther was torn between feelings of elation — a job! Money! No late Fridays! — and fear: What would her mother say? Could she do it? Her degrees wouldn't help her now; she was on her own!

The children were playing listlessly in the yard, and her mother was waiting at the door when Esther returned.

"Ma, where were you?"

"Did you bring me anything? You said a dolly —"

"Estele! I was so worried about you; you said only window shopping, and it's already getting dark."

"Let's all go inside. I have great news to tell you." Esther was already hanging up her suit jacket and removing her high-heeled shoes.

The grandmother and the two children sat on the couch. Esther faced them; she was too nervous to sit.

"Listen, I have a job! And I hope," turning to her mother, "that you'll be able to take care of the children when I'm out. I'll do the shopping and the laundry," she was talking very quickly now, "and maybe we'll take in someone for the heavy work. Mom, what do you say?"

Her mother twisted the wedding ring on her finger and started to speak, but the children didn't give her a chance. "Oh, Nana, please do it! It was great today: the chocolate cookies and the pink lemonade and that great story."

"Nana, you promised you'll finish it tonight, soon as we're in bed. Want me to get into pajamas now?"

Well! Esther had been prepared for anger, tears, complaints, whining, but not this! And her mother! For the first time since they had arrived, there was a smile on her face.

"Estele, the *kinderlach* were so good, and they made me feel so good. So go to the job *gezunterheit, zol zein mit mazel!*"

Esther's relief was so great that she collapsed on the couch. "Oh, Mom, that's wonderful! Joshie, go next door to Mrs. Rubin and tell her I got the job. And ask for a pint of strawberry ice cream — here's the money. Tonight we're celebrating!"

The factory was even noisier than Esther had anticipated. Mr. Roth took her to the second floor, where the sound of dozens of machines whirring constantly was punctuated by the clacking of bobbins and the grinding of wheels. Each worker had a great pile of sweater parts at her station: sleeves, collars, backs, and fronts, and was busy sewing them together, barely looking up when Mr. Roth showed Esther the various machines and introduced her to the workers.

"Rosita, this is Esther. You need anything, just tell her."

So it went around the huge loft; the women and girls spared her only brief glances, intent on their work.

The next floor was quieter. Here sat many older women, embroidering designs in bright colors of wool, sewing buttons, and finishing seams by hand. Here was also the packaging department; the finished sweaters were labeled, folded, and sealed into plastic bags. The women murmured softly to each other while they worked. Here and there Esther caught a phrase in familiar Spanish or in a Haitian patois — not classical French as taught in school, but quite intelligible to her trained ear.

And what did they talk about? The same concerns that Esther had, and that women have the world over: children, health, making a living, husbands, elderly parents. It came as a shock to her to realize that these Puerto Ricans or Cubans or Haitians had the same dreams, the same hopes as she did. There, among the piles of sweaters, Esther experienced an epiphany; she felt at one with the hard-working women, and wanted only to work, to do a good job, to help them and herself to a better life.

The day passed quickly as she dashed from one station to another, bringing whatever supplies were needed to keep the machines humming, to push out the work. And there was a satisfaction in seeing the finished piles of colorful sweaters, neatly bagged in plastic, mounting higher and higher. She had loved the academic life, loved reading about and researching abstract subjects, but there was a feeling of solid accomplishment here which she had not experienced before. Yes, the job was turning out better, much better than she had expected.

Back home, the children greeted her happily. Nana had taken them to the park, had bought them soda, had made their favorite corn on the cob for lunch, and another story was promised for after supper.

All was well in their little world.

Esther had not realized how deeply her financial problems had affected her attitude toward her children and even her relations with her mother. Worrying about money, buying food, and paying for utilities had pushed everything else out of her mind. Now, with a paycheck coming in every week, she was able to attend to all the things she had neglected since the *shivah* — first and foremost, registering the children in a Jewish school.

"Strange," she thought. "This whole thing started because I wanted to have Josh and Sharon in a better atmosphere, with better friends. And I came just when Mom needed me most. And now I have the responsibility of earning a living, of raising the children alone, of helping my mother get over her loss. Am I better off? Yes, a hundred times yes! May Hashem give me the strength I will need."

The following Sunday, Esther took the children to the Beth Chinuch Hebrew Academy. Here too, just watching the students playing outside, she found the calm order that she had noticed back in the L.A. Jewish school. This would be a peaceful haven for her youngsters, and would help them forget the scenes of anger and violence with their father.

Yaron, after several letters and telephone calls from her, had sent her one letter: "I am willing to take you back, on my terms. You know what they are: The children are to be brought up according to my rules, and you are to behave in a normal fashion, like my family and friends. Forget those religious superstitions. You have a month to decide."

No money had been enclosed.

She had crumpled the letter and thrown it in the wastebasket. It hurt too much, but she hadn't really expected anything else. Then she retrieved it and stored it in the bottom drawer of the dresser. One never knew ....

After a long wait, the secretary motioned her to enter the principal's office. Rabbi Gordon was a pleasant middle-aged man who listened to her story patiently. Josh and Sharon were on their best behavior, not fidgeting or complaining about being bored. They seemed to sense how much this interview meant to their mother.

The principal briefly questioned the children. He said they would be accepted, but that additional tutoring would be needed, since they were not on the level of their respective age groups.

"How much will it cost? I can't afford anything extra right now!" Esther was frantic. Would she have to send them to public school after all?

Rabbi Gordon considered for a moment. "We'll arrange free tutoring with some older students; they do an excellent job. But minimal tuition must be paid. Is your husband able to contribute?"

"Able, but not willing." She did not wish to reveal more before the children's searching eyes.

Rabbi Gordon sent the children to the secretary's office and asked Esther for her husband's telephone number. She gave it, but warned: "It's no use. I know —"

"I'm willing to try."

Yaron answered after the first ring. The principal identified himself and requested that Dr. Adams pay his children's tuition. The response came, fast and furious — so loud that Esther was able to catch words and phrases: "Arrant nonsense ... insane mother ... ruining my son ... crazy cult ideas ...," ending with a crash that seemed to shake the room.

"Well, I guess we have his answer," said Rabbi Gordon, "but I'll call him again right now!"

"It's no use, Rabbi Gordon, I told you. Why bother?" Esther was trembling.

"It's about something else entirely. You see —"

Again, Yaron's response was immediate. "Harassment ... I'll sue you ... How dare you ...."

The principal remained calm. "I see you're not interested in supporting your children or paying tuition. So why not arrange a divorce and give your wife a proper Jewish *get*? Then you have no obligation ...."

Again furious screaming issued from the receiver, ending in a big bang.

It was fortunate that at this point the children were not in the room; Esther did not want them to hear and to hate their father.

Rabbi Gordon told her that Josh and Sharon were accepted at a minimal tuition that she could afford, to be supplemented by a scholarship grant.

"Tell the secretary to give you a list of supplies, and they'll start tomorrow, *b'ezras Hashem*."

Happy and relieved, the three walked home together, stopping only at a stationery store to buy school supplies. Nana greeted them with a delicious lunch: pancakes, scrambled eggs, and chocolate milk, "because you're starting school tomorrow." When Esther told her about the call to Yaron, she became visibly upset.

"He wouldn't give anything? I knew it! You never should have married that no good...! But, at least he should give you a *get,* like the rabbi said."

"Mom, please, not in front of the kids."

The subject was closed, but now Esther had another major worry that kept her awake at night, and intruded into her thoughts even during her hectic workday at the knitting factory.

Would she ever be free? Would she ever be able to remarry? Would the children ever have a normal life, with a father and a mother?

Esther did not want to upset her mother, and bringing up the subject of Yaron and a divorce would upset her terribly. But she had to talk to someone, had to pour out her troubled heart, even if no solution was forthcoming.

Yes! The next-door neighbor, Mrs. Rubin! She was the one! Hadn't she helped her from the first moment back home, with the children, and with finding work, with her daily cheerful greeting? Of course!

Mrs. Rubin was busy, as usual. She was making marmalade from the orange and lemon peels she had saved, but was not too busy to listen to Esther while she cut the peels into long, fragrant shreds. While Esther related what had happened at the school and spoke about Yaron's continued refusal to support the children, Mrs. Rubin continued to work quietly, her expression non-committal.

"So, tell me, Estele, did you ever *ask* him for a *get*? First you got to ask, then see what he says."

"But Mrs. Rubin, I'm afraid to ask; he just yells. I did write to him about it twice, but he ignores my letters. I know it's hopeless. But what I'm really afraid of is that someday he'll try to grab the children. Right now it's not convenient for him to take them, but they're growing older and he's getting richer; and as long as we're married he still has power over them … and over me."

"You're right. Something has to be done." Mrs. Rubin stopped slicing. Esther could almost see the gears meshing behind the elder woman's calm forehead.

"Listen, Estele, I have an idea. My niece Sorale's boy is marrying in L.A. and we are all going, the whole family. Of course, my nephew Yontel, the rabbi from the Emunas Tzaddikim, is also going. Everybody listens to him, he's so smart, he knows everything just like *der haylige zeide* Yontel, *olov hasholom,* that he's named after. So he'll know what to say to that no-goodnik. So let's see, the wedding is in three weeks," and Mrs. Rubin marked her large calendar from the fish market: "Tell Yontel to talk to Esther's no-good husband."

Rabbi Yom Tov Freedman loosened his tie, took off his glasses and his shoes, and flopped down on the hotel bed. A small smile played around his mouth, as he thought about the last few hours and his dynamo of a *tante,* Mrs. Rubin.

"Yontel, what took you so long? I was really getting worried, and the children are waiting on *shpilkes* for us to call them, like we promised. And you look like the cat that swallowed the canary!" His wife tapped her foot impatiently. "So what happened with that big shot, Dr. Adams?"

"Big shot? You better believe it! I took along the *Tante,* she's bored doing nothing in a hotel, and I figured it wouldn't take long, and afterward I would take her sightseeing. We came to his office building — you never saw anything like it, all chrome, glass, and marble, with two receptionists in two separate waiting rooms before you get to see the big man. The *Tante* says she'll wait outside, she doesn't want to look at a *roshe,* so she sits in the waiting room with her *Tehillim,* whispering — you know her whisper, you can hear it a block away. Everybody's looking at her, but she doesn't care.

"'Nu, go in already,' she tells me. 'I'll just have that poor Estele in mind.'

"So I go in. He's sitting behind a desk, about an acre wide, smoking a fat cigar.

"'What can I do for you, Rabbi?' he says, giving me his hand, with polished nails, I think.

"'You can't do anything for me, Dr. Adams, but I'm here to do something for you,' I tell him.

"'And what may that be?' he retorts, with a fishy look out of his fishy eyes.

"'I'm giving you a once-in-a-lifetime opportunity at a *mitzvah* that only you can perform.'

"'I'm not in the habit of doing *mitzvahs*,' he says, really sarcastically. 'What's in it for me?'

"So I tell him that he should give his wife a *get* and a legal divorce. It'll be good for him — no more calls from her, no more obligations to her or to the children if his lawyer handles it right, and he can remarry, and so on. Well, he jumps up and starts screaming like a maniac.

"'You rotten rabbis! You troublemakers! Get out of here or I'll have you arrested.' You know, I was really getting scared.

"*Tante* in the other room hears him yelling, and she comes storming in. She takes one look and tells him, 'Shut up, sit down, and listen, sonny boy!'

"And guess what? He does just that!

"She walks right up to him — and you know how short she is — standing she's as tall as he is sitting. She leans over him and stares him in the eye:

"'Listen, mister' — the only doctor she knows is the one she goes to for her bunions — 'you know what happens to you if you won't give Esther a *get*? *Der heilige zeide,* Reb Akiva Eiger, also had a rotten customer like you. So the rebbe says to him, "There's two ways a woman can get rid of a no-good husband: either divorce or he drops dead." You're laughing? That no-good also laughed. On the way home he dropped dead like a doornail!'

"Adams gets white as a sheet. He grabs his chest. She's still standing there, staring at him.

"'You see?' she says, and she's smiling!

"He's gasping for breath and waving his hands. After a while, he gets control and gives a *krechtz*, 'Okay, okay — you win! She can have it!' And he makes with his hands, like 'Just get out of here!'

"So right away we go to the L.A. *Beis Din*. We had all the

papers along; the *Tante* was that sure I'd be able to persuade him, but believe me, without her it would never have worked. They got everything ready, and all he has to do is grant it to her. So we take the papers and the *sofer* and two witnesses — these guys know all the big shots in L.A. — and we go back to his office. The receptionist tells us, 'Dr. Adams is not seeing anyone,' but before she even has a chance to finish, the *Tante* pushes through. We all crowd in after her, and we're in his room.

"He yells at the secretary, 'Didn't I tell you I'm not seeing anyone?' but when he sees the *Tante*, he gets all pale again.

"She tells him, 'Just do what the rabbi tells you, or maybe you won't see anyone for a long, long time.' He takes one look at her face, and he falls down in his chair like a bag of *shmattes*. So I get everything set up and the *sofer* does his thing, and the witnesses do theirs, and all the time the *Tante* is staring at him like a snake charmer. He's afraid to look at her, but he's also scared to look away. So it's finally all set, and I told *Tante* she could be a rebbe, but she says she's too busy."

"Mazel Tov! Mazel Tov!" Rabbi Yom Tov Freedman came in, waving the paper like a flag. "We got it! It's right here — take it!"

And he handed Esther the precious document, the piece of paper that meant freedom for her and for her children.

Her mother was ecstatic, but when Esther explained to the children what all the excitement was about, they were not thrilled, as she had imagined they would be, but quiet and subdued; and she thought she saw tears in Joshua's eyes.

Rabbi Freedman told Esther that children hate change, sometimes even if it is a change for the better. Secretly they hope that their parents will reconcile and that they will all be together again; even if there had been problems in the past, even violence, well, they were used to it.

Mrs. Rubin had been watching quietly. She put her arms around the children.

"Come, *kinderlach,* we'll have a little ice-cream party at my house. I have chocolate and strawberry and pistachio — did you ever taste it before? You can go over right now. I'll be there in a jiffy." The children, hand in hand, eagerly trotted off next door.

"*Mit a bissel essen vert alles fargessen* — how do you say that in English, Yontel?"

"'Some yummy food can change the mood — you like my poetry? And *Tante,* besides being a rebbe, you also are a psychologist. So what do you prescribe for Esther?"

"Of course, she should find a good man and get married. But it won't be so easy. She is picky, right?" Turning to Esther, she continued, "But you deserve a good life; you went through enough already."

"It's true," Esther thought. Her failed marriage, the difficulties with her children, and then her father's sudden death and the struggle for a livelihood — all had taken their toll. Right now she felt an overwhelming exhaustion, a desire just to sleep and sleep, to stop all worrying and planning for the future.

"Thank you, Mrs. Rubin," she said aloud. "I wish it were that simple, but I'm not getting married so fast. I'm just happy that I'm free. And I can't thank you enough!"

"Nu, *baruch Hashem, men halt shoyn du,* so let's all be happy. Estele, your eyes look like burnt holes in a blanket, so go to sleep. I'll keep the *kinderlach* busy for a while and your Mama will put them to bed."

Mrs. Rubin hustled her nephew and Mrs. Feinberg over to her house to join the ice-cream celebration, and Esther dragged herself to her room. She lay down, her eyes closed, and in minutes she was fast asleep.

Life goes on. Esther went to the factory every weekday,

and became accustomed to the noise of the machinery and the rapid pace of the work. She befriended the women employees — her knowledge of Spanish and French put them at ease and made it easy for them to confide in her; often she was able to assist with their problems with children, with schools, with doctors, with the Immigration Department, with all the complicated facets of American life.

She found that she truly liked these women and felt at one with them. In the past — and how far away it seemed now! — she had thought of herself as a liberal, a friend of the working class, but it had been a sham. Inside, she had felt superior; after all, she was a highly educated American, while they .... Her liberalism had been only a reflection of the attitudes and opinions of her academic surroundings. Now she was faced with the realities of life, the daily struggle for existence. Now she understood many things of which she had never been aware.

With both children in school, Nana was a bit at loose ends. She got excited when Esther told her that she might have some work for her at home, hand-embroidering the neck-bands and sleeves of Mr. Roth's most successful design, which was copied from a Paris original.

The next day, Esther arrived home with a box of sleeves, accompanied by Margarita, the most skilled needleworker in the shop.

"Here, you see, Senora, you start by the seam. Don't let the thread twist. Like that, good, good!"

Nana caught on quickly. Hadn't she embroidered countless tablecloths, pillowcases, and napkins in her youth?

So now there was another source of income, and life became somewhat easier, less strained. The children improved in their schoolwork, and did not need tutoring any longer. At the PTA meeting, Sharon's teacher mentioned that the child spent too much time in fantasyland. Esther had been the same at that age, so she decided to ignore it. Brother and little sister played nicely together most of the time, they were polite to their elders and very solicitous of their grandmother, which gave her a secret delight, though she protested, "I'm not 100 yet! Don't treat me like an old lady!"

On pleasant Sunday afternoons, Nana often joined them on trips to the park, to the zoo, and to museums, replicating Esther's childhood days. The hours before Shabbos were devoted to cleaning, cooking, and polishing the small silver candlesticks, the only objects that reminded Esther of her previous life in California.

One day Esther received a letter written on heavy cream stationery. It was from the law firm of Coleman, Brown, and Lazarus. Their client, Dr. Yaron Adams, was prepared to pay all divorce costs under the following conditions: Esther was to relinquish all rights to alimony and child support, now and in the future. Her husband also wanted regular visitation rights, at his discretion.

Her mother said, "That low-life! He's just trying to get away with it. He's loaded with money; don't give in! And who knows what he'll do with the children!"

Mrs. Rubin advised, "Sign it! What does he care about visiting the kids? He never gave them a nickel; he just put that in to torture you, so you should be upset. I would be surprised if he ever shows up at all. So don't make a fight; this way you'll have your divorce in case you meet somebody."

Esther firmly told Mrs. Rubin that she was not interested in remarriage, "and besides, do you think that there are many men interested in a tired woman with two children, no money, and an elderly mother?"

"Never mind, *bubbele*, you need only *one*!" Mrs. Rubin had an answer for everything.

Esther tossed and turned all night, weighing the merits of the conflicting advice she had received. The next morning, she called Rabbi Freedman and explained her dilemma.

"Well, Mrs. Adams," Rabbi Freedman responded, "I feel

you should sign. You know your husband is not really interested in the children, and he probably wouldn't pay alimony or child support even if you took him to court. If you don't agree to his terms, the case may drag on for years."

"But Rabbi Freedman, shouldn't he contribute *something*? My mother says —"

"Besides, if my *Tante* advised you to sign, you probably can't go wrong — she's *always* right!"

Esther laughed a bit uncertainly, and sent out the signed papers that very day.

In due time, the divorce papers came through. Yaron sent a letter from his office, signed by his secretary, stating that he planned to take his children to Palm Springs for their winter vacation. Not knowing what to do, Esther did not reply, and spent the next three weeks worrying. But she did not hear from Yaron or his lawyers again.

Mrs. Rubin kept hinting about this or that well-to-do widower or fine bachelor or lonely divorced man, all members of the Emunas Tzaddikim *shul*, which automatically made them eligible. But Esther refused to listen.

"When I'll meet the right one, that'll be the time," she said.

"But how will you ever meet anyone if you just go to work and come home at night? You got to go out a little bit, weddings, *simchas* ...."

"Thank you," Esther said. "I'll try." But she didn't.

Winter turned into spring, spring into summer. The children spent a few weeks in camp. They returned sunburned, full of excitement about new friends, new songs, new activities. The Shabbos table became more cheerful; even the candlelight seemed brighter.

Esther fell into a monotonous routine — work, home, work, home — but she was content. At Mrs. Rubin's urging, she had met some "prospectives," but, as Mrs. Rubin said,

"It's a gleicher shidduch"; she was not interested, nor were the men she had met.

Esther was doing well at work, and had received two raises. On one of his frequent inspection tours, Mr. Roth, the boss, noticed her speaking Spanish to the Latin American women. He was surprised.

"Why didn't you tell me you can speak Spanish? And what about the Frenchies? You can talk to them also? And where you learned all this?"

Esther told him that it was a long time ago, in a different setting, but "a language once learned comes back when you hear it every day."

Mr. Roth was impressed. "So I have an idea. We have lots of Spanish customers. Half the time they don't know what I'm saying, and three-quarters of the time I don't know what they're talking. You'll talk to the buyers, and if you sell more than we did before, you'll get a commission on the extra."

"But Mr. Roth, I don't know anything about selling. I only did it once; I was 8, and it was my lemonade stand: five cents a cup, straws free. I lost money."

"Don't worry, Mrs. Esther" — he was unfailingly formal – "You'll do very fine. Anything you don't know, just ask."

Now, in addition to supplying the women on the two upper floors, Esther was occasionally called upon to speak to the foreign-language buyers. She did well, and slowly the commissions started to mount. She had decided long before that any extra money would go toward the children's tuition; it was a happy day for her when she was able to send almost double her standard monthly payment.

The next day, there was a call for her from Rabbi Gordon, the principal of Beth Chinuch. Esther was certain that it was in reference to the increased payment. When she called back, she was surprised at the troubled note in the principal's voice.

"Mrs. Adams? I'm calling you at work because I don't

want your mother or your children to overhear. There's a problem with Sharon —"

"But I thought she was doing so well!" Esther remembered the report cards of the past year, and the PTA meetings. No, there had been no hint of trouble.

"Yes, she's doing well academically and socially. But she seems to be drifting further and further into fantasyland. Does she tell lies at home?"

"No, never! But why do you ask?"

"Mrs. Adams, let me read you a composition she handed in yesterday. By the way, you *are* divorced now, aren't you? And one of the reasons was your husband's opposition to a religious upbringing for your children?"

"Yes, that's right." Esther couldn't breathe. Where was this questioning leading?

"The topic assigned by Mrs. Perl was 'My Family.' Sharon described you and your mother and Josh very accurately. Then she wrote, 'My father is very religious. He *davens* three times a day and learns at night. He is very handsome and a little taller than my mother. He has a short brown beard and gold glasses. He brings treats for us when he comes home from work, especially Friday afternoon. He's the kindest, nicest daddy in the whole world.' Does that describe Dr. Adams?"

Esther was speechless. When she was finally able to answer, she said, "No, of course not! Just the opposite! Anyway, she barely remembers him and never talks about him."

"Does Sharon know anyone like that? Perhaps an uncle or a neighbor that she might have fixed upon as a father figure?"

Esther tried to think, then answered, "No, there's no one. We don't know anyone fitting that description. Tell me, has she told any other — er — untruths?"

"I spoke to Mrs. Perl and several of her former teachers. They all said she's dreamy and imaginative, but essentially truthful."

"So then —" Esther was vastly relieved. She had tried so

hard to instill honesty in her children, and had been shocked and hurt by Rabbi Gordon's words.

"So we'll consider this a passing aberration. However, you should be aware of Sharon's tendency to — er — fantasize. The sooner that's corrected, the better. There's another call coming in now. Goodbye, Mrs. Adams."

It was difficult for Esther to concentrate the rest of the workday. Should she say anything to Sharon? To her mother? No, better not. Whom could she consult? Probably Rabbi Freedman; he seemed to have an instinctive understanding of children.

Late that night, when her mother and the children were fast asleep, she called Rabbi Freedman's number. When his wife answered, Esther said that she must speak to the rabbi; it was urgent. The rabbi was unavailable, but his wife assured Esther that he would call back as soon as possible.

"Good evening. It's Rabbi Freedman. What can I do for you?" He had called back sooner that she expected.

"It's Esther Adams, Rabbi Freedman. I'm just so broken up. Rabbi Gordon from the school practically accused my daughter of being a liar," and Esther broke into loud sobs. Everything she had held back all this time suddenly came to the surface, and she bawled like a baby.

"I can hear that you're very upset." Rabbi Freedman's voice was soothing. "Can you tell me what Rabbi Gordon actually said?"

Esther was ashamed of her outburst. A few more sniffles, and she was able to control her voice.

"Well, Rabbi Freedman, the class had to write a composition about 'My Family' and Sharon wrote a description of her father, as religious, kind, generous, brown beard, glasses … You've met Yaron. Does that sound like him?"

"Yes, I had the pleasure. No, it's not like him at all, of course, not in appearance, not in character."

"So what does it mean? Why should Sharon write something so … so far-fetched?"

"Well, Mrs. Adams, a young child's mind works differently from an adult's. The imagination is very active; even dreams are often confused with reality. Children at that age often can't tell the difference. As long as Sharon is generally truthful, there's nothing to worry about. You are doing a great job with the kids; keep it up! G'night —" Before Esther had a chance to express her thanks, the connection was broken.

Despite Esther's difficult schedule and many responsibilities, this strange incident continued to trouble her, nibbling at the edges of her consciousness. After a while, she decided to place it at 99 on her worry list. There were so many more urgent matters to consider.

Mrs. Rubin had a list of candidates she wanted Esther to meet: a doctor, a lawyer, a chef in a kosher restaurant. None of them appealed to her. But was she too picky, as Mrs. Rubin often said?

The children were getting older. They would soon need a bigger place; her childhood home, with only two bedrooms, was getting very crowded. Perhaps she should start looking ….

One day Mr. Roth, out of the clear blue sky, asked her to do something she hadn't done since her college days: take a trip to Paris!

Admor Knitwear had been relying on expensive representatives in the fashion center of the world to relay the latest designs, which had to be adapted to the realities and costs of mass production, he said; he felt that Esther could do the job far more effectively and at lower cost.

Since by now she was familiar with every aspect of the business, from spinning the yarn to the finishing touches, Mr. Roth just *knew* she could do a better job than the French stylists who designed for a custom clientele.

Trying to persuade her, Mr. Roth argued, "Look, Mrs. Esther, they don't know over there what kind of problems we got here. From a pretty picture, we got to make something that sells, we should make a profit on it. You already know everything from working here so long. So why should I pay some Frenchie a fortune when you could do a much better job? Anyway, it'll be a change for you, a *shtikel* vacation.

"You can't decide so fast? Okay, so let me know tomorrow. It'll be worth your while, believe me."

Mr. Roth was an irresistible force, and Esther was not an immovable object. Her mother also urged her to go, in almost the same words as Mr. Roth.

Mrs. Rubin gave her usual speech. "Go, *mammale,* maybe you'll meet some nice man there."

Esther smiled. "Let's see, Mom will watch the kids; I'll have to renew my passport, buy good walking shoes and a couple of skirts to go to with the best of Admor's knitwear, order a ticket to Paris — I'll do it!"

She was ready in less than a week. A little scared — her last time on an airplane was when she had escaped from Yaron — but exhilarated, too. At lift-off she felt like a schoolgirl on holiday: young, unfettered, looking forward to the charm and novelty of this journey.

She had made reservations at a mid-priced hotel near the Jewish section of Paris. Her days were crowded: rushing from one fashion house to another, trying to include as many shows as possible, staring at the elegant Parisiennes, searching for and finding ideas to bring back with her.

Esther felt she had made excellent progress. Her sketchbook was filled with drawings of what could best be adapted to the American taste; she had swatches of material and colors, and ideas enough for a year. Mr. Roth would be pleased.

Although she hadn't done as much sightseeing as she had hoped to — there hadn't been time for the Louvre or the Champs Elysées — she felt she had accomplished a great deal. Now to purchase a few gifts for Mom, the children, her co-workers, and of course Mrs. Rubin, and she would be home in good time for Shabbos, as planned.

"Let's see: confirm the reservation, do last-minute packing, make sure nothing is left in closet or drawers, have the concierge call taxi to the airport — check!"

Esther's mood was as springy and hopeful as her step when she entered the crowded elevator. Stepping out at the lobby level, she felt a shove against her shoulder. Her heel caught in the small gap between the elevator floor and the stone paving of the lobby and she pitched forward — into blackness.

When she came to, she was lying on the terrazo floor with her arm oddly angled beneath her; waves of pain radiated through her body and her brain.

"*Qu'est ce-qu'il est passe*? What happened?"

"*C'est une étrangère - vite, a l'hospital*! It's a foreigner — quick, to the hospital!"

"*Ah, la pauvre* .... Oh, the poor thing ...."

By now, the pain was so intense that she only wished to lose consciousness again, and to escape the curious faces peering down at her, but instead she felt herself being lifted onto a stretcher and placed in an ambulance. Esther opened her eyes in the emergency room of the hospital. A gray-haired man in a white coat stood at her side.

"*Vous êtes Americaine*? I am Dr. Samuel Bermain. I regret to say that you have suffered a compound fracture, a cracked rib, and a slight concussion. We will apply a cast and —"

"But doctor, my plane is leaving in two hours! My ticket ... my job ... my children — I must make that plane!"

"*C'est impossible, madame*. You cannot travel in this condition. Perhaps tomorrow afternoon —"

"That's Friday! I can't stay here. I must be home for the Sabbath!" Esther was crying by now, from frustration as well as pain.

"*Ah vous êtes juive,* you are Jewish, I presume. I understand. But now, no more talking."

Another doctor and a nurse rolled in a complicated apparatus. Dr. Bermain approached Esther with an anesthetic injection, and soon all was blackness again.

When Esther awoke, she was propped in a wheelchair with a huge cast on her right arm, which throbbed inside the plaster. Dr. Bermain entered briskly.

"*Comment ça va?* How do you feel, *madame?*"

"Better, I guess. But I've got to get out of here; I can still make the next flight."

"*Je regrette, madame, mais c'est ne pas possible.* But I have consulted with Mme. Bermain, and we have agreed that you will be our guest this Sabbath. You will rest here tonight. Kosher food will be provided and tomorrow afternoon I will drive you to our home in Hière. The family is so looking forward to meeting you. Rest assured, *chère madame,* that you will enjoy a Sabbath most agreeable."

"But doctor," Esther wouldn't give up, "I must return — my children ...."

"I will notify them. *Alors,* it is settled. You come to us for the Sabbath. *Bonne nuit!*" The closing of the door sounded final.

Esther felt hot tears run down her face. She had enjoyed the trip so much! Maybe this was a punishment for running away from her responsibilities? And now she was injured, alone in a strange country, forced to accept the hospitality of strangers ... and her arm was starting to throb again.

Finally, sleep came.

At 11, they woke her to give her a sleeping pill. A cordless phone was brought to her room, and Esther called her mother, who was full of sympathy.

"Darling, please don't worry. The children are fine and so am I. Just come home safe and sound. But how can you travel alone, with your arm in a cast? Maybe they'll provide someone to help you on the plane."

Esther reassured her mother, although she felt far from brave. How *would* she manage? The plane, the luggage — oh, it was too much to think about. Why had she ever agreed to this trip? But no use regretting — *hettach pettach,* as her father used to say, could have, should have ....

"Good-bye, Mom! Lots of love to Josh and Sharon." She was too exhausted to continue talking. Esther fell back on the pillow and drifted into an uneasy state of semi-consciousness.

Friday morning was a flurry of nurses and interns taking her temperature and checking her cast, practicing their English on Esther. When she demonstrated her French, they lost interest. In the afternoon, Dr. Bermain came to check her chart and then her cast.

"*Très bien, madame.* I shall return shortly. And do not worry about your things at the hotel. We will retrieve them later."

The Bermain home struck Esther as comfortable, cozy, and somehow familiar. The bookshelves, the pictures, even the flourishing green plants reminded her of home. Mme. Bermain gave her a warm welcome and introduced her to assorted family members.

The glowing candlelight, the cheerful faces around the table, the festive meal — it was turning out to be quite a pleasant experience. Mme. Bermain, in a mixture of French and English, showed such sympathetic interest that Esther soon told her all about her circumstances, about the great change in her life since she had left her husband, about her worries for the future, about the "prospectives" she had met and the failure to connect, about her eagerness to get home and her fear of the trip. How easy it was to confide in someone she would never see again.

"*Ma chère,* do not be afraid. We will take you to De Gaulle Airport and arrange for a good seat. And also someone to meet you in New York and drive you to your home. Perhaps my young nephew, Jacques — Yaakov — I will tell him about you. Yes, I am certain that he will be available."

Esther was reassured, and passed the rest of Shabbos in a calm and hopeful frame of mind. It was the first time in years that someone was taking care of her. For too long it had been the other way around.

By Sunday morning everything was arranged, and the Bermains took Esther to the airport and right onto the plane — doctor's privilege.

"I have called Jacques with your flight number, and told him all about you. He said he would take care of everything. He asked how he would know you, and I said you probably would be the only charming lady with a cast on her right arm, but do take my yellow scarf just in case. We will call him again to make sure that all goes well. *Au revoir! Au revoir! Bon voyage!*" The Bermains were still waving as the plane began to ascend.

The hours of the flight passed quickly. As the shores of America came closer, Esther felt herself getting tense. Perhaps this Jacques would be late, or not show up at all? Young people were so unpredictable and forgetful! But how would she manage then? Dreadful scenarios passed through her mind — alone in Kennedy, losing her precious notes and sketches — how would she ever get home?

But minutes after the plane landed, she was paged: "Jacob Bermain to meet Mrs. Esther Adams." Afraid of being jostled in the crush, Esther hung back until everyone had left the plane.

As she entered the terminal building, she saw a good-looking man of medium height, about her own age, with a trim brown beard, gold-rimmed glasses, and an exceptionally sweet smile.

"You are Mrs. Adams? Esther Adams? I have waited so long for you ...," he said.

What Do You Think?

HELEN NEEDED A NEW SEWING MACHINE, EVERYONE in her family agreed. The old portable she had received from her aunt as a wedding present had stitched innumerable dresses for herself and her daughters; it had repaired hundreds of ripped seams for her husband and sons; it had sewn curtains and linens, baby outfits, and bedspreads — but now it was erratic, exhausted, ready to give up.

Sewing, for Helen, had become a tangle of broken threads, skipped stitches, and seams opening at the most inconvenient times. A new sewing machine was an absolute necessity, that's all!

But what about the cost?

This time, Helen had decided, she must have a machine in a cabinet, preferably a big cabinet with many drawers. Lifting the heavy "portable" was becoming more and more difficult, and the dining-room table that she had used all these years for her sewing projects was getting shaky; any day she expected to find it with a broken leg, and the machine smashed on the floor. No, it had to be a good sturdy machine in its own cabinet, with a free arm for mending sleeves and pants, and maybe with a few fancy stitches. That wasn't too much to ask, was it? Especially since she had used the old *klutz* for the past 23 years without complaint.

Only one problem: The machine she wanted cost over $1,000 new — she'd checked all the stores in the area — and that was way beyond the amount they had budgeted for this essential purchase. So it would have to be a secondhand Singer, and for months Helen had scanned the classified ads, hoping to find her heart's desire at a reasonable price. But no such luck; every ad she answered was a disappointment. Junky machines in worse condition than her own, battered cabinets, missing accessories, plastic parts that dropped like fall leaves when the machine went fast. Helen had almost given up hope.

One evening, Sarah, her good friend and neighbor, was shopping at the Mall, when she met Helen, whose smile stretched from ear to ear.

"Listen, Sarah," she said, "I found it! And it's ex-act-ly what I want!"

"What ever are you talking about?" Sara had never seen her friend so excited, even when she had announced that baby Dov was finally trained, at age 4.

"Well, you know how long I've been looking for a sewing machine? And this one — I was looking for material, and there it was, staring me in the face — this one is just perfect, with all the features I need, and some more besides! And it's only $75 more than we figured to spend. Oh, I can't wait to start using it!"

"So did you put down a deposit?" asked Sarah.

"No, I told them I'd have to ask my husband; of course Yankel will agree, and anyway they only want cash-and-carry. But I told them I'll call them first thing in the morning, when the store opens. I'm so excited ...," and Helen ran off to catch the last bus home.

The next day, Sarah called Helen: "So why don't you

invite me over to see your new machine? And does the cabinet fit that corner in the dining room? I'll bring doughnuts to celebrate, and you put up coffee."

Helen did not answer.

"What's the matter? Didn't you hear me? Helen ...."

There was a sound of suppressed sobs. Then Helen started crying in earnest.

"Sarah, they sold it! They sold it to someone else! When I called this morning, they said it was gone. Some man bought it for his wife. Oh, oh, oh –"

Sarah searched for words of consolation.

"Helen, you'll find another one, maybe even better than that one, and if it costs a little more, I can lend you – "

"No, no, no! That machine was just exactly what I wanted! And the cabinet matches my dining-room furniture, and it would have fitted in just right. Oh, now I'll never have it – boo hoo, boo hoo — "

Sarah tried to calm her friend, but it was no use. Helen kept crying as if her heart would break. Sarah tried to end the flow of tears by promising to look for another sewing machine or to rent one for her, but Helen kept saying, "I only want that one! Why can't I ever have what I want?"

At three that afternoon, Sarah's phone rang. It was Helen and she was ecstatic.

"Sarah! Guess what — that sewing machine was delivered to me 15 minutes ago, with a great big gold bow on it and a card. Here, I'll read it to you, 'To my dear precious wife — happy sewing! Yankel.'"

"Oh, Helen! I'm so glad! What a sweet thing to do! I never thought that Yankel was the type for such gestures. I guess when you told him how much you wanted it, he decided to go to the store and pay for it and have it delivered as a surprise. It's so – so romantic!"

"Yes, isn't it? Come on over, Sarah we'll have that party now!"

That night, Sarah told her husband all about the exciting events of the day.

"How come you never think of things like that? Now it means so much more to Helen, with all the suspense, and then getting it after she had already given up on it. I never knew that Yankel had it in him, he's always so serious and sober. And Helen is in seventh heaven now – "

Sarah's husband walked up and down, stroking his chin.

"But Sarah, look what she went through in those few hours, thinking she had lost her heart's desire, that she would never get what she wanted. Do you really think a golden bow and a card can make up for that agony?"

Sarah and her husband are still — not arguing exactly — but discussing the matter.

What do *you* think?

◦⊱ A Very Careful Man

Mendel Deutsch came out of the side exit of the Kopolner Yeshivah after *Shacharis*, carrying his *tallis* bag, umbrella, and raincoat. The gray, misty skies of early morning had cleared, so he figured he would leave the coat and umbrella home; he wouldn't need that them on this sunny, humid day.

As usual, he stopped for a moment to plan his schedule. Oh, yes, Edna had asked him to bring home rolls, milk, and a jar of instant coffee for their breakfast, and the giant box of Honey Raisin Wispies for the children. The grocery was across the street from where he had left his car parked, just a couple of blocks from the *shul*. He deposited his burdens in the car and entered the store with a cheerful greeting, and a request for a big box of Wispies.

"Mr. Deutsch, didn't you just buy that same cereal yesterday? Your kids sure must love it!"

Joe, the clerk, always displayed a friendly interest in his

steady customers and their purchases; while Mendel was busy picking out the four freshest rolls and a bottle of milk with the latest date, and the coffee, he also tried to keep up his side of the conversation.

"No-oo — I guess it was last week, but you're on the right track; it seems they can't get enough of this stuff. My wife and I never touch it …. Well, be seeing you, Joe."

Mendel paid for his purchases, accepted his change, and with a brief good-bye nod, left the store.

During the 5-minute drive home, Mendel reviewed his appointments and plans for the evening. He was a careful person, and he nodded with satisfaction. His day was under control.

He parked neatly in front of his house and brought in the bag of groceries, the raincoat, and the umbrella. But there should have been something else — oh, of course! — his *tallis* bag!

Mendel went back to the car to bring it in, but it was not there.

"I'm quite sure I put it in the car after *davening*," Mendel told his wife. "In fact, I'm almost positive."

"But I remember another time when you left it in the yeshivah and you thought you took it home. Anyway, who'd steal a *tallis* bag? You'd better go back to *shul* and look for it. I'm sure it's there."

"Edna, I'm positive —"

"Look, Mendel, it's not in the car, so it must be in *shul*. Just go back there — it's only a couple of minutes — instead of worrying over it."

"I guess you're right. I'd hate for anything to happen to my *tefillin*. You know I got them from *Zeide* Chaim Pinchas, and he had them made special, and they cost a fortune even then. I can still remember."

"Mendel, it's getting late. Don't you think you'd better go?"

"Okay, okay, I'm going! Just give me a thermos of coffee and some of Mom's honey cookies. I'm late already."

Back in the car, Mendel searched the floor in the back. He had been so sure that he had put the *tallis* bag on the seat — maybe it had fallen down? No, nothing there. Maybe in the trunk? No, of course not, only the spare tire and the jack and a few deposit bottles. Mendel prided himself on his neatness, but now the clean barren space was a reproach. Where was the *tallis* bag?

"Like Edna said, it must be in *shul*."

Mendel marched in, straight to his usual seat by the east wall. The bag was not there, but he was not too concerned; probably the *shammes* had moved it while straightening up the tables and benches. Where was the man anyway? Why wasn't he ever around when he was needed?

Well, Mendel decided, he would search the room himself, methodically, from front to back. Nothing! The shelves from top to bottom — nothing! The coatroom — frantically now — nothing!

Maybe one of the *bachurim* had found it and put it away for safekeeping? Yes! That must be it!

Relieved and hopeful, Mendel went upstairs to the *beis hamidrash* where rows of tables were occupied by dozens of young men swaying back and forth to the familiar cadences of Talmud study.

Could he interrupt them with an announcement? No, that wouldn't be right. He decided to write a note: "Has anyone found a black *tallis* bag with initials M.M.D.? Please call 376-2431. *Yosher Koach*. Mendel Deutsch."

Mendel was starting to feel faint. He realized he had eaten nothing that day. He went back to the car and drank the entire contents of the large thermos. Maybe the strong black coffee would help him think.

Leaning his aching head on the steering wheel, he remembered that he had left his car unlocked when he ran into the grocery store. Oh, why had he wasted so much time looking for the Wispies, picking out the crispest rolls, shmoozing with Joe? Yes, that's when it must have happened! Whoever took it probably figured there'd be something valuable inside that gold-embroidered velvet bag, and when the *goniff* saw only black boxes and leather straps and a length of black-striped white wool with fringes, he probably dumped it someplace.

Mendel got out of the car and started to search the dark doorways and halls on both sides of the street. The houses were mostly dusty and deserted. Occasionally he encountered an old man or woman who peered at him suspiciously. He found nothing.

Maybe in the battered garbage cans placed at the curb for this morning's collection? He thought he heard the pickup truck rumbling in the distance. He lifted each lid, releasing clouds of flies — nothing!

He would have to report his loss to the police.

At the precinct, he tried to explain — two black boxes with leather straps, a religious object, very valuable, in a black velvet bag — but the desk sergeant only yawned.

"Well, mister, I don't know, call back in a couple of days. We'll hold it for you in case somebody turns it in."

"Well, at least I tried," Mendel consoled himself.

He had missed breakfast and all his morning appointments. There was a hammer pounding inside his head, and his knees were trembling. What more could he do? Where else could he search?

Mendel decided to go back to the yeshivah. Maybe there was some corner, some cubby he had overlooked. And maybe, maybe there would be an answer to his note.

In the hallway he met his older brother, Shaya, whom he had last seen at *Shacharis*.

"Shaya, I don't know what to do! I lost my *tallis* bag with *Zeide's tefillin* inside."

"I know," said Shaya.

"What do you mean, you know? Edna called you?"

"Just a minute, Mendel. Wait right here!"

His brother dashed upstairs and returned a minute later, bearing a black velvet *tallis* bag.

"Shaya! What's this? Wh-where did you ...?" Mendel stuttered.

"I'm the one who took it. When I saw your car standing unlocked with the *tallis* bag inside, I thought I'd teach you a lesson. *Zeide's tefillin* — I know how precious they are — and you just left them like that! Well, I just couldn't stand it. So ...."

"Shaya! How — how could you do this to me?" Mendel was almost crying.

His brother hesitated. "I thought I'd return the bag right away, but then you disappeared. *Zay moichel* — please forgive me!"

What do you think? Do you think Shaya did the right thing? What would *you* have done in his place?

✐ David's Dilemma

This was the fourth time that David Glantz had met with Debbie Wendel. He had been hesitant at first, when his uncle had suggested the *shidduch*. Although the girl's family had an excellent reputation in Baystown, they were not over-endowed with worldly goods, and their background was a simple one: not a rav or a rosh yeshivah or a millionaire in the family, at least for the last few generations.

His parents had urged him; they were close friends of the Wendels, and had watched Debbie grow up. She was sweet, bright, pleasant and cheerful, and they felt there was no girl better suited to their David. In fact, they had regarded her as almost a daughter long before she reached marriageable age. They were happy when, after the second meeting with Debbie, David reported, "She's nice! I feel so good when I'm with her. And she's really *frum* without being *farchnyokt.*"

They had wanted him to say more, but one mustn't pressure.

So a third meeting was arranged. The young people talked about childhood experiences, about teachers, favorite and unfavorite, about their parents, grandparents, brothers, sisters — rather, Debbie did, since David was an only child. They had friends and even relatives in common, and the conversation flowed easily. Debbie thought she was beginning to know David well, and he thought the same about her. Each hoped that the other would agree to a fourth meeting, and both were thrilled when it turned out that way.

The fourth time, they discussed more serious matters — their ambitions, their hopes for the future: yeshivas, jobs, good places to live. David felt he was ready for the next step: a proposal of marriage, but his more experienced friends had said that one should meet at least seven times before taking such a momentous step. David had always thought highly of his friends' judgment and depended on their approval, so he now turned the conversation away from the personal to neutral subjects — a *vort* on the *parshah,* an explanation of the situation in Eretz Yisrael, the latest album of *zemiros.* Debbie was surprised but carried her side with grace and intelligence. They parted amiably, both looking forward to another meeting in the near future. However, Debbie's brother was getting married the following week to a girl in Cleveland, so with the preparations for the *aufruf,* the traveling, the wedding, the week of *sheva berachos*, it would be a while until they could meet again.

They set the date for two weeks later, when things would have returned to normal.

The next day, David's *chavrusa,* Reuven Greenblatt, did not show up at *davening,* nor at breakfast, nor at the morning *seder.* At lunch recess, David headed for the public phone. "This is David Glantz. Can I speak to Reuven, please?"

"I'm sorry, he's sick and he has to stay in bed for a few days. He has a sore throat and he really shouldn't talk."

"Well, can I come over to see him tonight? Maybe we can catch up on a bit of learning." And I'll have the *mitzvah* of *bikur cholim*, visiting the sick, David thought.

"Just a minute, I'll ask my brother." A moment later, the voice was back on. "Yes, Reuven will be happy to see you; around 9:30, okay?"

"Fine. What's the address? 18 Van Velder Drive, the corner house? Thank you."

That evening, David took a bus straight from the yeshivah. It was quite a distance, and as they traveled, the streets became wider, the houses taller, the lawns and trees thicker and greener.

Number 18 was a red-brick mansion, rather old-fashioned, with white marble steps and a shiny brass knocker on the front door. It was opened by a tall girl.

"Oh, you must be David. Reuven is waiting for you. I'll show you to his room."

She led David through a wide hall, past several rooms to the bedroom where Reuven lay, looking eagerly toward the door. "I'm so glad you came, David," he whispered.

"Reuven! What's this? You're not supposed to be sick; remember, we made up to learn a *blatt* a day?"

"Yeah, I know, I know. The doctor says I have to stay in bed at least two weeks. So maybe you'll come every day, we shouldn't fall behind?"

Reuven spoke casually, but David detected the plea in his friend's voice, so he agreed to come for two hours every night.

The learning went well. David met the parents; the father was a substantial businessman, well versed in learning. The mother was seldom home; she had a responsible position in a lawyer's office. Usually the door was opened by Reuven's sister, and David went straight to his friend's room, where a snack was already laid out. Sometimes Reuven would ask about the doings in the yeshivah, about the latest engagements and weddings, but most of the time they learned seriously, without a break.

So David was surprised when Reuven asked, "Maybe you know a boy for my sister? She's a real good kid; she's 20, graduated from seminary, and she's ready to get married."

"Well, there's Chaim Waldman, you know he's looking for a while now. And Levi Singer, but he's probably too short. Oh, and what about 'Shorty' Grossman? He's at least six two, he should be just right, and he's a great guy."

"No, she's not interested in any of them. When I asked her, she said — well, she said that someone like you would suit her just fine."

David turned all colors. He had not told anyone about his involvement; his parents insisted that a *shidduch* should not be spoken about until its happy conclusion.

"Well … that — that's very nice, but …."

Reuven did not let him continue. "And my parents like you, too. Dad said so from the first time you came. So what do you say?"

"Well, all this is kinda sudden. I'll have to think about it and speak to my parents, I guess. Oh – " looking at his watch – "I have to catch my bus! See you tomorrow!" And David dashed into the hall and out the door.

All night he tossed and turned. True, he had met Debbie four times, and he really liked her. But did that obligate him in any way? And what about his learning, his future? Surely Mr. Greenblatt could do more for him than Debbie's parents, with their modest income. He'd be able to study many more years without worries about *parnasah*.

Still, wouldn't this hurt Debbie terribly? He tried to recall every word they had said to each other. Had he made any commitment? No. Had she? No, or at least he did not think so. And what about his parents? They liked Debbie so much and had been hinting about her for years.

By now, dawn was breaking. David decided to get dressed and go to the yeshivah. His oldest and closest friend, Velvel Lando, was sure to be there. The jokesters in the *kollel* said that he came extra early to escape the crying of his twins, but that was not true; he was the biggest *masmid* of the group and learned best in the early hours of the day.

Velvel was there, his *sefer* open before him on the *shtender*. David told him everything: his dates with Debbie, his parents' fondness for her, Reuven's suggestion about his sister, the worry of not being able to continue learning.

Velvel listened quietly, occasionally interrupting with a brief question.

"David, do I have it right? You met this girl a few times. You did not discuss your feelings or anything personal. You did not propose. So I really think you don't have any obligation toward her, and if you want to learn a good long time, there's really no choice. The other girl's father, Mayer Greenblatt, is one of the richest men in town; they say he owns millions in real estate. You owe it to yourself and to your future as a *lamdan*. So forget about that other thing, and go for this."

"But Velvel, I can't just drop her like that. And what will my parents say? No – I can't!" He was almost in tears.

"Listen to me, Reuven; I know what I'm talking about. You think it's fun when the rent is due and you can't pay? And your wife needs a new dress for Yom Tov and you can't afford it? Don't throw away your future! With this *shidduch* you can *shteig* and *shteig* — you have it in you to become a rosh yeshivah. With the other ...," and Velvel made a dismissive gesture and turned back to his *shtender*.

David usually ate breakfast in the yeshivah, but that day he came home to catch his father before he went to his job. When they were seated at the kitchen table, he told his parents the same thing he had told Velvel, and asked for their guidance.

His mother was the first to answer, and her words were like a slap across his face.

"David! Is this the boy I brought up to know the difference between right and wrong? You go out with a wonderful girl — one, two, three, four times. You like her and she likes you, and Papa and I feel she's perfect for you — and now all of a sudden, just because that other one is richer, you're ready to drop her? *Vey, vey iz* mir — " His mother dropped her head in her hands and started crying.

"But Mama, Papa — it's not that way at all! You don't understand! I'll be able to *shteig* if I don't have all those *parnasah* worries. Don't you want your son to be a rosh yeshivah?"

"I understand very good," his father muttered. "You think with money you'll be able to learn better. Ha! You'll be busy catering to her — 'Take me out I'm bored! Do the shopping, I'm tired! Watch the kids, they get on my nerves!' Sure, you'll have a fancy wedding, but what happens after that? And where's your *bitachon* that you're always talking about?"

"You don't understand, Pa! You don't even want to listen. Just because you're friends with her parents and you'll be embarrassed .... I'm sorry, Pa, I'm sorry, I didn't mean that!" His parents' faces had turned to stone.

"I'm sorry," David said again. How he wished he could take back those last words! He knew that his parents were deeply hurt and he tried to make amends.

"Well, maybe you're right. Maybe I should forget about all this and settle for Debbie. That's what you always wanted, isn't it?"

"Don't do us any favors — or Debbie either, David. *You* have to decide. It's your *achrayus*."

His parents went out and David was left sitting alone at the table. What should he do now? What should he do?

WHAT DO *YOU* THINK?

This volume is part of
THE ARTSCROLL SERIES®
an ongoing project of
translations, commentaries and expositions
on Scripture, Mishnah, Talmud, Halachah,
liturgy, history, the classic Rabbinic writings,
biographies and thought.

For a brochure of current publications
visit your local Hebrew bookseller
or contact the publisher:

Mesorah Publications, ltd

4401 Second Avenue
Brooklyn, New York 11232
(718) 921-9000